THE COMING OF THE WOLF

ELIZABETH CHADWICK

sphere

SPHERE

First published in Great Britain in 2020 by Sphere

This paperback edition published by Sphere in 2021

1 3 5 7 9 10 8 6 4 2

A CIP catalogue record for this book is available from the British Library.

ISBN 978-0-7515-7765-5

Typeset in BT Baskerville by
Palimpsest Book Production Ltd, Falkirk, Stirlingshire
Printed and bound in Great Britain by Clays Ltd, Elcograf S.p.A.

Papers used by Sphere are from well-managed forests
and other responsible sources.

Sphere
An imprint of
Little, Brown Book Group
Carmelite House
50 Victoria Embankment
London EC4Y 0DZ

An Hachette UK Company
www.hachette.co.uk

www.littlebrown.co.uk

Great Britain
0
50
100 Miles
0
50
100
150 Kms
N
SCOTLAND
North Sea
York
Atlantic Ocean
Chester
Oxley
Nottingham
Fletesbroc
Stafford
Irish Sea
WALES
ENGLAND
Ashdyke
Hereford
Milnham on Wye
Striguil
London
Hastings
English Channel

A Cast of Characters

A list of the characters peopling *The Coming of the Wolf.* Actual historical characters are marked with an asterisk.

The English

Christen – Lady of Ashdyke, wife of Lyulph, an English thegn
Lyulph, son of Wilfrid – Christen's husband
Osric – Christen's rebel brother
Hrothgar – Osric's friend and second in command of his warband
Wulfhild – Christen's maid
Leofwin – An English soldier in the pay of the Normans
Father Aelnoth – the village priest
Caelwin – a cloth merchant
Edward – constable of the castle of Milnham-on-Wye
Mildrith – Edward's wife
Golding and Freda – two villagers of Oxley

Wulfric – lord of Oxley, Christen's grandfather
Bonde and Gythe – husband and wife, villagers of Oxley
Eric – a village boy at Oxley
Wenfled – A refugee taken in by Christen
Eadric Cild – An important English rebel, who has a deep impact on what happens in the story, but does not make a personal appearance

The Normans

Miles le Gallois – half-Norman half-Welsh scout and soldier for King William, Lord of Milnham on Wye
Odo FitzWilliam – Norman mercenary in the pay of the Earl of Hereford
Guyon le Corbeis – Marshal and protector to Miles le Gallois
*William FitzOsbern Earl of Hereford, related to King William
Aude – sister in law to Miles le Gallois
Emma – Miles's illegitimate daughter
Hodierna – nurse and aunt to Miles's daughter Emma
Etienne FitzAllen – a knight in the entourage of Miles le Gallois
Gerard FitzRenard – Half-brother to Miles
*King William – also known as William the Conqueror and William the Bastard
Alicia FitzOsbern – daughter of William FitzOsbern

The Welsh

Dewi - a serjeant in Miles le Gallois' employ
Cynan ap Owain – a young well-connected Welsh lordling
Siorl ap Gruffydd – uncle to Miles
Olwen – a Welsh midwife

Author's Note

I was fifteen years old when I wrote my first historical novel. I had been telling myself stories about all manner of things since infancy – usually verbally, talking the tales aloud to myself. In my teens, though, I fell for a medieval hero in a children's TV series titled *Desert Crusader* and started writing what I suppose today would be called 'fan fiction'. That phase swiftly evolved into something else as I travelled further into my own imagination and began researching the historical background. My writing took off in new directions with fresh ideas, although with medieval settings.

By the time I had completed that first novel – over the course of a year – I realised that what I wanted to do for a living was write historical fiction. It took me more than fifteen years and eight full-length novels to achieve that goal, but I got there in the end when a leading London literary agent read that eighth novel, *The Wild Hunt*, and offered to represent me. Several publishing companies ended up in a bidding war for it and the rest, as they say, is history. *The Wild Hunt* went on to win an award and is still in print today, thirty years after its first publication. I had the career I wanted.

However, before *The Wild Hunt*, there was its prequel – *The Coming of the Wolf*. It had been rejected on its first and only outing. In my innocence, I managed to send it out to a publisher dealing in erotic fiction, because I took the terminology of 'adult' fiction to mean something more mainstream than it actually was! When I received a rejection letter, I shelved *The Coming of the Wolf* and got on instead with *The Wild Hunt*. My new agent asked if I had written anything else. I diffidently mentioned *The Coming of the Wolf* and she asked to see it. She loved it, and passed it on to my editor. The latter also thoroughly enjoyed it, but felt that *The Wild Hunt* ought to be the start-off novel for my career and that a prequel at this stage in the game did not quite fit the agenda. Fair enough, I thought, and shelved it again.

I had written *The Coming of the Wolf* before the days of software programmes such as Word. I had used an Amstrad Green-Screen to write the novel and that system and software gradually died a technological death. As my career progressed, I sometimes thought about *The Coming of the Wolf* and its near-miss, and eventually decided to type it into Word so that at least I would have an up-to-date electronic copy of the work. I embarked on the project in spare moments, and as I transcribed, I edited the novel at the same time. It was a labour of several years, widely spread out. Finally finished, I put the first couple of chapters on my website as an extra for the readers. It still needed more editing I felt, but was at least presentable. The response was immediate and requests for more of the story came piling in.

I edited the novel again in my spare time and showed it to

my current agent Isobel Dixon, and my editor at Little, Brown, Viola Hayden. They both felt that the time was now right to publish the work to accompany *The Wild Hunt.* A couple more edits followed and now, here it is – not only the prequel to *The Wild Hunt* but its catalyst.

1

Manor of Ashdyke, Welsh Marches, August 1069

Lying in bed, Christen listened to the birdsong. The rippling sequcnce of a thrush, two blackbirds in competitive harmony, the bold chirping of sparrows, and the raucous cawing from the rook colony in the ash trees beyond the stockade.

Grey daylight poked through the gaps in the shutters and stole across the skins on the bed to touch the bare shoulder of the sleeping man at her side. She turned her head to look at him. The muted light was kind to his years, gentling the lighter wrinkles and smoothing the crêpey skin on his throat and arms. Since the arrival of the Normans, three years ago, Lyulph had lost his prime and become an old man lacking the spark and vigour that had kept him vital and strong even though he was well past his fiftieth winter.

In the days before the Normans, in the time of King Edward, Lyulph would have been busy husbanding these estates from the first streak of dawn until the last quench of sunset. In his moments of leisure he would have been out hunting, or exercising his weapon skills. In the evening he would have presided over the household in the great hall, dispensing food and drink to the dependants at their board, making toasts with his silver-chased drinking horn, while taking shrewd note of everyone and everything. As strong as an ox, but never bovine. And kind, she thought, swallowing grief at what he had become.

It was so difficult for Lyulph now. He had travelled north with King Harold Godwinson to face the invasion forces of Hardrada of Norway and had been badly wounded in the great battle at Stamford. He had been unable to march back down the country with Harold to face the new threat from William of Normandy. Instead, he had spent the day of the second great battle for England's throne burning with fever from an infected gash in his thigh. The wound, a stab from a Norse spear, had saved his lands and his family. Christen often thought that for Lyulph it would have been a mercy had he died in Harold's shield wall at Hastings, rather than surviving to swear his allegiance to King William and live each day ravaged by guilt and bitterness.

The birdsong was growing more insistent and the grey light brightening with gold. Lyulph slept on, his breath fluttering through his thick silver moustaches. Christen slipped from his side, drew the bed covers back over him and silently donned her gown and chemise. She combed and braided her heavy flaxen hair and with deft fingers pinned it up and donned her wimple, covering her head as a decent married woman should. Sitting down on a low stool to put on her shoes, she glanced again at her sleeping husband with a mingling of worry and sadness.

They had been married for five years and she had recently entered her twentieth summer. Lyulph was thirty years her senior. Her land and her marriage had been in King Edward's gift

– she had become the King's ward when her father died and Edward had bestowed her on Lyulph who had been a fit and powerful warrior, capable of defending her lands on the troublesome border between England and Wales. She had never thought of Lyulph as an old man in the early days, but rather as a solid bulwark and protector. A man of gravitas, strong and dependable, with a ready laugh, who treated her with kindness and a little indulgence. Her situation in an arranged marriage could have been so much worse and she was grateful.

She had conceived twice. The first pregnancy had ended in a miscarriage before the baby had quickened; the other had resulted in a still-born daughter in the year the Normans came and the week before Lyulph set out to war. They had not lain together as man and wife since. He said he would not bring a child into a land suffering under the yoke of rapacious wolves, chief among them their close neighbour William FitzOsbern, Earl of Hereford, a powerful Norman warlord and the scourge of the area. He was William the Bastard's kin and one of his chief advisers.

Christen tip-toed from their bedchamber and entered the adjoining hall. A yawning maidservant was poking the fire to life under the cauldron at the central hearth and the hall's other occupants, roused from slumber, were rolling up their sleeping pallets and preparing to face the day. Christen went out into the yard. Two women were drawing water at the well and a third was washing her face and hands in a bucket of water. A mouthwatering smell of baking loaves wafted from the bread oven next to the hall, making her stomach clench with hunger. In the dairy, the women were churning butter and making curd cheese to serve at the breaking of fast. She paused to supervise, saw that all was as it should be, and continued on her way.

It was pleasantly cool now, but bid fair to be a hot end-of-summer day once the sun had gained height – ideal for dyeing the skeins of wool spun from the manor's flock of sheep at shearing time and now awaiting her attention. The yarn would set and dry swiftly in the warm air. She entered the storage hut where the dye vats were kept. On two rows of shelves stood neatly arranged jars and bags of mordants and dyes – madder root for red, weld for yellow, and balls of dried woad for blue. Less of the woad, because it was expensive and she kept a shrewd, housewife's eye on the purse strings. There was less to go round since the Normans had come.

A movement in the shadows touched the corner of her eye, but before she could turn, a hard arm clamped around her waist, and she was lifted from the ground and spun into a lung-constricting bear-hug. Crying out with what breath had not been squeezed from her body, she strove to break free.

'Christen, it's all right, it's me!' A whiskery face loomed over hers and planted a rough kiss on her cheek.

'Osric!' She stared in shock and not a little dismay at the brother she had not seen since the rebels had raided Hereford last year. 'Dear God, what are you doing here?' The rings of his mail shirt imprinted the flesh of her cheek, and the hard edge of a sword pommel jutted against her ribs. Recovering, she pushed herself out of his arms, and glared at him, knowing of old that his great, solid body was the only dependable thing about Osric.

'Don't look at me like that.' He gave a tense laugh and dug one hand through his thick, fair hair.

'How should I look at you?' she snapped. 'A year passes without news, and then you leap on me out of nowhere, squash me half to death, and expect me to be overjoyed. Are you still with the rebels?' Even as she asked the question she knew the answer.

He had fought on Hastings field but had survived by fleeing from the final slaughter. The fight was not over for him, and would never be. He dropped his hand. 'The free English,' he said stiffly.

Unimpressed, she folded her arms.

Osric opened his mouth to remonstrate, but changed his mind and gave her an imploring look from wide hazel eyes. 'I need your help,' he said.

Christen wanted to throttle him. Wherever Osric went, mayhem invariably followed, and his schemes were always detrimental to anyone foolish enough to become caught up in them. It had been that way ever since childhood. She made a brusque gesture, devoid of welcome. 'You had better come to the hall and break your fast. Lyulph is still abed. I . . . who are they?' Her gaze shot to six men gathered furtively near the stable enclosure.

Osric shrugged and affected nonchalance. 'My warband. We are on our way to rejoin Eadric Cild west of here.'

Eadric Cild, as Christen well knew, was an English rebel, determined to oppose Norman rule to the last, bitter drop of blood. After an unsuccessful attempt to take Hereford from the Normans, he had retreated over the border into Wales, and no one was ever certain where he would strike next. Neither he nor William FitzOsbern cared what they destroyed if it stood in their way.

'Well, keep them away from our horses,' she snapped. 'God knows, Lyulph has had trouble enough keeping them out of FitzOsbern's grasp without you seeking to "borrow" them from us.'

'Christen!' Osric gave her a look drenched in reproach.

'I have grown up,' she said wearily, 'and Lyulph has grown old before his time. We are beyond riding on the back of glory into death. You may bring them into the hall for food and drink, but you cannot stay here or use us for your refuge. I will go and rouse my husband.'

Lips pursed, Christen served her menfolk with bread, curd cheese and new ale.

'So you go into Wales to rejoin Eadric Cild?' Lyulph studied his brother-in-law from faded blue eyes.

Osric broke a crust of bread, pushed it into his mouth, and spoke around it. 'If we can break through the Norman net, yes. It should not be difficult; we have already shaken off one band who were on our tail.'

'Then you are hunted?' Lyulph raised his brows.

Osric hunched his shoulders defensively. 'We lost them in the forest last night. You know I would not bring danger down on your heads.'

'I know no such thing,' Lyulph said. 'Your very presence here puts us in peril.'

Osric swilled down the bread with a gulp of ale. 'They weren't a large troop. We would have turned and fought, but they had horses and we were on foot. It was easier to use the dark to slip away. We won't stay here long, I promise.'

Christen glanced apprehensively at Lyulph. He met her gaze steadily, but his mouth was down-turned and grim. Osric's pursuers could not be far away unless they had given up the chase and turned back.

'I am glad to hear it,' Lyulph said, and gestured Christen to leave them to talk.

She went outside to supervise the dye tub and to tell the kitchen servants to prepare extra food for the midday meal. She knew exactly how it would go between Lyulph and her brother. Osric would ask for spears, axes and horses to take them into Wales and Lyulph would agree in order to have them gone from

Ashdyke. Exacting tribute, she thought with tight lips. Why couldn't Osric leave them alone? They had enough to contend with already.

She was stooping over a vat of stewing madder root, skeins of wool at the ready, when Lyulph emerged from the hall to speak to her, his gait heavily favouring the wounded leg. As a sop to his pride in the presence of her brother, he was not using his stick but she could see he was struggling. 'Set seven more places at our table,' he said gruffly, 'and serve dinner early. Osric will ride out afterwards.'

'*Ride?*' She stepped aside to let a woman empty another pail of water into the bubbling cauldron. 'We cannot spare the horses, you know we cannot.'

Lyulph's mouth hardened. 'He is kin. We are obliged.'

'Precisely the reason he is here. He knows we are obliged.'

'They cannot win,' he said heavily. 'There is no one left of King Harold's mettle lest it be William of Normandy, and him we already have whether we like it or not.' He rubbed his palm across his face. 'Your brother will not listen, but then at his age I would have been the same. Indeed, far more recently than my youth I would have joined him and gone to the rebels because he is weaving his fate and not sitting with empty hands and a broken body at the loom of his life.'

Impulsively she reached up to stroke his silver beard and smiled at him with concerned, sad affection. 'I am not sure Osric's weaving will ever prove fruitful,' she said. 'I would not have you follow my brother's road.'

'And at his age I would have been of more use to a pretty young wife,' Lyulph said with a rueful grimace, and his eyes clouded with pain.

Swiftly she covered his lips with her palm. 'I will not hear you say such words. I am content, my lord.'

He took her hand and lowered it from his mouth. 'Are you?' He searched her face.

'Yes.' Christen's throat tightened. She would give him the part that was truth and avoid the other. 'You are a good and considerate husband. Had King Edward bestowed me on one of his young warriors, there is no certainty that my life would have been any more fulfilled. He would not have had your wisdom and patience.'

He sighed and shook his head. 'Those are not always the traits that a young woman would put above others.'

'This one does!' Christen said stoutly. 'I thank God every day that King Edward did not give me in marriage to such a one as my brother.'

'I see your point,' he said with pained amusement and leaned forward to kiss her cheek before limping away to the stables to order the release of the horses they could ill afford to lose. Christen watched his laboured progress, a cold hand squeezing her heart. His step held a heavy finality – not of defeat, but of weary endurance.

Her eyes became dry with staring and began to smart. Abruptly she returned her attention to the dye tub. The sooner Osric left, the better. He had been reckless before the slaughter at Hastings, but since the battle, the recklessness had changed and become a dark and dangerous bitterness within him.

They were seated at the long table in the hall, Osric waving a chicken leg around on the point of his knife and regaling them with an exaggerated tale of his deeds among the 'free English', when the Normans hit them in the summer noon like a bolt of lightning. One moment Christen was directing a servant to refill Lyulph's cup, the next there was a golden splash of ale across the trestle and down her skirt as the men leaped up in answer to a terrified shriek of warning. Lyulph rose and made an awkward turn to grab his battleaxe off the wall behind his chair and stepped in front of Christen to defend her, shouting orders to his startled retainers.

There seemed to be hundreds of attackers, although Christen later learned there were no more than twenty, but enough to overcome a small English community that had lost its best fighting men in the north against Hardrada. Osric was neither a martyr nor, for all his boasting, the stuff of which great leaders and heroes were made. As the Normans poured into the hall, he leaped over the trestle, seized a burning brand from the hearth and set light to the rushes carpeting the floor. As smoke and stench arose amid small soft teeth of flame, he ran to the window at the side of the dais and scrambled through the aperture, his so-called warband deserting in his wake.

Coughing, Christen drew her veil across her nose and mouth.

'Go, get out!' Lyulph shouted at her. 'Run to the woods and hide until I come for you!'

'I'll not leave you!' she answered fiercely, then coughed so hard into the linen that she retched and could only see him through a stinging blur.

'There is no time to argue, do as I say!' He gave her a vigorous shove.

Christen stumbled on her gown, righted herself, stared down the hall with smoke-torn eyes at the mail-clad figures striding through Osric's flimsy barrier of smoke and fire, then fled.

In their bedchamber, she grabbed her cloak, stuffed her jewellery into a cloth bag and ran to the window, then recoiled with a scream as a Norman soldier straddled the sill. The man leaped down into the room and advanced on her, his sword raised, light gleaming along the blade. Outside someone screamed in English and was answered by an exultant bellow in Norman French.

Christen backed away from the man, in terror, her knees almost buckling.

The Norman advanced on her, lips parted in anticipation. Christen hurled the cloth bag at him and he caught it with a laugh, and then whirled as Lyulph staggered into the room, his axe blade dyed crimson, dark trickles running down the haft and staining his hands. Roaring with rage, Lyulph launched himself on the Norman and, in the heat and desperation of the moment, fought as he had fought at Stamford. Christen felt wet heat spray her face before her attacker fell at her feet, his jawbone shorn from his body.

She screamed and ran to Lyulph. He held her hard for the space of a heartbeat before spinning her round and bundling her towards the window, pausing only to snatch her jewels from his victim's still-twitching hand and tie the string through her belt. 'We were betrayed,' he panted. 'Gyrth the blacksmith sought the Normans and told them we were harbouring rebels, and opened the gates for them. Can you reach? Quickly now.'

He lifted her, fingers digging painfully into her hips, finding the strength out of desperation. Christen did not need to ask why Gyrth had gone to the invaders. They were the ones with the good horses and the custom these days, and they paid hard silver for information. Gyrth had been sullen ever since Lyulph had dealt him a fine for drunken brawling last month.

'Meet me at the Hundred oak,' Lyulph said as she gained the sill. 'If I do not come, make for the nunnery at—'

Christen screamed a warning and Lyulph whirled, the axe already swinging through its bright arc. The Norman howled as the blade sheared through his shield as though it were made of butter, and opened his leg to the bone. Lyulph tried to balance himself to strike again, but his leg gave way and a second Norman following on the heels of the first took advantage and struck Lyulph in the side, the sword biting deeply into his flesh.

Still grasping his axe, Lyulph stared incredulously at the blood saturating his tunic. He twisted towards the window, to Christen, but no words came from his mouth, only an eruption of blood, and the Norman struck him again as he fell.

The first soldier threshed about on the floor, screaming in terror and agony as his life bled away. As his companion turned to help him him, Christen swung her other leg over the sill and dropped to the ground. The landing winded her and sent pain jolting through her ankles and knees, but she was not injured. Dry-sobbing with fear and shock, she stared round, her fingers tightly gripping the drawstring cord of the jewel bag.

The hall was ablaze, the timbers having dried out in the long summer days, and the Normans were doing nothing to douse the flames. She saw the sprawled bodies of Lyulph's men and the male servants, cut down as they fled, and others, running for their lives, but being caught and slaughtered. Her people, and she could do nothing for them, and there was no escape. Everything was fire and blood and harsh, triumphant voices exulting in French. And Lyulph . . . Lyulph was dead.

A troop of horsemen entered through the open gates and thundered across the compound, straight towards her. The lead stallion was upon her so quickly that she was flung from its broad, dappled shoulder like a child's straw doll. Sprawled face-down in the dirt several yards away, dazed and barely conscious, she was aware of the roar of flames and the vibration of hooves on the ground against her cheek. The screams and pleas, the butchery, the roars of triumph, and excited laughter.

She lay very still, not daring to move, praying to God and the Holy Virgin for mercy and succour against the minions of Hell.

Guards had secured the gateway and more Normans were riding into the compound on their stocky warhorses, disciplined now and purposeful. She watched them dismount and knew there was no way out, although for now the killing appeared to have ceased. She should do something, but she did not know what. In her mind's eye she kept seeing images of Lyulph being struck down in front of her eyes. The thrust of the sword, the look on his face the moment before he died.

Nearby, two Normans were arguing. One she recognised as the man who had killed Lyulph. He was tall and thin with a prominent red-stubbled jaw and he was gesticulating furiously with a clenched fist, his voice a raw snarl. His opponent stood as still as a stone and his own voice never rose above the same level pitch, although it was obvious that he was equally determined to have his way. Christen understood a little French, for her father had traded with Norman and Angevin wine merchants in more peaceful times. Indeed, for a while he had even considered wedding her to one such, although it had never come to pass. Her father had died, and King Edward had given her to Lyulph.

'Yes, you got here first,' said the quiet one, distaste evident in his voice. 'There was no need for this.'

'They were harbouring rebels as you well know. The old man killed Sir Everard with a battleaxe, and you say there was no need?'

'Hah, knowing Everard de Nantes, I would say the English lord was more than justified.'

The belligerent Norman reached to his sword, and the quiet one made his first move, his hand streaking out to clamp on the hilt of the half-drawn blade. 'That would be unwise. My men would not delay in the least to kill you, and I am more certain of them than you will ever be of yours. I am assuming command here.'

The man's eyes flickered. 'I'll take this up with the Earl of Hereford,' he threatened, snatching his wrist free. 'He gave the order to take this place and deal with it. You have not heard the last of this, le Gallois.'

'Take it up with the Pope himself, only get out of here now while you still have the wherewithal to walk and beget sons.'

'If Sir Everard were not dead . . .' The mercenary turned to his horse and set his foot in the stirrup.

'I would kill him myself, that is a promise.'

Christen watched one group of Normans ride out, taking with them a couple of pack horses laden with the corpses of five of Osric's companions, slung like dead deer across their saddles – presumably as proof in order to claim a reward from the Earl of Hereford. The remaining Norman leader studied their retreat with narrowed eyes, hands on his hips, and she saw him mutter something under his breath.

'What's to be done with these two, sire?' A soldier kicked a pair of bound captives to their knees in front of the Norman, and Christen saw with horror that it was Osric and his close companion Hrothgar.

'Hang them,' the knight replied with contempt. 'It is all they deserve.'

'No!' Christen cried, leaping to her feet, all thoughts of self-preservation forgotten. She ran out to put herself in front of the bound men, arms outspread. Her ankle, sore from her leap out of the window, gave way and she fell at the Norman's feet. 'In the name of our saviour, have mercy, I beg you!'

He considered her. It was hard to read his expression because the nasal bar of his helm concealed the nuances. 'Why should I do that?' he demanded.

'Osric is my brother.' Christen swallowed and tried to steady her voice. 'He is the only family I have left. You have killed my husband who was lord here, and my home is burning. I have lost too much already.'

'Do you know what he and his "warband" did to one of my villages yesterday?' he said contemptuously.

'They learn by Norman example,' Christen retorted, gesturing around the devastated compound. The hall was still on fire but his soldiers had formed a bucket chain leading from the well to the hall, and the remaining people of Ashdyke were part of that link also.

'Perhaps they do, but sometimes I doubt they need prompting.' He nodded acknowledgement to a soldier demanding his attention, and began to turn away.

'I beg you . . . if you have any mercy in your soul, spare him.'

He gave her a hard look. 'I am not sure that I do.'

'But I heard you tell that other man there was no need for all of this . . . and I thought you might have more Christian decency. He . . . he was the one who killed my husband. Please – I . . .' She bit her lip. 'I will make it worth your while.'

His lip twisted in what might have been distaste. 'I do not think that your brother is worth *your* while,' he said, 'but I will think on what you have said and advise you not to make assumptions about me in any way, be it of Christian decency, or how much I am open to offers. You would likely be wrong.' He stooped and drew her to her feet, gave her a brusque nod, and walked away to his men, his step lithe and agile.

Christen gazed at her brother's smoke-grimed face and swollen black eye, and felt a mingling of pity and disgust. 'Why did you raid his lands?' she demanded.

Osric's hazel eyes widened in astonishment. 'He's a Norman! What other reason do I need?'

She looked over her shoulder at the burning hall, still on fire despite the best efforts of the bucket chain, and thought of the gleeful hatred taken in the plundering. They were two sides of the same coin. 'You had better think of a better one quickly, or you will hang. You brought this down on us. Think on that.' Without giving him a chance to reply, she went to assist in laying out the dead and helping the wounded.

Osric and his companion were taken to the bucket chain and, under the watchful eye of a dour guard, put to work.

The onslaught had been swift and brutal. Most of Ashdyke's remaining warriors had died with Lyulph. Goddard, who had fought beside his lord at Stamford and helped him from the battle when Lyulph took the spear in the thigh. Edwin his cousin, with the merry laugh and his over-fondness for dice games. Now he would never sit at a gaming board again, or tease the maids, or carve little wooden figures for the children. Asmund the cook was dead, and the two youths who worked with him. Nesta, the Welsh goose girl, fourteen years old, had been struck a crushing blow to the back of her skull and had died instantly, beside her scattered bowl of poultry scraps.

Christen washed Nesta's body with a wrung-out cloth, wiping away the blood and grime. She folded her arms on her breast and covered the girl with the cheerful red cloak she had always worn about her duties and of which she had been so fond.

When the fire in the hall and adjoining chamber had finally been controlled, the bodies were brought out, some of them blackened and contorted but most still recognisable, and dead of wounds long before the smoke and fire got to them. Lyulph was borne out on a table in the mellowing mid-afternoon sun.

Christen fetched fresh water and washed him as best she could. She had her antler comb in her jewellery bag and she groomed his hair and beard, smoothing their gold and silver wiriness. She kissed Lyulph's cold cheek and folded his hands upon his breast across one of the terrible wounds he had taken while protecting her. Strong hands, beginning to knot with their years of use. Firm on the grip of an axe, but gentle at her waist. Hail and farewell, Lyulph son of Wilfred, King's huscarl. Her eyes grew dry gazing upon his body, but no tears came. For the moment she was beyond tears. Her grief was too deep. The dead were dead and no amount of wailing would bring them back, even though she knew she must eventually mourn. It was the living that must concern her now, and their survival.

'I have brought you a blanket for him,' said the Norman leader, and handed her a woollen cover. It was a good-quality Welsh plaid with a braided edge.

'Lyulph,' she said. 'His name is Lyulph.' Not 'was' but 'is'. 'He should be covered with his own cloak.'

'Yes, but that is not possible.'

Christen took the blanket from him in silence and draped it over her husband's body. It was not fitting, but it would have to do. And at least the Norman had given it to her rather than performing the deed himself. She could not have borne that.

'The priest will come in the morning,' he said.

She nodded to show that she had heard and prayed that he would leave. Eventually he did, but she did not hear him go. She lifted a corner of the plaid and held its softness to her cheek, gazing upon Lyulph's closed eyelids that a few short hours ago had still been open on the world.

2

In his dream, Miles checked his mount on the hilltop and watched a blood-red sunrise lift out of the October morning mist and sweep colours across the slope below him. Bodies sprawled as far as the eye could see, caught in the swift indecency of violent death. The fighting elite of King Harold's English – the mighty axe-wielding huscarls – with a high toll of their Norman enemies scattered among them. A breeze wafted the pennons upon abandoned lances and stirred the feathers of the carrion birds that hopped among the dead and perched on stiff shoulders and unmoving breasts to feast.

In the distance, a group of dark-garbed women searched among the slain – King Harold's mistress and mother, seeking on Duke William's orders for their lord's war-butchered body.

Miles's stallion swung its head, the bridle accoutrements jingling. He was so overwhelmed by the terrible sight below him and so drunk with exhaustion that he did not see the bloody shreds of something once human rise up behind him and swing an axe at his spine until it was too late.

His eyes jerked open and he awoke sweat-drenched and rigid to the liquid note of a thrush and the distant nickering of a horse, the battle cry of the wounded huscarl a fading illusion. He lay gasping, disorientated, terrified. A cloak-wrapped figure beside him grunted and turned over, shifting to a more comfortable position, and moments later started to snore. Miles drew a long, shuddering breath and exhaled slowly. Hastings was three years over and still, occasionally, the dreams seized him. It was not the first battle in which he had fought – he was experienced – but never had he come so close to dying as in the seconds before he had spurred Cloud out of range of the axe, and the English warrior had fallen dead on the blood-soiled turf.

He took another breath and grimaced as he tasted smoke. Such stupid, wanton waste. The punishment meted out so gratuitously by FitzOsbern's men was half the reason the English were so difficult to tame. Rape and pillage were hardly the tools with which to come a-wooing, but then the Earl of Hereford knew no other manner or courtship. Although in this particular instance, from what he had been able to glean, the near-disastrous blaze had been started by the two English prisoners currently tied to the post in the compound.

Miles threw aside his blanket, stood up and stretched. The sky was paler in the east and would soon bear the pink flush of dawn. A guard was stirring a fire to life under a small cauldron. Miles nodded to him, yawned and, rubbing his shield arm to ease a lingering stiffness, strolled to the midden pit to relieve himself before climbing to the walkway on top of the palisade.

The strengthening light afforded him a view of the immediate settlement and lands. Below the natural escarpment on which the manor was built, the River Wye glinted like a new-scaled snake. Beyond its convolutions, the Roman road drove east towards Hereford and west towards Wales. Between road and river fertile fields, some ruched by the plough, filled his view. Cattle grazed the water meadows and sheep the higher, craggier ground between village and manor.

Miles looked over his shoulder at the fire-damaged hall and beyond it the rear palisade, fringed in the near distance by deciduous forest, and his eyes narrowed in concentrated thought. Several times over the next half hour as the sky changed from bruised pink to tawny-gold his gaze flicked between river, road and fields, before coming to rest again on the palisade and the charred building it defended. Finally, as the sun spilled a line of burned gold over the rim of the horizon, he left the wall walk and made his way back down into the compound.

Christen was so stiff and bruised when she awoke from her most recent bout of fitful slumber that she could scarcely move. With an effort, stifling a groan, she struggled upright and took the cup of ale that Wulfhild, one of the surviving maids, was holding out to her. The light had not yet reached the bloom of full dawn, but she could see enough to tell that Wulfhild appeared to be inordinately interested in the men at the Norman campfire.

'Something pleases you about them?' Christen massaged her stiff neck with her free hand.

The girl tore her gaze from the soldiers. 'These are good men, my lady. They mean us no harm. I know they do not.' Her cheeks were flushed and her blue eyes sparkling. Wulfhild had always been nothing if not resilient.

'I suppose one of them told you,' Christen said, taking a sip of ale.

The sarcasm sailed over the top of Wulfhild's head. 'Yes, my lady. He's an Englishman called Leofwin, born and bred near Wigmore, and his lord is Miles le Gallois, lord of Milnham-on-Wye. He's native-born too.'

'He certainly spoke like a Norman yesterday,' Christen said sharply, but her interest was kindled by the difference between her assumption and Wulfhild's information.

'There's no English in him, my lady,' Wulfhild said, eager to tell what she knew. 'His father was one of those Normans that settled here in old King Edward's time to protect the border against raids from Wales and his mother's of Welsh noble blood.'

Hence 'le Gallois', Christen thought, which was Norman for 'the Welshman'. Glancing towards the soldiers, she saw a stalwart young man with shoulder-length light-brown hair grinning at Wulfhild and could immediately guess the source of her information.

'That's him,' said the maid. 'That's Leofwin.'

'You wasted no time.'

Wulfhild looked hurt. 'Not all stories are the same – my lady,' she said. 'These men are not like the other group.'

'They have swords and spears and shields,' Christen answered bleakly. 'They have not ridden away, but do not tell me that they are here for our own good. They are not staying to protect us, but because it suits their plans to be here.'

Wulfhild shrugged. 'They saved our lives,' she said simply. 'Without them, all the men would have been killed and we would have been raped and probably murdered afterwards, or sold. Look at what happened before they arrived and saw the others off. And they helped to put out the fire.'

Christen looked over at the row of shrouded corpses she had helped to lay out the day before, Lyulph's among them, marked out by the plaid blanket. She looked at the huddled survivors, many bearing injuries, and acknowledged to herself that Wulfhild was right. If she took it back further, then the root cause was sitting tied to a post near the dung heap. It was difficult and painful to think in that direction. She knew what Osric was, and yet he was her brother and her kin. There were moments in the past when he had been amusing and loveable. Wild and irresponsible it was true, but that spontaneous element had been endearing. She still felt a sense of duty towards him, and responsibility. She had to, because he had none himself.

She watched Miles le Gallois arrive at the Normans' fire and, crouching on his heels, accept a cup from the one called Leofwin. He wore no helm or arming cap now, and Christen saw that he had short coal-black curls and an olive complexion. His features were fine and set in a habitual expression of composure, for his manner was no different now than it had been when confronting the enraged mercenary yesterday. He said something briefly to Leofwin and received a reply that made him arch his brows and smile in the women's direction, particularly at Wulfhild. He finished his drink, stood up, and came across to them.

'Lady, if you please, will you walk with me?' He extended his hand.

His voice was pleasant but it was still a command spoken as a request. After a moment's hesitation Christen placed her hand in his and allowed him to draw her to her feet. His fingers were fine like the rest of him, but strong and hard, and as he closed them on hers she had to resist the urge to pull away. She brushed down her rumpled gown with her free hand, and seeing with sharp awareness the brown bloodstains and the smears of soot, felt sick. These clothes were all she had. The chest holding her spare gowns, chemise and shoes had not survived the fire.

In silence he led her across the compound towards the

palisade. His grip was light, but she received the impression that it could tighten in an instant if necessary to hold her fast.

'Some of my men have gone into Ashdyke village to bring the priest to attend the dead and bear them to the church,' he said. 'They shall be given a full funeral mass and be buried decently.'

'Thank you,' she said, finding that she could manage the words this morning when she could not yesterday. 'And thank you for Lyulph's covering.'

'It was the honourable thing to do,' he said. 'I have asked my men to bring the villagers as well as the priest.'

'The villagers?' She stared at him. The early morning light was full in his face and his eyes were a vivid, blue-flecked green. 'Why the villagers? What are you going to do to them?'

'Nothing to their detriment,' he replied. 'They need to be told the full story of what happened last night, and what the consequences are to themselves.'

'What do you mean "consequences"?' she asked with sharp and fearful suspicion.

'Nothing untoward, I promise you. I have lands of my own with English and Welsh settlers – since before the great battle.'

She gave a cautious nod. 'I have heard that it was so.'

'They will also be witnesses to the other morning's business,' he said.

'What business?' She felt as if a stone had lodged in her stomach.

'That depends on you.'

They had reached the stairway to the palisade, and he removed his hand from hers and ushered her up on to the wall walk. Then he swung his arm wide to encompass the land spread to their view. 'Look,' he said. 'Look around.'

Mystified, Christen did so, and saw only the usual vista. 'Since Stamford and Hastings some of the plough lands have reverted to waste for want of men,' she said, and her expression grew bleak. 'Still, there are not the mouths to feed that there were.'

He gave a questioning look.

'Lyulph did not care,' she said softly. 'His body was maimed at Stamford, and his soul at Hastings, even though he did not fight in the great battle. What was left after that was little more than a shadow. Why should he work the land when to him there was no longer a purpose and when so many of the husbandmen he knew were gone?' Her throat closed. She looked down at her hands.

'Even so, the neglect is superficial. These lands are rich.' When she did not respond, he continued, 'You are a young widow with assets and I am not the only man with a soldier's eye. This is a perfect place to build a keep to command the approaches to Hereford and the Welsh border, and as long as it is controlled by a strong hand, the King and the Earl of Hereford will not much care who it is.'

Understanding widened Christen's eyes. She would be forced into marriage with Ashdyke's claimant to legalise his possession, and it would not matter who he was, save that he served the interests of his Norman masters. 'I would rather die!'

He shook his head. 'I hope there is no need for that. I have the custody for now, and no intention of giving it up. I have the King's ear, and my family is well known to the Earl of Hereford. There might be some harsh words spoken and some hard bargaining involved, but I believe I have enough credit with both men to be given permanent command of this place. If you will agree to wed me, then it will make my tenure secure on all sides and safeguard your future.'

She stared at him in shock. 'Wed you?'

'If I am to build up this place and enrich it, I need a mediator whom the people will trust.'

She shook her head and took a step away from him, appalled at the notion.

'I intend having Ashdyke,' he said doggedly. 'It would be easier for me with your cooperation, but in the end, it comes down to the fastest sword, and the greatest cunning. If you accept me, you may live as you lived with your former husband. The domestic arrangements will be yours to command, the military ones mine.' He flicked his gaze to a laden cart creaking into the compound through the main gateway. 'If you refuse, then you and your people face an uncertain future, although I suppose you might find a nunnery to take you in.'

Christen stared queasily over the palisade. Marriage to a man of whose existence she had been unaware until last night, a man of whom she knew nothing except the scant information told to her by Wulfhild a few moments ago? She was watching this happen to someone else. In a moment she would wake up in bed with Lyulph still sleeping beside her and the birds chirruping their morning chorus. But the moment passed and she found herself still standing on the palisade next to this man. She tried to think, but it was like wading through fleece. Her choices were stark. Marriage to him, marriage to someone else, or taking a chance on the road. She had an estranged grandfather in Staffordshire who might take her in, but it was a slim chance, and she would have to make her way there first along dangerous, robber-infested roads. Perhaps this was the best of several unpalatable choices.

'When would the wedding be?'

'The quicker the better. Say, the day after tomorrow?'

'So soon?' She shot him a look filled with dismay and caught the eager glint in his expression.

'It is necessary, unless you would rather see the likes of Odo FitzWilliam seize the tenancy.'

'Who?'

'That mercenary I faced down last night and sent away. One of the Earl of Hereford's hirelings.' His lip curled with distaste. 'He did not take it well, and I have no doubt he will be reporting to his master as fast as he can ride.'

Christen swallowed, feeling sick. 'You give me no time,' she said. 'It is indecent.'

'Because there is no time,' he said. 'And yes, it is indecent, but no more so than the alternatives.'

She gazed at the fields and trees, the glint of the river, reflecting blue as the morning brightened. If she looked behind her, she would see the charred remains of the hall and the life she had led. She would see Lyulph's corpse on a bier. Before her, however harsh the choice, was life and what she might make of it. If she chose the path he offered, she might be able to influence other lives and outcomes, whereas there was no gain from refusal.

'Very well,' she said stiffly, 'I accept, but from necessity.'

A slight flush warmed his face and further brightened his eyes. He gave a brisk nod. 'The priest from the village can draw up the contract this morning while he is here and have copies made.'

'And what of my brother?' Christen asked. 'Does my consent buy his freedom?'

Miles rubbed the back of his neck and looked away. 'It is not that simple. If I release him and his companion I know full well they will hasten to join the rebels over the border. From what I hear, it was your brother who started the fire in the hall and brought all this down upon you.'

'The fire was a diversion,' she said, defending Osric out of old habit and loyalty.

'It may have been, but see what it has wrought, and before that he raided my lands without provocation. I have the right to hang him.'

'I do not love my brother at the moment, but if you think that riding him on a gibbet is a fitting wedding gift that will buy my compliance, you are mistaken.'

He lowered his hand. 'I said I had the right, but not that I would do it. As a sign of goodwill to you, I will release him and his companion, but they must know before they leave that all actions bear consequences.'

Christen swallowed, for his tone was ominous. 'What will you do to them?'

'Sire, the priest is here!' Leofwin bellowed up at them through cupped hands. 'He doesn't speak French.'

Miles le Gallois waved in acknowledgement and turned back to Christen. 'I promise I will not hang him, and that he shall go free. We are agreed in principle?'

Christen nodded, but still felt apprehensive. His reply, despite reassurances, had been ambiguous.

'Good, then we shall talk later.'

He led her back down to the compound, then bowed and departed to his men. She watched his confident, lithe walk and clenched her hands, for the future, far from being settled by his offer, was an open door into God knew what.

Father Aelnoth was at first doubtful and extremely wary of the mail-clad Normans, particularly since yesterday's departing troop had wantonly torched several dwellings in the village and killed a pig, but as he learned more about what had happened, and discovered that Miles spoke reasonable English, some of his trepidation dissipated. He was sufficiently pragmatic to realise there was nothing to be gained from raising objections to the proposed marriage between the lady and Miles le Gallois. Indeed, the Norman was something of a blessing in disguise. God help them all if either the lady's wild brother or that rabble from

Hereford had been left in possession. The village seniors were also prepared to accept Miles as their lord, because none of them wanted FitzOsbern's mercenary captain building a castle here and taking command.

Miles dismissed out of hand the blacksmith who had betrayed Lyulph by running to Hereford with tales. He wanted no such disloyalty in his household, nor did he ever want to ride a horse shod by the man, partly from a lack of trust and partly from superstition. Miles allowed him to take his tools and his pack horse, and he was seen out of the gate peremptorily but without violence.

'I do not believe you are going to wed that bastard!' Osric growled with contempt when Christen came to tell him the news of her impending marriage. He was still tied to the post, although he had been brought bread, water and a pisspot. 'Your grief over Lyulph was short-lived indeed!'

'Lyulph need never have died were it not for your stupidity!' she retorted. 'Look into your own mirror before directing me to mine. I have no time for grief. If not this man, I will be forced to marry another, perhaps a thousand times worse. He has promised me that on our wedding day he will set you free.'

Osric's eyes filled with incredulity. 'And you believe him?'

Christen thought of Miles's comments on the wall walk about consequences, and her stomach clenched, but she showed none of that trepidation to Osric. 'I believe him more than I will ever believe you again,' she said. 'The Normans may have come as destroyers, but you arrived here first.'

Osric ignored her words. 'I expect he intends to follow our trail, thinking we'll lead him to our allies,' he said scornfully. 'In which case we'll dance the Normans through the woods like a pair of will o' the wisps.'

Christen arched her brow. 'As you danced them to Ashdyke when you said you had lost them in the forest? You are the foolish one, Osric. He has your measure. Indeed, he has the measure of every one of us here.'

'Not mine,' Osric said stubbornly.

Christen turned and left him, knowing nothing she said would make a difference.

Caelwin, the travelling cloth trader, whose cart she had seen while up on the palisade, was waiting to speak to her.

'The lord says you are to choose such fabrics and threads as you need to make good the garments you lost in the fire,' he said, an avid gleam in his eyes as he indicated the cloth bales that his apprentice was setting out on a trestle beside his cart. He removed his hat. 'I am sorry to come to Ashdyke in such tragic circumstances. I will pray for the souls of those who have died. The lord Lyulph was much respected by all, and he will be greatly missed.'

Christen murmured a fitting response, knowing well that while Caelwin might indeed be sympathetic and sorry for Lyulph's death, he was a merchant to his bones, and was also thinking of future profits. 'And did the lord say who would pay?'

'Himself, my lady. As soon as his reinforcements arrive.' Caelwin clucked his tongue against the roof of his mouth. 'The roads are becoming too dangerous to travel these days. I was saying to the lad just now that we should consider staying closer to Hereford after this.'

Christen nodded absently and thought that Miles le Gallois had wasted no time in sending for more men, plainly leaving nothing to chance.

She followed the merchant to the trestle where his apprentice had arranged various bolts of cloth. There were some plain russets and greys, and beside them some pieces of local homespun lengths from Hereford in undyed cream and dark-brown wool but woven with an interesting diamond pattern. There were various bolts of Flemish cloth, the weave fine and smooth, dyed in various colours including a warm red and a forest green. Beside them were piled some soft, checked plaids from Wales, in subtle shades of green and gold. There was also a piece of expensive woollen cloth of the kind called scarlet, but Christen did not look at that. Of the nobility she might be, but not of such estate that she could afford to spend her time in idleness in order not to ruin her gown.

She chose some soft, bleached linen for chemises, the finest that Caelwin had because it was a false economy to buy coarser fabric to wear against the skin. That was easily settled, but in selecting the material for outer garments, Christen was less sure. She did not know how generous her future husband was with his coin or how much he had to his name. He had bidden her choose of her own free will, but that had to be governed by the funds available, and men, even the generous ones like Lyulph, always put horses and weapons above clothing in terms of their expenditure. In the end she made do with a length of grey wool, some of the russet, and a piece of the cunningly woven plaid for a cloak.

Horrified at the lack of profit, the merchant tried to interest her in a special length of apple-green wool-damask, which he presented with a surprise flourish, but to Christen it appeared garish and tasteless with the blackened hall and the shrouded bodies as a backdrop.

'It is not as if we are going to entertain the King to dinner, and even if we were, I would not want him to think we could afford to clothe ourselves in such finery,' she said with a firm shake of her head.

'But the cost is not high, my lady. I bought it in Bristol for a bargain price from an Italian merchant who—' He stopped and bowed, rubbing his hands.

Miles glanced at the pile that Caelwin's lad had folded to one side, taking in the fine white linen and the coarseness of the other stuff, then he eyed the puddle of green cloth opened out across the back of the cart. Christen blushed poppy-red.

'Master Caelwin thought I might be interested, but I told him it was not fitting,' she said in halting French.

'You have leave to choose whatever you desire,' he answered evenly. 'If the green is to your taste, then have it.' He looked again at the meagre pile of sober fabrics she had chosen. 'Admirable for working garments, but what do you intend for your wedding?'

'There is no time to stitch a gown,' she said, remaining crimson.

'Nonsense! If that girl of yours is as quick with a needle as she is with my men, and if the village women help, you will grace the altar as befits your rank . . . and mine.'

She saw his gaze dart again to the green, and a muscle twitch in his cheek.

'Put that away, Master Caelwin,' she commanded, swallowing her chagrin. It was not as if she had been about to purchase it.

The merchant bowed, and with calculating eyes produced instead another damask, this time a rich tawny with a paler gold under-pattern.

Miles eyed Christen with a lifted brow and the merest twitch of his lips which raised a treacherous answering spark of amusement in herself. It was a very fine cloth, but the colour would make her look bilious.

'No,' she said.

'But, my lady, see how it catches the light, and is subtler than the green.'

'Sire, Father Aelnoth desires to know what lands you apportion the lady in the event of your death before hers,' interrupted the priest's scribe, a quill between his ink-stained fingers, another behind his ear.

Miles turned to look at the trestle where the priest was poring over the portion of the marriage contract already written. 'My lands are in the King's gift, so any settlement will have to be in terms of silver.' He washed his palm over his face and sighed. 'Tell the Father I will come as soon as I have settled this business here.'

The scribe acknowledged and departed. Miles lowered his hand and turned to discover that the gold damask had been replaced by a handsome length of sea-dark silk, its surface shot through where the light struck with shimmers of sapphire and malachite. Christen's fingers were wistful on the cloth, but she was biting her lip.

'It is too expensive,' she said. 'And when would I wear it?'

'My lady will have the blue,' Miles said decisively to the merchant. 'And a length of this too.' Leaning forward, he tugged free a bolt of the Flanders twill, darker than wine, almost brown. The colour would light a garnet glow in her brown eyes and set off her flaxen hair to perfection.

'It is too much!' Christen gasped.

'The blue for your wedding,' he said curtly, 'the red for other days when you need a good dress.'

'But the cost!' she protested.

'Hang the cost!' he snapped, then smiled and shook his head and said in a softer voice, 'Hang the cost, but haggle if you must. I recall that it was one of my mother's foremost pleasures, the driving of a hard bargain. Count it as your wedding gift. Count it as compensation.' He nodded brusquely to the slack-jawed merchant, and strode off in the direction of Father Aelnoth's trestle.

'I will require needles and thread,' Christen said faintly, and wondered if she would have the wit to haggle. Usually it was an occupation she relished, but she was in no state to concentrate, and she was aware at the end of not having done full justice to her usual skills. Certainly, Master Caelwin wore a half-moon smile as she left him and his apprentice busy with their shears, while she went in search of women who could sew.

The rest of the day was spent clearing up and checking and shoring up the defences. The dead were borne away to the church in the village where a funeral mass was conducted with solemnity before the bodies were taken to the churchyard and interred in freshly dug graves.

Standing in the little church with Wulfhild and the other survivors, still Christen did not weep. It was almost as though the fire had evaporated her tears to leave her eyes dry and burning. At the gravesides she watched and prayed and listened to the soft thud of moist soil as the grave diggers shrouded the bodies in a blanket of earth.

Miles le Gallois attended the ceremony with his men and remained quietly in the background, for which Christen respected him, although doubtless his reasons for attending were as calculated as those that had led him to propose marriage to her. But still, it showed a level of decency. Osric and his companion Hrothgar had been escorted down to the church, still with their hands tied and under close guard. They said nothing, but stood with their heads bowed. For once Osric was neither sneering nor truculent. He reminded Christen of a chastised child that knew it had done wrong, was accepting the consequences, perhaps even feeling chagrined, but whether a lesson had been learned was debatable.

3

The following evening, shortly before dusk, Christen heard the guards on duty call a warning, and her heart began to pound. Even after Leofwin shouted a reassurance, it took her some moments to gather enough courage to leave her makeshift shelter and find out what was happening.

Miles was greeting the leader of a troop of about twenty men, his voice hearty with relief and welcome. A mail-clad giant swung down from a glossy black warhorse and Miles clasped him briefly, before turning to assess the soldiers and ask a swift question. The giant responded with a shrug and a sparse reply that nevertheless reassured Miles into an approving nod. A fawn mastiff dog the size of a small horse stood at the newcomer's side and he casually clipped a leash on to its wide leather collar.

Christen hesitated and started back to her shelter, but Miles had already noticed her, and called her over. Warily, she went to him and his companion, avoiding the dog, which was wagging its tail in a friendly fashion but its jaws were foamed with slobber.

'My lady, this is my marshal, Guyon le Corbeis,' Miles said in English, with a smile. 'Guy, I present to you my wife as of tomorrow – Christen of Ashdyke.'

'Sire,' Christen murmured, keeping her gaze politely lowered after one assessing glance that took in a full dark moustache stranded with grey, and alert, dark eyes. His nose was high-bridged and bony, his jaw powerful, and his cheeks pitted by smallpox scars. And all of it frozen in a moment of stony shock.

The man inclined his head to her and muttered a salutation.

Miles turned to Christen and indicated Wulfhild, who was hesitating off to one side. 'Your maid wants you, I believe,' he said.

Christen excused herself and turned to deal with Wulfhild's query.

The exchanges had been in English, but now Guyon switched to the more familiar ground of French, unaware of Christen's knowledge of the language. Wulfhild's query, although essential, about the wedding gown, was answered and clarified upon the moment, and Christen was able to hear and understand what the men were saying.

'Not your usual kind,' Guyon remarked, and signalled his second-in-command to deal with the horses and organise the pitching of tents. He tugged on the leash and made the hound sit.

Miles chuckled. 'How many types of wife have I had before?'

'You know what I mean. You like them wild and well endowed. This one's skinnier than a winter cow and hardly looks as if she's going to be mettlesome between the sheets.' He cocked his head. 'Still, she might put on more meat to please the eye once she's in calf, and it does not matter when the land is all.'

Christen propelled herself vigorously away from the men towards her shelter, Wulfhild scampering in her wake.

'She speaks enough French to understand,' Miles said neutrally.

Guyon grimaced. 'I have two left feet,' he confessed. 'Both of which should be jammed firmly up my backside. How was I to know?'

'You might have considered the possibility before you opened your mouth.' Miles sighed and shook his head. 'No matter. I daresay matters can be mended with a bit more diplomacy. And for your further information, I do not find her displeasing to look upon at all.'

'Well then, that is all to the good,' Guyon said gruffly. 'But it is a sudden decision, although I hardly think it was love at first sight – unless of the land. It is a fine location to build a castle. Nothing wrong with your strategy, but you should beware the English. They are not yet entirely defeated and resentment is rife.'

'I know what I am doing,' Miles said, glancing at his marshal with irritated amusement.

'I hope you do,' Guyon growled.

Miles drew him over to the prisoners. 'I need this place made secure as quickly as possible to discourage raiders such as these.' He gestured with distaste at Osric and Hrothgar.

'Planning some especial punishment?' Guyon enquired. 'I take it they belong to the raiding party that burned down our barn at Milnham?'

'Yes, indeed. The others are dead and of these two sorry specimens, the one with the fair hair and the vainglorious pout is their leader and happens to be my future brother-by-marriage.'

Guyon's brows drew together in a deep frown. 'Dear God.'

'Do you think I chose him on purpose?' Miles growled. 'The fool came here seeking shelter and supplies for his warband.

One of the villagers betrayed him to the Earl of Hereford and Everard de Nantes was sent here to put down the "rebellion", and you know what his methods are.' Miles sent a disgusted gaze around the charred compound. 'As they hit the front gate, we hit the back. De Nantes was killed in the first onslaught and his second-in-command decided not to engage with me. I sent the pack of them back to Hereford with their tails between their legs.'

'Hah, I understand now why you stressed the need for haste in your message. God grant you have not bitten off more than you can chew!'

Miles shrugged. 'I can handle the Earl of Hereford.'

Guyon was unimpressed. 'Let us hope that you can, otherwise we are all in the fire.' He handed the dog to his squire and told the lad to give it a drink.

Miles made a dismissive gesture. 'With the English under Eadric Cild stirring up trouble along the March, he is not about to begin a feud with me because he needs my support and my skills. Mercenaries like Everard de Nantes are ten a penny. I possess a higher value.'

'Modest!' Guyon snorted, but a glint of humour lit in his dark eyes.

'Never underestimate your opponent, and never underestimate yourself. Duke William taught me that lesson himself, and now he's a king.'

'By the skin of his teeth,' Guyon qualified, unimpressed. 'Keep your feet on the ground, lad.'

Miles shot him an irritated look, saw the smile curving beneath the full moustache, and softened his own expression. 'I have no choice; they are made of clay.'

'So just what are you going to do with this brother-by-marriage of yours?'

Miles rubbed the back of his neck. 'I was going to hang him, but I made a promise.'

Guyon raised his brows, and Miles told him exactly what he was going to do.

'Still busy?'

Christen looked up from her sewing to see Miles standing in front of her. She narrowed her eyes into the darkness behind him, but there was no sign of the tall oaf who had ridden in earlier. 'I have almost finished, my lord. And you?'

'Nearly. There are a couple of matters still to attend to, but I wanted to speak to you before you retired.'

His gaze went to the other women sitting nearby. Christen took the hint of his silent signal and gestured for them to take their work elsewhere.

Miles crouched with feline ease and watched her needle fly in and out of the fabric. 'I apologise if Guyon offended you,' he said. 'He is unaccustomed to the gentleness of women in our lives.'

Christen rested her needle and considered him. 'I was offended at first,' she admitted, 'but then I realised he was not to know I spoke some French, and eavesdroppers never hear well of themselves, do they?'

'That is true,' he said with a half smile.

Christen smoothed the blue cloth under her fingers. Women might judge the great ox worthless, but Miles le Gallois clearly valued him and she supposed every person had their function. 'It seems to me that you must have known him for a long time?'

'Since I was twelve and my father employed him to guard and train me at one and the same time. I owe a great debt to his perseverance. He struggled to tame me when everyone else had thrown up their hands in despair.' He grinned. 'He almost succeeded. *Cais ffrwn gref I farch gwylit*, as my mother would have said. Seek a strong bridle for a wild horse.'

'And he is your bridle?'

'I trust him with my life.'

Was that a warning, Christen wondered, or had she just imagined an edge to his voice? She did not think he quite trusted her. But then again, perhaps she did not quite trust him. She did not know him beyond the surface of a first acquaintance made in violent and desperate circumstances.

'I hope you and he can be friends,' he continued. 'It behoves me to have my wife and my marshal in harmony. Guyon may be rough around the edges, but he is honourable and true to his core. I want you to know that. He guards me with his life, and he will do the same for you.'

Christen took up her sewing again, and wondered if the last part of his statement was over-optimistic. 'I would not deliberately make him my enemy. It would not be in my own best interests to do so. I know how vulnerable I am and I will not make matters more difficult than they have to be.'

'Then I am glad, and thank you. I will not make matters more difficult either.'

She paused her needle a second time and gave him a direct look. 'One thing I will have is the full respect that is a wife's due,' she said. 'I had it from Lyulph and the men of his hall, and I will have it in this marriage from every man or woman who sits at the board in the hall.'

'On that we are agreed,' he said.

Christen resumed her sewing. He shifted position several times, but made no move to leave, and at length she was drawn to ask him if there was some other purpose to his visit.

He rubbed the back of his neck in a mannerism she was already coming to recognise. 'Well, yes, there is, and I have been wondering how to broach the matter so I suppose I had better say it straight out. As soon as we are married and the feast celebrated, I intend taking you to my own keep at Milnham-on-Wye.'

A jolt of shock flashed through her and she put down her work. 'Why?'

'This place is too vulnerable to attack at the moment. We need to raise the height of the palisade, build a gatehouse, and replace the gates with reinforced oak. Milnham is more secure and comfortable. You do not really wish to dwell here in a tent while the labourers toil around you and enemies threaten from every side? To spend your wedding night in a blanket on the ground?'

'If I said that was indeed my preference, would you give me the choice?'

He kept his hand at the back of his neck and looked away.

'I thought not,' she said. 'And again, I know I have no choice, but I tell you this. If you take me away, the people here will be less inclined to cooperate. They will be ready to believe the worst of you, and perhaps I would agree with them.'

'What you say is true, but it cannot be avoided. Milnham is not far and it would only be until the main defences are strengthened and the hall refurbished. I swear to you on my soul that you can return as soon as the work is complete.

'Besides,' Miles added with disarming candour, 'Milnham is in sore need of a mistress. The undercroft is foul and the kitchens and dairy would benefit from some strict overseeing by a capable wife. The place hasn't owned a chatelaine since my mother died four years ago – not an official one. My sister-by-marriage is visiting, but she arrived just as I set out to chase the raiders. My needs are entirely practical.'

Christen busied herself threading her needle, mollified despite her misgivings by his appeal to her domestic abilities. 'You said Milnham was more comfortable, but it sounds as if there is much work to do to make it thus.'

'It needs a woman's touch, I admit,' he said, 'and that woman as mistress of the household. But it will certainly be more comfortable than what is here at the moment.'

'And how will your sister-by-marriage react to you bringing home a wife?'

'Aude?' He looked briefly nonplussed and then shrugged. 'She will welcome you, I have no doubt, and give me short shrift for living on the wild side. She is my brother's wife and a practical woman. I think you will like each other.'

'Even though I am English and she is Norman?' Christen asked doubtfully.

'Aude has spent half her life living in battle camps and lodgings and has had dealings with people from Scotland to Outremer. You will find many things in common as women – including exasperation with the ways of men.'

His tone was rueful but Christen was not entirely appeased. She recognised his diplomacy for what it was. 'I have no doubt of that,' she said after a moment. 'As long as there is truth between us, I agree.'

'Truth?' he said. 'Is that your price?'

She said nothing, unable to ask how she would know if she was being paid in false coin. Before truth, there had to be trust.

He brushed her cheek with his fingertips, and she gave an involuntary shiver. 'I swear to you on the cross of Jesus that I will not lie. If I cannot tell you the truth, then I will say nothing.' He leaned towards her, but Christen recoiled as Guyon le Corbeis arrived and stood over them, taking the light from the lantern and quenching it with his shadow.

'Champing at the bit, eh?' he said with a grin, although his gaze was uneasy and the look he cast at Christen verged on the hostile.

She lowered her gaze, avoiding his piercing scrutiny.

Miles eyed Guyon with wry exasperation, and stood up. 'Not so much that I require your intervention for the sake of moral decency,' he said curtly. 'Still, you remind me that it is late and I have things to do.' He bowed to Christen. 'I should go,' he said, 'before the dawn catches me on my feet.'

'Indeed,' she said. 'And I have a wedding dress to finish by then.'

A short while later, Guyon le Corbeis returned. He had the great dog with him on its leash and Christen drew back warily.

'Paladin won't harm you,' he said. 'Soft as melted grease he is, unless you happen to be an enemy.'

'Paladin,' she repeated faintly, and had no desire to extend her hand to its slimy dewlaps.

'Shortened to "Pal",' Guyon said. 'I have had him since he was whelped.'

'He looks like a fine guard dog,' Christen offered in an effort to be sociable.

'He is. Nothing passes him.' Guyon cleared his throat. 'I should not have spoken as I did earlier within your hearing, and for that I am sorry, and my lord has rightly taken me to task. It will not happen again, I promise.'

At least not within her hearing, she thought, but did not say so. After all, she and this man were supposed to be allies and her safety might depend on his formidable strength. 'Thank you, sir,' she said. 'I think we both know where we stand.'

He nodded brusquely. 'Yes, we do,' he said, and walked off, the enormous dog panting and padding at his side.

Christen sighed pensively and resumed her sewing, wondering what she had set upon herself.

4

Christen's marriage to Miles le Gallois took place in the porch of Ashdyke's small village church so that everyone could witness the irrefutable binding of their lady to the Norman lord. There was much muttered speculation as the deed was pronounced and the groom kissed his wife briefly on the lips, before entering the church, his arm over hers, to attend the wedding mass, as the day before yesterday there had been a funeral one. At the side of the church, the mounds of fresh graves formed a sober backdrop, which some of the more pessimistic villagers viewed as a portent of things to come.

Although Christen's gown had been hastily stitched and awaited further embellishment, the iridescent blue-green enhanced her fair complexion and brown eyes, and accentuated her height. She found it impossible to raise a smile, but she held her head high and stepped proudly, not just for herself but for all the people watching, and she made her vows in a firm, steady voice. Miles produced a ring from his pouch, of plain gold and of a size more suited to a woman's finger than a man's, and as he slipped it over her knuckle she steeled herself to accept it, and with it the promise to obey him and be a good wife.

Her new husband wore his mail shirt and his sword, although the latter was tied in the scabbard by a peace knot. His own expression held pride and satisfaction, but no smugness, for which she was glad. For both of them the risks of this marriage might yet outweigh the advantages. His hand clasping hers was warm and dry; her own was clammy with tension.

'My brother,' she said to Miles as they emerged from the church. 'Will it please you to release him now?'

A groom led forward the piebald gelding on which she had ridden down to the church. The reins had been adorned with small tinkling bells, and some lengths of red ribbon, bought yesterday from Caelwin the cloth merchant, had been braided into its silky long mane. Christen was not a natural rider, but the horse was a placid beast and stood still as Miles boosted her into the saddle, before turning to his own more spirited grey.

'Soon,' he said. 'Once we have settled the debt he owes me for raiding my lands.'

Christen stared at the man to whom she had just sworn lifelong obedience. 'You said that you would show him mercy!'

'And so I did, by not hanging him, which he justly deserved,' Miles replied. 'Did you really expect me to set him free unscathed?'

Christen swallowed, filled with fear, all too aware of the danger. She was walking on eggshells and this man could do exactly as he chose. 'What will you do to him?' Perhaps he intended to release Osric only because what was left of him would be nothing but a bloody shadow. 'If you take me away from here and wreak your vengeance on my brother all in the same morning, you will court more trouble than any of this is worth.'

Guyon le Corbeis made a sound of contempt. Miles silenced his marshal with a raised palm and looked at Christen. 'Not vengeance, but justice,' he said. 'I give you my word that your brother and his companion will be perfectly capable of riding out through Ashdyke's gates and going on their way.'

Perversely, his reassurance only increased Christen's worry.

Christen bit her lip until the blood came and with it the pain that kept her upright, silent and unmoving, as her brother was roughly helped into the saddle of a stocky dun gelding and Hrothgar on to a star-faced bay. They had cut off three fingers from Osric's right hand and two from Hrothgar's. It was impossible to believe that it had happened, but the impassive-faced Norman at her side had commanded it, watched it carried out, and the moment the bleeding had been staunched had commanded the provisioned horses to be led forward.

Tears of shock and pity blurred Christen's eyes as her brother's mount made a sudden lunge and the thickly wadded remnants of his hand jarred against his thigh. 'You devil!' she choked at Miles.

'I'd have been within my rights to have his head for what he did,' Miles said curtly. 'Some of my men think I should have done just that. Be thankful that he still owns palm, finger and thumb to make the limb useful. What did you expect me to do – deal him a whipping as if he were a mischievous child caught thieving my orchard?'

'Osric is like a child!' she sobbed, knuckles pressed to her mouth to stifle her anguish.

'Then it is past time he became a man!' Miles retorted. 'Had he been a common raider, he would now be dead and his flayed corpse nailed to the nearest castle door for all to mark. He has his life, which is more than can be said for Milnham's potter who leaves his wife and four children without a provider. More than can be said for the people we buried yesterday, including your own husband. Save your pity and grief for them. He has escaped more lightly than his just deserts because of the boon you asked of me. Go to him if you will and bid farewell, and let it be an end.'

Christen compressed her lips, and having flung him a single dagger look, stalked from his side and over to Osric.

He was groaning softly to himself, his good hand gripping the reins, his other one nursed against his chest. Behind him, his companion Hrothgar waited, his teeth bared and his face grey with pain.

'I'll see that Norman whoreson in hell before the year's end, I swear it, Christen. If it's the last thing I do, I'll release you from this unholy farce of a marriage.'

'The attempting probably would be the last thing you did,' she hissed. 'Osric, as you value your life, never come back this way. You do not have his measure, but he most surely has yours, and everyone else's down to the last hair.'

Osric's hazel eyes narrowed. 'I almost believe you are glad to have married the whoreson,' he sneered.

'I must be glad of a strong hand to rule Ashdyke and protect it from raids,' she said. 'I will not see my home go up in flames again, and if marriage is the price, then I will pay it.'

'Do not be so sure!' Osric warned. The last word was lost in an agonised shriek as Hrothgar, as if by accident, sidled his mount against the dun and gave the beast a surreptitious kick in the belly that sent it skittering through the gateway.

'God go with you!' Christen cried after them.

'No place for us but hell, my lady – you are the one who

needs God,' Hrothgar replied, and with a curt salute he followed Osric down the track in the direction that led towards the Welsh border.

Christen watched them for the space of ten heartbeats then turned away, eyes dry, and rejoined her new husband.

'You will come to regret what you have done,' she said stiffly.

'I agree with you,' he said, 'but it was part of our marriage bargain that I let them live.'

He looked round and nodded to one of his men – a slender, dark-haired Welsh soldier dressed in a quilted jerkin and forest-coloured tunic and hose. The man nodded in return and went quietly towards the horse lines, picking up his bow and a sheaf of arrows as he went.

'That is not what I meant.'

'Yes, I know.' He turned to look at her. 'These are harsh and difficult times and I have to find a way through for all. Your brother should have been hanged, but I stayed my hand because of my vow to you. And that is as far as I am prepared to go.'

Christen swallowed. 'You have made your position very clear.'

He gave a curt nod. 'Then let us put it behind us and go on from here. It cannot be with a clean slate, but at least let us draw a line.' He offered her his arm, and after a moment she took it because she had no choice.

The wedding feast was a simple outdoor affair provided by the villagers and paid for in silver by Miles. Christen accepted his hand and sat down at the long trestle bench. The plain scrubbed wood had been covered by a length of Master Caelwin's linen cloth. Father Aelnoth blessed the food and a couple of village women filled wooden drinking bowls with the local ale and cider.

'Thank God the weather has remained bright,' Miles said.

'They have gone to much trouble and it would have been a pity if rain had spoiled their efforts.'

Christen sipped cider from her bowl and watched him from the corner of her eye. There was enough food to fill bellies, but it was plain fare, lacking the embellishment one might expect of somewhere so close to Hereford and the busy trade route of the river Wye. Mutton pottage and coarse bread.

He looked amused. 'Do they think too great a show of largesse will cause me to run amok with greed and double their rents and obligations?'

'Perhaps they have no reason to think otherwise,' she replied, thinking that he saw everything, and through it. 'Perhaps they think if they make any display of wealth, you will take it all from them by force.'

'Time will tell, won't it?' he said flatly. He looked at her over the rim of his bowl. 'Are you still angry with me over your brother?'

'Would it matter to you if I was?'

He ignored her counter-question. 'Are you?'

'A little perhaps, but he has polished the art of driving away even those who would have at one time succoured him. I am relieved that he has gone.' Relieved because she did not want him to forfeit any more than fingers on his right hand in payment to this man. She held out her own hand and regarded her new wedding ring. 'It was fortunate that you had this with you,' she said.

He put his bowl down. 'It was my mother's,' he said, 'and since I am her only son – her only child in fact – it came to me as part of her effects. The gold is Welsh and rare.' He smiled at her and the light enhanced the blue flecks amid the sea-green of his eyes. 'It looks like a plain gold ring, but it is not.'

'What was your mother's name?' she asked, made curious by this revelation and the softer note in his voice.

'Heulwen,' he said. 'It means "Sunshine". My father married her in order to seal peace with his Welsh neighbours when he arrived to serve King Edward in these border lands.' He gave her a sideways look. 'It was a match of convenience to solve a problem, and so it did. I hope in turn to build on that tradition.'

Christen felt her cheeks grow warm. 'Then I must hope for that too,' she said, 'because it would be foolish to do anything else.'

'I am glad we agree on that.'

'Was your mother happy?'

'She made the best of what she had. My father . . . was my father.' He gave her a rueful look. 'He was most at home on the battlefield, but the lands here were well run and they prospered. I learned a lot from him – what I would be, and what I would not.'

He lifted his bowl to drink but set it down again as Guyon came striding from the direction of the gates where he had been keeping watch.

'FitzOsbern,' he said tersely as he reached the table. 'My eyesight is not as good as it was, but I would say he has your brother-by-marriage and his henchman in his custody.'

'God's balls!' Miles stood up. 'I did not think he would be so quick.'

'Well, he's here, so you had better think of something fast,' Guyon said.

Miles swore again and grimaced in the direction of the gate. *Never underestimate your opponent.*

'My lord?' Christen stared up at him, her face drained of colour.

Miles set his hand gently on her shoulder. *Never underestimate yourself.* 'It seems that the Earl of Hereford himself is about to honour our wedding feast. The King's own cousin and senior wolf in the pack. Take your lead from me. Do as I say, and we may yet come unscathed from this. No,' he added as she started to rise, 'stay where you are and say nothing unless spoken to – whatever happens, whatever is said. Our lives may depend on it – understood?'

She nodded and began to shiver, feeling as if a chill wind was blowing through her bones.

William FitzOsbern, Earl of Hereford, Earl Palatine, lord of the Isle of Wight, of Breteuil and Paci, rode through the gateway into the compound, his gaze flicking to the left and right to absorb and memorise everything. With unthinking ease, he reined his strong roan stallion to a halt and turned in the saddle to speak to his nearest companion. When the horse jibbed, he drew the bridle taut through fists the size of hams until the roan's muzzle was forced down, emphasising its sweating, arched neck.

'My lord, it is a great honour to welcome you to my marriage feast,' Miles said, sweeping a bow. 'The fare is by necessity frugal, but will you share?'

FitzOsbern grunted. 'I doubt that welcome is the word since you sent me no invitation,' he said, and dismounted, throwing the reins to his squire.

'There was no time, sire, and besides, I knew you would receive the tidings of my acquisition almost immediately.'

The Earl looked round at his men, Odo FitzWilliam scowling in their midst. 'Oh yes,' he said neutrally. 'I had the tale from my mercenaries by Tuesday dawn. Indeed, were it not for the doings of Eadric Cild, I would have been here a day sooner.' He removed his helm and arming cap to reveal a thatch of crinkly grey-speckled hair, slightly receding from his temples, and regarded Miles with hard, shrewd eyes. 'I was told that Eadric Cild might not be the only rebel with whom I had to deal.'

'Sire, Ashdyke was held by the old lord directly of the King,' Guyon spoke out. Leashed at his side, Paladin bared his fangs in a warning growl. 'This business is not your concern.'

Miles threw a warning look at his marshal, but even as he prepared to pour diplomatic oil on the statement, FitzOsbern burst out laughing.

'Hah, I did not realise le Corbeis still held himself responsible for wiping your backside!'

Guyon opened his mouth. Miles elbowed him in the ribs and sent him to find accommodation and refreshment for the extra men.

'My pardon, sire. You know my marshal's failings and I hope you will excuse them.'

'He is without diplomacy,' FitzOsbern chuckled. 'But he is a fine soldier, I grant you. You have a formidable guard dog there – indeed two of them!'

He unfastened his cloak and gave it to his squire. The movement caused him to notice and be recalled to the two rebels they had picked up on the road and brought into Ashdyke. FitzWilliam had dragged them off their mounts, hands tied, and thrown them down in the dirt near one of the cooking fires.

'Indeed, le Corbeis is as straight as an ash lance,' FitzOsbern continued, 'but you, Miles, are of a more devious nature. I could ask your giant, but I doubt the reply would be half as entertaining as your own. FitzWilliam swears that these two were part of the rebel group I sent him to hunt down, yet I find them free upon the road, astride good horseflesh with food in their packs and swearing that you had released them to go their own way with no harsher punishment than the odd missing finger.' He rubbed his grizzled chin. 'Would you care to add to the tale?'

'The one with the mouth happens to be my wife's brother.'

'Ah.' FitzOsbern nodded. 'You disappoint me, Miles. What do a woman's wishes and sentiments matter?'

Miles thought it a wonder that FitzOsbern's wife had not salted her husband's dinner with monkshood before now. 'I am killing two birds with one stone, sire,' he said. 'By sparing the life of my wife's brother, I foster good relations with these people, which has to be of benefit. But the main profit is that her brother will almost certainly make tracks to Eadric's lair, and whatever makes a track, either myself or my man Dewi can follow – as well you know. You would not have noticed Dewi when you took those two prisoner, but he is out there.'

FitzOsbern grunted and swatted at a fly. The reply was not particularly entertaining, but bore the ring of well-reasoned truth. Whether it was truth in fact was a matter on which he reserved judgement. 'You know this land is forfeit to the King.'

'Indeed, sire, and that is why I have sent a messenger to him with a copy of the marriage contract and begged his leave to establish myself here.'

'You warn me that the place is already claimed?' FitzOsbern narrowed his eyes.

Miles returned the look steadily. 'I would not presume, sire. I do not wield the power to contest your will.'

'No, but you have the gall to snatch the place from beneath my nose!' FitzOsbern's expression was half infuriated, half amused.

'It might yet have been in your hands, sire, had not your hirelings shown such a wanton desire for destruction. It was that which prompted me to meddle. It was the action of imbeciles. Now everything will have to be rebuilt, and where is the profit in that?'

FitzOsbern pursed his lips and gave a judicious nod. 'You are right,' he said. 'It was mishandled.' He turned to Odo FitzWilliam and gestured at Osric and Hrothgar. 'Return their horses and let them go.'

'But, sire, they are proven felons and rebels!' Odo spluttered, his face reddening with righteous anger.

'And as le Gallois says, they can be followed to their master's lair. Let them go – do it now. That's a command, not a point of discussion.'

Glowering, FitzWilliam stumped off to perform the unwelcome task of bundling Osric and Hrothgar back on to their horses and escorting them out of the gates. He made sure, however, to be rough in his handling, and Osric cried out as his damaged hand received a kick.

Miles gestured at the trestle where Christen sat in demure silence, eyes lowered. 'Will you join our wedding feast? The cider is good, and so is the cheese.'

The Earl inclined his head and accompanied Miles, who made a peremptory gesture to Christen. She rose and made a deep curtsey to FitzOsbern, and bent her head.

The Earl raised her to her feet and, pinching her chin between forefinger and thumb, lifted her face to examine her as though studying a horse for sale. 'Plain and meek,' he said, cocking a speculative eyebrow at Miles. 'No meat on her, but at least her hips are wide enough for breeding.'

Miles shrugged. 'She has borne one child dead at birth and miscarried another, but I do not foresee any difficulty. Her husband was elderly and crippled. Poor seed rather than poor soil.'

'And if she belies your word and is already in whelp to the dead man?'

'Her maid says they have not lain together in over a year and she finished her flux on the day before we arrived. Any child that comes from her body nine months from now will be of my siring.'

'That red-haired firebrand you had with you back in Rouen – now she had a body worth dipping your bread!' FitzOsbern's man-to-man grin was expressive. 'I do not suppose she is still with you?'

Miles had seen Christen's revulsion at FitzOsbern's touch, and had watched her colour fade until she was as pale as a sheet, but now it returned in a wash of deep pink that stained her forehead, cheeks and throat. He gave her a nudge with his hip that threw her off balance and commanded her brusquely to fetch a fresh flagon of cider for their guest.

She made a strangled sound in her throat but went to do his bidding, walking gracefully, her head carried high. Miles watched her recover herself, and was filled with both admiration and foreboding, especially when he saw the look she cast at the girl Wulfhild, the source of his information.

'Felice died in childbed on the eve of Hastings,' he replied to FitzOsbern. 'I have no mistress currently warming my bed to keep me from my duty.'

The Earl grunted. 'Duty indeed,' he said, and with a dismissive glance at Christen, sat down at the trestle and waited to be served.

Tight-lipped, Christen waited upon the men who treated her as if she was of no more consequence than the board at which they sat. Several times Miles sent her away on some trivial pretext and she overheard him saying to FitzOsbern that it was unwise to let her hear too much since she understood a reasonable degree of French.

'God's bones, lady, mind your face before the Earl of Hereford lest you ruin us all with your black looks!' Guyon le Corbeis warned her as she shot a fulminating glance at William

FitzOsbern while fetching yet another jug of cider for Miles and his guest.

'I am a bitch, a brood mare, a ewe to be tupped!' she said through clenched teeth. 'I would rather crack this jug over both their heads than smile them fair.'

'You should open your eyes, and then you might see,' Guyon growled. 'He is playing for our lives and you had best pray that he wins. He did warn you.'

Casting another glare at the men, she watched her new husband laugh at something the Earl had said, shoulders shaking, mouth open. And then he looked in her direction and met her gaze, and for an instant she caught the spark of desperation before he looked away, lifted his bowl and drank.

FitzOsbern eventually departed with Odo FitzWilliam grumbling at his heels and receiving short shrift for his complaints while Miles received a hearty clap on the shoulders and salacious wishes for his wedding night.

Miles watched until the hindquarters of the last horse had disappeared down the track, his stance rigid. And then he strode away from Guyon and Christen to the midden pit where he was violently sick.

Guyon raised a knowing eyebrow and went to see to the men and to arrange the guard duty.

Miles returned, his step unsteady and his complexion green. 'I am not accustomed to matching the Earl of Hereford drink for drink,' he explained to Christen. 'He is so much bigger than I am that whatever goes down his gullet only has half the effect.'

He reached out to her, but Christen stepped back, her lip curling with disgust.

Miles sighed and rumpled his hair. 'I do not have the military strength to defy the Earl of Hereford,' he said wearily. 'I have to persuade him it is to his advantage to let me keep Ashdyke, and that means paying lip service if nothing else to his code. The cider was not the only reason for my curdled stomach.'

'Then I pity your weakness, my lord. My first husband might have been injured and no longer able to defend his holding, but he had twice your strength and he was a dozen times more honourable.'

'I daresay he was, and now he is dead.'

'And my life with him reduced to an accounting of fluxes and couplings by men not fit to speak his name!'

'If there had been another way, I would have taken it,' he said with determined patience, brittle at the edges. 'Women in FitzOsbern's household rank below the status of his hounds and horses. He would have thought me a soft fool had I behaved any differently.'

'And in your own household? How do women rank there?' She thought of the Rouen whore FitzOsbern had mentioned with such offhand amusement. A red-haired firebrand, he had said.

'They are respected on their merits. If you wish to be a martyr that is your privilege, but I had credited you with more sense.'

Christen clenched her teeth. If she did not run with the invading wolf pack then she became its victim. 'I am unaccustomed to being insulted, even for the sake of keeping a roof over my head,' she said. 'Lyulph would never have said such words to a woman for whatever reason.' She was close to breaking. The storm was almost upon her and she was fending it off by lashing out.

A muscle twitched in his cheek. 'As I recall, his death did not prevent FitzOsbern's mercenaries and your zealot brother from almost razing this place to the ground and murdering half the people inside. Without my intervention you and your people would now be either dead or enslaved. How does that weigh in the scales against a dozen times more honour?'

She saw the leashed anger within him, barely contained, and made a final effort to draw back from the brink. 'Was it worth it?' she asked, in a quieter but still bitter voice. 'Was FitzOsbern convinced by your deception?'

He shrugged. 'He was convinced enough to do nothing for the moment. He even brought himself to declare me a more suitable candidate to rule Ashdyke than someone like Odo FitzWilliam. FitzOsbern has me marked down as a useful but expendable tool. He is content with my tenure because I will have the work and expense of rebuilding this place and keeping the rebels at bay. He may well try to claim Ashdyke for himself at a later date if it suits his plans.' He gave her a humourless smile. 'I dislike gambling with loaded dice but I lack the will to say no to the lure of the prize.'

'Then you are a fool, because death is the outcome,' Christen said.

'Well then, you will be rid of me soon enough.'

'And all this will have been for nothing.'

'I would not say that. Your brother has gone to join his friends across the border and has his life and his freedom. If I die, you can join him in Wales and enter the Church – although I shall do my utmost to remain alive and make the most of the time that God gives me on this earth.'

She looked at him. 'It is about survival,' she said.

'Yes, which is what I said earlier in so many words. Go and make yourself ready and I will see to the horses and baggage. We should be leaving for Milnham soon if we are to reach it before full dark.'

He reached for her again and this time she let him take her

hand and gently squeeze it before he released her and walked over to the horse lines.

Rubbing her hand, still feeling the sensation of his touch, Christen found Wulfhild busily making a final check on the meagre baggage they were taking to Milnham, including the recently purchased textiles. The maid's cheeks were fire-red with chagrin.

'My lady, I—'

'I thought I could trust you,' Christen said, 'and now I find that you have told the Normans the personal things about my life with Lyulph. How could you?'

Wulfhild's eyes filled with tears. 'My lady, I did not wish to cause you grief, I swear it. Leofwin seemed so kind and interested and wanted to know about all of us, not just you. I should not have spoken, I know that now, but at the time I did not think.'

Christen looked at the maid with exasperation. Wulfhild was younger than her by a couple of years and until his death at Stamford, her father had been the keeper of Lyulph's stables. Lyulph had thought she would make a good maid for the hall and bower. She was cheerful, warm-hearted, swift and efficient. She was also an excellent seamstress. However, she took too many situations and people at her own honest face-value.

'No matter,' Christen responded wearily. 'Done is done. If not from you then my lord Miles would have gained his information elsewhere.'

'My lips are stitched together from now on, I promise,' Wulfhild declared with guilty fervour.

'There is no need for that,' Christen answered with a pained smile, 'just be careful and measure your words before you speak.'

'I swear I shall, my lady,' Wulfhild said, and then asked in a slightly downcast voice: 'Does that mean I should not talk to Leofwin any more?'

Christen shook her head at the girl. ‘Talk to him if you will,’ she said, ‘but not of me.’

Wulfhild’s eyes filled with relief. ‘Thank you, my lady, I promise,’ she said, and tackled her work with fresh enthusiasm.

Watching her, Christen wished that everything could be so easily fixed.

5

Castle of Milnham-on-Wye

Dusk was falling by the time Miles and Christen arrived at the settlement of Milnham. The sky was tinted amber and pale green in the west and pinned by the brooch of a rising white sickle moon. Christen saw no one in the village clustered around the base of the keep, but was aware of being watched from doors cracked open the merest sliver.

'It is market day tomorrow,' Miles remarked with a knowing nod as a door hinge creaked to their left. 'The stalls will be busy with folk thirsting for knowledge, never mind provisions.'

Christen murmured a vague response and tried to relax her grip on the reins as her mount sidled, sensing her tension. She was an indifferent horsewoman at the best of times, and this was not one of them. They had set out in the middle of the afternoon and the muscles of her inner thighs were strained and aching. She had a vile headache because her spine was improperly aligned to her mare's gait. Her throat was dust-parched and she was so saddle-sore that she viewed her coming wedding night with dread.

A familiar taint filled her nose as they passed the gutted barn and the acrid remnants of the two dwellings that had stood beside it. Miles said nothing but she saw his mouth tighten.

Leaving the village, they climbed the slope to the timber keep standing above the village on Milnham Hill and behind a high palisade. Miles rode to the front of the column and shouted an order and the guards on duty hastened to open the heavy timber gates, allowing the troop to ride over the bridge across the water-filled ditch and into the bailey. The fortress on top of the mound was pricked out with haphazard glints of torchlight.

A watch fire burned in a brazier near the gate and soldiers kindled torches from this to light the area. Grooms and stable boys arrived to take the horses away to the stable block. Miles helped Christen to dismount from her piebald cob and set her on her feet. She staggered, and he braced his weight to support her. She felt the hard, cold rivets of his mail shirt, the tensile strength of the man, and steadying herself drew back.

'It has been a long journey for you,' he said.

She shook out her gown. 'Yes,' she agreed. 'I am not accustomed to riding for such stretches at a time, and usually I would travel in a cart – but needs must.'

'You have done well.' He gestured to the timber keep crowning the flattened top of the slope, accessed across another ditch by a hinged walkway that could be drawn up in times of siege, and then a set of steep wooden steps. 'Only one last part to accomplish.'

Christen raised her chin and steeled herself to endure. At some point, beyond all this she would eventually arrive at the welcome oblivion of sleep. 'It would greatly aid my comfort if I could bathe, if you have a tub,' she said as they began the climb to the top of the mound. She waited for the guffaw of disbelief, for the baffled query as to why she should want to wash the goodness from her body or dilute her essence. She had become accustomed to the sidelong looks and raised eyebrows at Ashdyke, although eventually folk had accepted that it was one of her peculiarities.

'Of course,' he said, his tone matter-of-fact. 'Indeed, they should be preparing one, but I did not think that you . . .' He looked over his shoulder and issued a command to one of his men, who squeezed past them on the steps and ran ahead towards the keep. 'It has long been one of my vices,' he admitted. 'I badly wrenched my knee a few years ago and regular bathing greatly eased the pain. Since then it has become a habit of mine – and a pleasure. Guyon says I am mad, but I can live with his opinion and without the lice.'

Christen was gasping by the time they reached the top of the steps, and so hungry that she felt sick. Another stout palisade and a gateway surrounded the keep, and entering within, she pressed her hand to her side, gazing at the open iron-bound door and the middle-aged man limping out to greet them and usher them up the final set of outer stairs to the hall on the floor above.

'Edward, my constable,' Miles introduced him. 'Edward, this is Lady Christen of Ashdyke – my wife as of this morning.'

The man's eyes widened in surprise, but he swiftly recovered his aplomb and bowed in welcome. He wore his fair hair long in the English manner and he had a long beard and full moustaches. A constable Miles had called him, but he wore the leather jerkin of a soldier and the seax on his belt was no toy. 'Then may I offer felicitations at this unexpected joyful news,' he said with diplomacy. 'I had not realised when you rode out, sire, that you were on your way to be married.'

'Neither did I,' Miles replied with a wry grin. 'I will tell you what is needful in a while, but first things first.'

Christen followed Miles's constable up the steps and into the main hall. The room stretched away before her gaze, wreathed in gauzy layers of smoke. At the far end on the dais stood the lord's great oak chair and above it, on the wall, a triangular golden banner embroidered with the device of a snarling black wolf. In the middle of the hall, a serving girl was tending a cauldron over the hearth. An older woman stood gossiping at her side, but at the sight of Miles and Christen she ceased to slouch and murmured something from the side of her mouth. The girl looked up from stirring the contents of the pot and replied with some kind of admonition, for the woman shrugged and walked away, looking disgruntled.

Christen's lips tightened. Room for improvement there, she thought. She noted that the rushes underfoot were heavy and soft with age and gave off a rank smell that told her they should have been changed some time ago. In a keep full of men, she doubted anyone had paid much attention to such domestic matters. Doubtless they were out on patrols and away from the place half the time. The limewash on the walls was flaking and soot-stained, and the only hangings in the room were war-banners and shields.

'If it please you, my lady, the bath is ready.'

Christen turned to face a timid woman wearing a drab gown. Wispy strands of hair were escaping from her grey linen wimple which had once been white.

'My wife, Mildrith,' Edward said, giving the woman an irritated look.

'Go and make yourself comfortable,' Miles said to Christen. 'I have matters to discuss with Edward before I am free.'

She gave him a long look, but inclined her head and followed the trembling Mildrith towards the stairs.

Edward stroked his beard. 'If you will permit me to say so, it is long past time that Milnham had a new mistress.'

Miles watched until Christen was gone from sight. 'Rather the mistress,' he said softly, 'is going to be the owner of Milnham.'

The tub in the bedchamber gave off a fragrant, herbal steam. Someone had added rose oil and a handful of sweetbriar to the water. Christen dismissed Mildrith with the assurance that she and Wulfhild could manage, and asked her to bring food, for the ride had left her not only sore but ravenous. The woman scuttled away in obvious relief and Christen shook her head in disappointment. No stalwart ally here to uphold her purge of this place when it commenced. Indeed, having encountered the constable's wife, she could understand why Milnham's domestic arrangements were so neglected.

She removed her wimple and cloak and gave them to Wulfhild. The girl went to fold them over a dusty clothing pole then returned to help Christen out of her chemise and hose and pin up Christen's hair to stop it from getting wet. Christen stepped into the tub, which was a cut-down barrel caulked and lined with linen. She closed her eyes as the water lapped around her like an embrace. It was a little too hot, but it was bearable, and it did not matter for it served to cleanse and sluice away some of what had happened in the last few days – at least superficially.

Christen had left the bath and Wulfhild had just helped her don one of her new chemises when the curtain swished and a tall, angular woman entered the room bearing a tray holding a loaf of bread, a hunk of cheese and a jug of wine. Christen stared at the newcomer in amazement, for her gown was laced at the sides to show her body, emphasising breasts, waist and hips, before flaring out into full skirts. Her hair was dressed in two thick bronze-brown braids that fell to her waist, although covered at the top of her head by a light linen veil. Daring, but not indecent. Her face was pleasant and ordinary with strong bones and wide grey eyes.

'I beg pardon for intruding,' she said, 'but Mildrith was voiding her bowels with terror and in no state to attend on you.' She set down the tray on a chest by the window embrasure. 'I should have been in the hall to greet your arrival, but I spilled half a bucket of water down myself while readying Miles's tub and I had to change.' Coming over to Christen, she gave her a swift embrace and kissed her cheek. 'I am Aude FitzRenard, Miles's sister-by-marriage. Welcome to the family.'

'Miles did make mention of you,' Christen said, and taking a comb from Wulfhild began to tidy the tangles from her hair and smooth it down. 'But I did not expect . . . well, your gown . . . Forgive me, but is that the fashion for Norman ladies?'

Aude glanced down and plucked at a heavy fold of her skirt. 'Not all Norman ladies,' she said, 'but it is the style of the court and many wear it thus.'

Christen raised her brows. 'My lord has given me some good dark-red cloth to make a gown in the Norman style – but I am accustomed to looser garments, not laced at the sides and pulled to the body.'

Aude smiled, revealing a gap between her two front teeth. 'I can certainly help you make one like mine!' Her eyes sparkled with enthusiasm and she gave Christen a considering look. 'Red will suit you, I think. Miles notices such things and that is unusual in a man. My Gerard would not see the difference were I to enter his presence robed in sack cloth!'

'Lyulph was the same.' Christen caught her breath, suddenly torn by the vision of her first husband going down beneath a Norman blade, and the hunger in her belly turned to nausea.

Aude, affecting not to notice, went to pour Christen a cup of wine. 'I am staying with Miles while Gerard is with the King in the south. We have no lands of our own save a few acres outside Rouen.' Her voice was matter-of-fact. 'When you are the youngest of six sons, pickings are slim when it comes to inheritance.'

Christen was puzzled. 'Then Miles is older than your husband?'

'No, younger by seven years,' Aude said. 'He is the only child of Renard's second marriage, and inherits the lands of that marriage. Miles's mother was Welsh – Heulwen uerch Owain.'

'Yes, he mentioned her to me,' Christen said.

Aude wrinkled her nose. 'It was a match to protect the lands and they did not dwell in domestic harmony. Welsh women live by different laws. She would rather spit in Renard's face than submit to his will, and eventually he took Miles away from her and sent him to be raised in Normandy with the rest of us, away from her influence. When our father died, Miles came straight to England and paid homage to King Edward for Milnham, and was reunited with his mother. Lady Heulwen was mistress here until a fever took her the year before the great battle, God rest her soul, even though I never knew her. By all accounts she was a formidable lady – she would have to be to stand up to Miles's sire.'

Christen made the sign of the cross as a mark of respect, and wondered if Aude's words about a marriage of convenience with no love lost was a portent of her own fate. She had asked Miles if his mother had been happy and he had evaded the question, with good reason it seemed.

Her parents would turn in their graves if they could see her now. Her grandfather in Staffordshire too, although perhaps he still lived. She had heard no word from him since her mother died, and the wind from Hastings had blown cold over so many graves since then. He had disapproved of the King taking over the wardship and matching her with Lyulph and had cut the ties. He would have been too old to go to Stamford and Hastings, although he might have sent men from the estate north and south to fight.

The curtain across the door hissed on its rings and Miles entered the chamber. His hair was a mass of tight, damp curls. Without the padding of his quilted tunic and mail shirt, he was lithe and graceful, like a prowling cat. He raised a dark eyebrow in greeting to Aude, and then let his gaze travel slowly over Christen.

Aude kissed his cheek and saw to the emptying and removal of the bath tub by two attendants. Bidding Miles and Christen a tactful goodnight, she withdrew. Christen sent Wulfhild out with her.

'Are you still angry with the girl?' he asked as the curtain fell. 'It was not her fault; Leofwin can charm the birds down from the trees if he so chooses.'

'Wulfhild is not without skill in that area herself,' Christen replied. 'What if it had been the other way round and Leofwin had revealed all the skeletons jangling in your own stable?'

He shrugged. 'There are too few bones to rattle. My past is no secret. You know my parentage and upbringing. What else is there to tell?'

'What of women?' she asked. 'I do not believe you have lived like a monk until now.'

'It is true they have drifted in and out of my life, some more than others, but without permanent arrangement. Surely they cannot matter now?' He traced her jaw with his index finger. 'You are my wife and you shall have all due respect in the household. Whatever you wish to know, ask and I shall tell you. And if by chance I cannot tell you, then I will not lie.' He touched her hair with light, reverent fingers. 'It is beautiful,' he said. 'Like ripe barley in the breeze.'

There was an echo in his words of something Lyulph had said on their wedding night, his gruff voice tender with compassion, and she shivering with fear and shock, a girl barely old enough to bleed. The wheel had turned full circle, only now it was not Lyulph but a wiry, dark-haired man with hungry eyes. Suddenly she was unable to prevent the shudders of reaction that tore through her body. A breath indrawn became a sob, and then another sob. Her control broke and she spun from his grasp and huddled weeping in a corner, shedding the first true tears since the ordeal of the attack and Lyulph's violent death in front of her eyes.

Miles stared at her in consternation, and then crossed the room to where she was curled in upon herself like a wounded animal. 'Come,' he said, crouching to her. 'I swear on my soul that I will do you no harm.'

She shook her head and choked, but the sobs kept coming, welling like blood from a deep wound. Somewhere there had to be an end to reason. She had thought to deal with this man in his own practical coin, and had discovered too late that it was impossible. 'Lyulph!' she sobbed. 'I am weeping for Lyulph and all that is lost!' She thrust away the hand he held out to her.

Miles frowned. Lyulph was an old man, they had said, old enough to be her grandfather, and lame from a battle wound. Perhaps her affections had been fixed when she was still very young. Perhaps she preferred older men. Perhaps, Miles, you are a fool.

'Lyulph is dead,' he said more harshly than he had intended.

'Tears will not bring him back to you; you must make the best of what you have.'

'It is your fault!' she accused, gulping. 'You said a similar thing to what he said about my hair on our wedding night and I . . . I cannot bear it.' She swallowed. 'I know my duty,' she added in a breaking voice.

'Yes,' Miles said flatly, 'I daresay you do. Go to bed. I'll return in a little while when I have spoken to the sentries.'

Christen bent her head and closed her eyes until he was gone and did not see his bleak expression. As the curtain dropped behind him, she was only aware of feeling sick and weary to death and full of the pain of grief. It had been that remark about her hair. Until then she had thought she could cope. Covering her face with her hands, she let the storm have its way, and sobbed out all the rage and tension and heartbreak.

Eventually, when the worst had passed, she crawled over to the bed and slipped between the sheets, feeling wrung out, exhausted, but much clearer in her mind. She used the corner of a sheet to wipe her eyes. The linen smelled musty, as if it had lain a long time in a chest, but it had been strewn with aromatic herbs. She recognised speedwell and amaranth to promote fertility, and wondered who had been responsible for their prickly blessing. A man needed heirs. Christen knew it was her marital duty to receive her husband, and she desired greatly to quicken with a child. She still felt the loss of her own babies keenly and had only to see another woman suckling her offspring to feel the pain in her own breasts. She might not be overjoyed at the notion of lying with her new husband, but she would do so as part of her marital obligation, and pray that she conceived swiftly, because once she was with child he would have no cause to lie with her.

The herbs were scratchy to lie on and she left the bed and

swept the sheet clean with her palm. The action further calmed her down and brought her back to practicality. When the sheet was clear, she climbed back into bed and pulled the covers around her body. She wanted Lyulph and the luxury of hiding behind his comforting bulk, but Lyulph was dead and she had to stand on her own feet. She thought of the golden banner in the hall above the lord's chair. A wolf's mate did not snivel; a wolf's mate snarled.

When Miles returned, he thought at first that Christen was asleep for she had snuffed the candle, and the only light came from the lamp he held in his hand, but when he extinguished the flame and slipped into bed beside her, he felt her turn her head on the pillow. It was dark, he could not see her face, but he sensed her surprise. He could smell the mustiness of the bedclothes, and over that the scent of her body, faintly perfumed with the rose water and herbs from the bath.

'I did not think you would return.' Her voice was thin but steady.

'Why should I not?' he asked. 'I meant what I said about dealing with the sentries, although I did give you a little more time alone.'

He touched her bare arm. She shuddered at the contact but did not draw away and so he brushed her face with his fingertips and found that her cheeks were dry. Clearly she had mastered her grief, but its effect still lingered. Miles found himself imagining that there were three of them in the chamber, that somewhere beyond his shoulder Lyulph's shade hovered and watched in outrage as the Norman who had claimed his home and his lands now set about claiming his wife too.

She was passive, neither welcoming his touch nor, after that first involuntary recoil, flinching from him, and he might as well have been bedding a lump of warm clay for all the response he received, while beyond him Lyulph of Ashdyke bore witness with dead, accusing eyes. There was a moment when Miles thought he might be unable to continue, but recent abstinence, his healthy young body and pure instinct brought him to his crisis and he gasped above her, surged hard, and was lost in a blinding moment of pure release when everything went away but the pleasure. However, when he returned to reality, he was aware of a hunger that had not been appeased and that the ghost of Lyulph continued to watch and disapprove.

She gasped as he withdrew from her body and he felt her tense.

'Did I hurt you?' he asked, stroking her hair. He wanted to see it again in all its silver-gold beauty, but knew that kindling a light would probably not be wise for either of them. There was so much he wanted to say, but he did not know where to start.

'A little,' she said. 'I am not used to sitting on a horse for hours on end, and Lyulph wasn't . . .' She broke off.

'Wasn't what?'

'As . . . as vigorous.'

Miles turned his head on the pillow. The scent of lavender came to him faintly from its stuffing. Being vigorous would be taken by many men as a compliment and proof of prowess, but he was not ignorant. 'I was too eager in the moment,' he said. 'Next time will be different.'

He put his hand on her arm and extended his thumb to lightly brush the side of her breast where the roundness curved into her ribs. She gave a small jump and her nipple stiffened.

'Do not fear, I will not trouble you again tonight. It has been difficult for both of us . . . Go to sleep.'

'My lord, I—'

'Go to sleep,' he reiterated. 'We will talk in the morning.'

She fell silent and turned her back. Her breathing was soft, but he heard the catch in it as she strove to control her sobs. Miles stared into the darkness and wondered what he had set upon himself, and wondered why it mattered when the land was the most important part of this marriage, as it had been with his own father and his reluctant Welsh bride.

6

Between spinning wool from distaff to spindle, Christen watched the women as they finished sweeping out the old floor rushes and their accumulation of detritus into a corner of the hall ready to be carted away to the midden pit. Now fresh rushes could be strewn in a thick layer and sprinkled with aromatic herbs to ward off vermin.

Servants were slapping limewash on the walls from a bath tub full of the white mixture and a carpenter was repairing and replacing the trestle tables. The constable's wife Mildrith twittered around like a sparrow with two heads, getting underfoot and being more of a hindrance than an asset. Aude was brisk and efficient. She was also more sensitive to atmospheres than the preoccupied Christen.

'Do not work them too hard,' she advised, pausing beside Christen to observe the toil. 'You will lose their willingness if you drive them.'

Christen blinked. Was that the impression she had given with her demands for this freshening? She had thrown herself into the work as an escape from thinking on other matters and her enthusiasm was clearly not mirrored by the servants who had to labour at her behest. 'You are right,' she said. 'It is time to make an end. The hall must be made ready for dinner. We'll finish tomorrow.'

Aude went to give the women instructions and Christen turned towards the chamber stairs. She and Miles had broken their fast at barely dawn and he had ridden out to patrol his domain. The lands were under constant threat from warbands both English and Welsh. She also suspected he was avoiding her. Since their arrival three days ago, they had lived on a knife edge of cool courtesy, and the tension between them was a taut thread.

A little girl in headlong flight hurtled into her, rebounded and sprawled her length upon the rushes. As she began to howl, Christen set aside her spinning and hastened to pick her up. About three years old, she guessed, with two dishevelled plaits of copper-red hair. Freckles of the same hue peppered her little nose. She sobbed, clutching a grazed elbow, and all Christen's thwarted maternal instincts flooded over their flimsy barrier. Drawing the child deeper into her arms, she soothed and cuddled her. 'Hush now, hush now, no tears, my sweeting.'

Aude returned from instructing the women and stopped abruptly, her expression wary. Mildrith wrung her hands, her tension palpable.

'What is your name?' Christen asked the mite in English, and when she looked at her blankly, repeated the question in French.

'Emma.'

The child sniffed and looked directly at Christen, who stifled a gasp. The green-blue eyes, the shape of her brows, her entire expression bore testimony to the direction of her siring.

Aude started forward but was shoved aside by the barging hip of the woman who had looked across the hearth at Christen with insolent challenge when she had first arrived at Milnham.

'Emma, come here, my sweet,' she commanded.

The child turned in Christen's arms, looked at the woman's outstretched hand and went reluctantly to her.

Christen stared at Emma's caretaker, at the sagging jawline and a rope of hair like rusty steel falling lankly over one shoulder and breast. The resemblance between her and the child was slight, mainly in the colouring, but still tangible. Dear God, was this a mistress? Surely not, and yet her air of defiance suggested she had an elevated position in the household, and she had certainly been scarce while the work was going forward.

'You should keep a closer eye on the child,' Christen said frostily. 'What if she had fallen into the fire?'

'Yes, my lady, I shall be sure to do so.' The woman's tone lacked deference. She hitched her ample breasts. What had Guyon said? That Miles preferred them well endowed, which this slattern certainly was. Christen longed to slap the insolence from the woman's face but was constrained by her dignity and the need to know more before she acted. She would ask Miles later, and in the privacy of their chamber. Aude might have told her, but Christen decided she would have it from Miles himself.

Miles strode into the hall, his curls windswept from his climb up the second slope and his expression guarded. His patrol had discovered nothing but the report of a minor raid on a herd of swine at one of the outlying settlements. The swineherd was a lazy oaf and Miles suspected he had concocted the tale to conceal his own shortcomings, and he had dealt with the matter summarily.

Such trivialities had not long occupied his mind and while he took his men on a wider sweep to the west, his thoughts had returned to the matter of his new wife like a sharp-edged tooth that could not be left alone yet drew blood at every touch.

Since that first night she had not cried. Indeed, she was outwardly placid and indifferent with no sign of the blazing spirit that had first brought her to his notice as she begged him to spare her brother's life. He knew he had made several mistakes in handling the situation, but he did not know how to go about rectifying matters when confronted by her empty brown stare and the compliance of lip-service replies.

He gazed round the hall, noting the improvements that only a few days of a resident chatelaine had already wrought. The smell of limewash was pungent in his nostrils and a large vat of the stuff stood covered and ready for further use. Fresh rushes gave off a grassy aroma under his boots. On the way home, he had seen people working by the river, cutting more reeds to bundle up and store in the undercroft. He noticed too that there was a certain alacrity to the way the trestles were being set up for dinner, from which he assumed that everyone was hungry and also being kept to their tasks by their new mistress. That at least was an indication that her spirit was unquenched, and surely it was a sign of more than mere duty.

Christen was sitting on the bed gowned in her chemise and combing out her braids. As she turned her head to the door, the light haloed her hair with silver. 'Did your patrol go well?' she enquired.

He shrugged as he unbuckled his sword. 'It was without incident except for putting the fear of God into a lazy swineherd.'

She nodded and put down the comb. 'I want to talk to you about Hodierna,' she said.

Miles manoeuvred himself out of his hauberk with a deal of

puffing and struggling, and when the mesh finally puddled on the floor, he looked at her warily. 'What of her?'

'Is the child yours?'

He folded and rolled the hauberk. 'Yes, she is mine. Surely you do not hold the child's birth against her?'

'Of course I do not, and it is not why I asked. She could have been born in a midden for all I care; she certainly looks as if she lives in one. Your daughter I will keep and nurture as I would one of my own, but you cannot keep me and that woman under the same roof. It is impossible.'

He shook his head. 'It is not as simple as that.'

Indignation flashed in her eyes. 'It is very simple indeed. I will not be disrespected by a woman who shirks her duties and looks at me as if I am dirt under her feet. You promised to honour me and I have seen very little of that honour so far.'

He raked his hands through his curls and sighed. 'Hodierna lacks a civil tongue, but there has been no time this summer to set my house in order. I have been in the field for weeks on end. I will speak to her as soon as I have unarmed.'

Christen put the comb on the coffer with a sharp rap. 'If you set so much store by that slut, then let her see to the ordering of your hall and the dinner. She has done precious little all day while everyone else has been working their fingers to the bone.'

'Christen, I don't—'

'And that poor child. Clothed like a beggar's waif and running wild like something out of the woods. Doubtless you think because you have given her sleeping space in your hall you have discharged your debt to her begetting.'

'That is enough,' Miles warned, anger beginning to burn in his blood.

'Not by far,' she flung at him. 'You said there should be truth between us but all you have given me are lies and evasions.

Lyulph was twice the man you will ever be. He would never have permitted his chance-gotten daughter to go about in rags. He would never have kept his whore under his wife's nose. But then he was not the baseborn follower of a baseborn throne snatcher!'

Miles took two steps forward and seized her by the shoulders, his fingers rigid. 'And would your precious, sainted Lyulph have done this?' he snarled, and silenced her mouth beneath his own in a hard, demanding kiss.

For an instant shock held her stunned, and then she began to fight him, biting, kicking, clawing, desperate to be free, and he equally determined to hold on to her. The wine flagon crashed on its side, red liquid puddling and soaking in the rushes. She groped, snatched up a cup and swung it at his head but he caught her wrist and the blow went awry, the cup striking the clothing chest and shattering into pieces. Her distaff came next and was dealt with in a similar wise. And all the time he forced her backwards, and she gave ground inch by inch until she could retreat no further and their bed caught the back of her knees and he pushed her down on to it. She writhed and struggled to escape him, but he held her fast.

'I am not Lyulph,' he panted. 'He's not going to return from the dead, so you had best grow accustomed to dealing with me. Even if I am only half the man, I am all you have.'

A furious sob escaped her before he kissed her again, parting her lips and caressing them lightly with his tongue, and the quality of the embrace changed. Her mouth softened, responding to his, and her hips undulated, meeting the downward thrust of his pelvis. There was a sensitivity to her skin; every touch of his lips or fingertips added exquisitely to a focus point of sensation at the juncture of her thighs.

'Ah Christen,' he said, and nibbled a line down her chin and throat until he came to the cleft of her breasts. His beard stubble scraped her flesh, but it was stimulation not pain that caused her to gasp as his lips found her nipple and he took it lightly between his teeth. His hand had travelled beneath her chemise, up her thigh, and now he began to tease inwards, seeking the core of the dull pressure with a touch as gentle as a feather. Christen arched with pleasure and parted her thighs. She clawed at his quilted tunic. The linen was scratchy and too great a barrier between them. She needed to feel the heat of his skin against hers, not this thick wadding.

Together they stripped their remaining garments, fumbling in haste and desperation, snatching kisses, touching, anger transmuted into lust on both sides. Avidly she drew him back down upon her and into her, and this time she welcomed the surge and took on the challenge. Whatever he felt for that other woman, he was obviously not thinking of her now. She locked herself against him, hips moving sinuously to his rhythm, breasts moulded against the wall of his chest, arms clinging tightly to his flexing back. There was a pleasure so sharply intense that it was almost a pain and she cried aloud as she was carried higher than she could bear. He thrust hard and quickly then, his fingers caught in her hair, his own voice breaking as his seed pulsed inside her body. Christen shuddered, convulsed by ripple upon ripple of sensation.

Slowly, reluctantly, her mind reconnected with her body. She was still experiencing small aftershocks of pleasure. Miles wore the stunned expression of a poled ox, his eyes heavy-lidded, and sweat curling the hair at his brow.

He gently touched a strand of her tumbled hair. 'I am sorry,' he said, 'but it is not a thing to be forgiven.'

She shook her head. The heat of rage had burned to ashes in passion. Now she felt a lassitude that would have been pleasant were it not marred by uncertainty caused by matters that lay beyond the chamber. 'Perhaps not,' she said, 'but I do forgive you, because I seem to think my own part in this has left much to be atoned for.'

'It was no more than I deserved. I should have told you about Emma and Hodierna.'

She raised herself on one elbow. His tone was rueful and matter-of-fact; certainly, he did not seem as if he were talking about a beloved concubine. 'Yes, you should! Emma is your daughter, that much is plain to see, and Hodierna is her mother?'

'Dear God, no!' A look of horror bordering on revulsion crossed his face. 'I'd sooner emasculate myself than share a bed with her!'

He rose and went to pour cups of wine from the jug set under the window.

'Then what is she to you?' Christen asked as he handed her a drink and got back into bed. 'Tell me!'

'Emma's mother died in childbirth. She was my mistress, in the year before the great battle between William and Harold – a mercenary's daughter from Rouen, and her name was Felice. Hodierna is her cousin. It is a matter of old loyalties.'

'The tie does not appear to bind both ways. Does not the state of your daughter's appearance give you cause to wonder?'

'In truth I had not noticed,' he said, and shook his head when she looked outraged. 'When Emma was born I was away in service to the King, preparing for the campaign in England, and did not return to Rouen until Felice had been a month in her grave. Hodierna had attended Emma's lying in and stayed to care for the baby. Her own man died in the great battle, and since she was kin to Felice and had nowhere to go, I took her in as Emma's nurse. It spared me the difficulty of finding someone to care for the child. They came to England just over a month ago from Rouen while I was away again with the King and I have had no time to turn around since and deal with matters. Poor excuses I know, but things will change.' He drank his wine. 'You say you do not mind taking Emma under your wing?'

'It would be my greatest pleasure, the poor little child . . . my own child still-born was a girl and would have been about her age now.'

He shook his head. 'I am not proud of what I said to FitzOsbern. Indeed, it sickened me. I spoke out of necessity, but even so, the taste of shame will remain a long time in my mouth. Again, it is no excuse, but it is a reason.'

'And I understand that reason,' Christen said. 'Even while it hurts, I understand. Did you love Emma's mother?'

He grimaced. 'It was not that kind of arrangement, but I was fond of her and she of me.' He captured Christen's hand and entwined their fingers. 'I did not use her, or if I did, that using was mutual. We were of a similar age and I was not her first man by far. Her father was a mercenary in the pay of Duke William and she was one of the women who frequented the court to serve the men. She needed a provider and I needed a woman's comfort – a means to forget and rest between my duties to the Duke. It began as a business arrangement but became more in the fullness of time. She did not expect to get with child – the women of the court have their ways and means of preventing such things – but it happened, and we were both content.' He looked at her. 'I did mourn for her when she died, and I acknowledged our daughter, but I have been remiss and you rightly take me to task.'

Setting aside their empty cups, he reached for her. 'I want to have peace and contentment in my household,' he said. 'I do not know if it can be achieved but I would like very much to put the past behind us – make a new start, if you are willing. I know there will be difficult times, and I have no doubt we shall argue more than once, but we can at least try.'

'Yes,' she said, her cheeks burning. 'I am willing.'

He leaned to kiss her, and she responded warmly, curving her arms about his neck.

As they embraced, Miles began to realise that despite having been a wife for several years, she had little knowledge of dalliance and love play. His imagination took fire as he contemplated the long autumn and winter evenings to come and the sensual pleasure of teaching her all that Lyulph had not. And this time he made sure to be slow, and tender and gentle.

'No,' he said, breathless and half laughing, putting his hand on top of hers to guide. He shifted his weight to fit his hips snugly within the saddle of hers.

'What about dinner?' she protested, but at the same time arched to meet him.

'It will be sadly late,' he replied and, nuzzling her neck, began to move at a leisurely pace.

'What are you going to say to Hodierna?' Christen asked some considerable time later as she plaited her hair into seemly order. She looked at Miles lying in the bed, head propped on his bent arm, watching her with sated appreciation, even as she watched him. The gleam of light on his skin. He was wiry, but still with strong muscles, and he had the coordination of a cat. She could barely fathom what had happened between them and needed time to reflect upon and remember the deliciousness of the sensations. The priest might frown and say that it was a sin to dwell upon the pleasures of the flesh, but she would confess later.

He pursed his lips. 'You are right that she cannot remain here, I see it clearly now. I will do what I should have done a long time ago – discharge my debt to her in coin and dismiss her. And you shall have responsibility for Emma. I will do it tomorrow before I ride to Ashdyke and check on the building work.'

Christen felt a small glow of warmth at the thought of taking the child under her wing. 'How long will you be gone?'

'Only as long as it takes to make my presence known and felt.' He grimaced. 'Guyon is honest but apt not to see the finer shades between black and white in any disputes presented to him, and I know FitzOsbern will be keeping an eye on what is happening. If he suspects that I have grown careless or lacking in my duty, he will be quick to intervene, and that is not desirable. Guyon will return here for a couple of days.'

Christen shuddered, remembering the man and the insults she had endured at his hand. His meddling was indeed not something to be desired, but she was not enamoured at the thought of exchanging Miles for Guyon. A few hours ago she had been wishing her new husband to perdition; now she was wishing his obligations there in his stead. How would they come to know each other properly if he was always absent?

Miles watched the various expressions flit across her face as she rose to put on her chemise and loose woollen gown, stitched from the everyday russet cloth.

'Why do you hide yourself away inside those baggy garments?' he asked.

She flushed. 'It is the English way, my lord. Gowned in the manner of a Norman lady of the court, I would feel indecent.'

'But a jewel should have a fit setting to display its lustre,' he argued, 'and you are beautiful. I have seen some of the well-born English ladies at court dressed the same – although of course you must do as you see fit.' He threw aside the covers and rose to his feet.

Christen hastened away from the bed, amused and slightly disconcerted. 'The more layers between us the better for now,' she replied. 'I fear that dinner is already dried up or burned with waiting.'

'We could eat bread and cheese in bed,' he suggested with a mischievous grin.

Christen shook her head and smiled. 'Much as I might enjoy such a thing, we quarrelled fit to set the household back on its heels. If we do not make an appearance in the hall suitably hand-fasted, people will think we have killed each other.'

Miles chuckled and reached for his clothes. 'You should not have such a temper,' he said. 'We could have discussed the whole thing reasonably in voices that would not have carried beyond that door. And to think Guyon said you were a nun. Nun's garments perhaps, but what lies beneath is certainly far too hot for a convent!'

Christen jutted her chin at him. She knew he was teasing, but it was a language of communication whose nuances she was still learning.

He donned his shirt and then drew her into his arms. 'Come,' he said. 'Do not be angry for a little jesting.'

'Should I then smile at your whim rather than for my own sake?' she retorted, but her hands stole up to press against his chest and feel the even thud of his heart and his sinewy strength and she was almost laughing. 'And I am not angry.'

'My whim is your sake,' he said with a grin, and bent to nuzzle her ear. 'If you had your wits about you, you would humour me until my leave-taking and then go your own sweet way.'

'I have humoured you twice already, my lord – grant me a little respite,' she retorted, and twisted out of his embrace.

Miles snorted with indignation but with a glint in his eyes. 'A respite,' he said softly. 'Very well, I will grant you a respite until dinner is over . . . and then you can humour me again before I leave.'

7

'Hodierna, you have no choice in the matter,' Miles said with laboured patience. 'As I have said, I will pay you enough to return to Rouen, and give you a pack horse for your baggage and sufficient to live on through the winter.'

Hodierna stirred her toe in the freshly strewn rushes – the laying of which she had avoided while the rest of the household toiled. Her eyes were downcast but she was far from submissive. She felt a mingling of resentment and hatred, the latter for the English bitch Miles had brought home, complete with a wedding contract. Her appearance had sounded a mort on Hodierna's life of slovenly ease. That long nose poking everywhere and finding fault. Those cow-brown eyes fixed with possession upon Miles and everything he owned – and especially upon little Emma.

Hodierna had been confident at the outset. They had all heard or heard of the raging argument between Miles and his

English wife. Hodierna had thoroughly expected to see Christen creeping around like a humbled mouse with satisfying bruises to show for not knowing her place, and it had been a nasty shock to see the newlywed couple emerge from their bedchamber hands linked, the woman's face rosy with embarrassment and the after-effects of satisfactory bed-sport. Miles had worn the look of a man equally satisfied and very pleased with himself. From his heavy eyes this morning, they had spent the night in a similar wise. Indeed, the moment she had been summoned to his presence, she had known what was in store, especially when the English bitch remained at his side.

'It is not fair on the child!' she protested. 'She has never known any mother but me, and I'm her own flesh and blood! I brought her to you from Normandy!'

'But you are not her mother, and you have neglected that charge,' Miles said. 'I am her father. I admit I have paid less attention than I should – to my regret. Emma is still young enough to accept change, and my wife is willing to accept her with an open heart. I intend to better fulfil my obligations from now on.'

'Obligations?' Hodierna sneered. 'You talk of Emma as if she were a parcel, while I have loved her and cared for—'

'A parcel of rags,' Christen interrupted fiercely. 'I suppose it was beyond you amid all your love and care to see her appropriately clothed and tended to. All that child is, is a means to an end.'

'That's a vicious slander, you English sl—'

Miles jerked to his feet and Hodierna took a stumbling backstep. 'Beg pardon now,' he growled.

Hodierna swallowed and lowered her head. 'I spoke out of turn,' she said, and pressed her lips together.

'My lord, let it be.' Christen held out her hand towards him.

'Make an end and let it go. There has been enough done and said of late.'

Miles sat down again, but his body was rigid. 'As I promised, I will give you a settlement. You shall also have a safe escort to Striguil, where you may find a ship or transport to take you further. Edward will arrange the details.' He nodded to his constable. 'I will see that you have a letter of safe conduct under my seal. You have three days' grace to prepare yourself. Go now and make ready.'

Hodierna withdrew, her lips set in a thin line, but she ceased to argue, for the offer was generous and not to be jeopardised – and she could not win.

'Hodierna would always say to me in excuse that it was useless for Emma to wear her best gown for romping in the hall and bailey,' Miles said. 'I gave her coin for my daughter's upkeep.'

Christen shook her head. 'Obviously she did not use it for that purpose. Look at her, my lord.'

She beckoned to the little girl who had leaped off Wulfhild's lap and come halfway towards them before stopping, fingers twisting together, blue eyes wide and anxious. Miles crouched and held out his hand and she approached him, shy as a deer.

Her hair was loose and had been combed until it shone like a sheet of molten copper around her narrow shoulders. Her little dress of leaf-green linen flirted the top of her ankles and the sleeves of her undergown stopped a good inch short of her wrists.

'Outgrown,' Christen said, 'and this is her best gown. Hodierna would have presented her in nothing less, knowing that your eyes would be upon her.'

Miles swore under his breath. 'I have been blind,' he muttered.

'I would see the smallest flaw in a castle wall, but I did not see this under my very eyes.'

Christen laid her hand upon his shoulder. 'And I would not have noticed the crack in the wall and thus given access to my enemies.' She crouched beside him to be on a level with the child. 'Come,' she said, 'I will not hurt you. I will be your mama.'

Emma hesitated for a moment longer, and then suddenly her face lit up and she ran to Christen and threw her arms tightly around her neck.

Miles stood up, making his movement slow and cautious so as not to alarm this little daughter of his that he barely knew, and was ashamed that it should be so. Emma craned her neck and he saw Felice again in the beautiful coppery hair and dainty freckled nose. 'I know which is the greater sin,' he said with a sigh, 'and to make matters worse I am now going to ride out and leave you.' He looked at Christen with genuine regret. Last night had radically altered their relationship, with vulnerabilities laid bare and knowledge gained. Now he was hungry to make new discoveries and spend more time with her – and yet, as always, there were obstacles.

Christen rose, Emma balanced efficiently on one hip. Miles thought that she would fight tooth and nail for what was her right, but he did not think she had it in her to be mean or vindictive. She had been furious about Hodierna, but it had been a bright, clean rage caused by the shock of mistaken identity and indignant maternal instincts.

'Guyon will be here before nightfall,' he said to her by way of reassurance to them both. 'Until then Edward has command of the keep.' He leaned round Emma to kiss her lips and then gave his daughter a parting peck on the cheek.

'God speed your mission,' Christen said.

'And God keep you,' he responded, and after a second, short, fierce kiss he left her before he jeopardised everything and took her with him at the risk of losing her to a Welsh raiding party or English rebels.

Christen climbed up on to the palisade battlements and watched Miles and his men ride out of Milnham and take the track that would lead them to Ashdyke. She gazed until they were no more than distant specks in the landscape.

'Gone,' Emma said. 'Gone again.'

'Yes, sweeting, but they will soon return, God willing.' She set Emma down. 'Come, we shall find you a cup of buttermilk to drink and perhaps put some honey in it? And then we shall seek out some cloth to make a fine gown for a fine little girl.'

Emma nodded with alacrity, and gripped Christen's hand tightly as they returned to the hall.

Hodierna was there, folding a red blanket into her baggage pack. She looked across the room to Christen, her gaze so malevolent that Emma whimpered and hid her face against Christen's skirt. Compressing her lips, Christen thought that the sooner Hodierna was gone, the better for everyone.

Guyon strode into Milnham's great hall and stopped dead, his eyes out on stalks as he took in the limewashed walls, the fresh, crisp rushes and the air of purposeful bustle. Usually if the bustle was put on to impress him or Miles, it was without purpose and died a death the moment their backs were turned.

Having recovered from the shock, he looked round for a culprit, and was not surprised to see Christen advancing on him, little Emma clinging to her hand.

'You are early, sire,' she said. 'We had not looked for you so soon, but I am glad you are here.'

He could hardly say that he had galloped all the way here because he did not trust his lord's judgement in this matter.

Bewitched he was, not his own master, and Guyon was both concerned and unadmittedly jealous. 'My lady,' he acknowledged stiffly. Looking at her in the full light of day, her manner more confident now, he had to admit that while not beautiful, she was strikingly handsome, and she certainly had a way with the child – and with his lord. Definitely she had changed Miles, who, arriving at Ashdyke, had been preoccupied and apt to smile into the distance when not engaged, although he had been alert and sharp on the salient points.

Guyon removed his belt and handed it to his squire with the instruction to check his sword and to polish the leather sheath. 'You have been busy, my lady,' he said. It was not entirely a compliment.

Christen eyed Guyon, more aware of his resentment than he knew, and commanded a servant to bring him wine. 'Stirring my fingers in the stew?' she said with a smile. 'Do not worry; I will season it so that it is palatable to all. How is the work at Ashdyke faring?'

'Well enough,' he answered, frowning. 'I would be more content if the Earl of Hereford would stop poking his nose into every corner and sending his soldiers to inspect.' He glanced down as little Emma tugged at the hem of his hauberk. 'How now, my young mistress,' he said. 'You are looking very fine today.'

'It's my new dress,' Emma said, holding out the cloth for him to admire. It had been cut from the green and gold Welsh plaid Christen had brought with her from Ashdyke. 'My new mama made it for me.'

Guyon's brows shot up towards his hairline at this piece of information. The servant returned and handed him a brimming cup.

'"New mama?"' Guyon asked.

'I assume Miles told you about Hodierna?'

Emma dashed off to pet Paladin who was nosing around the hall off the leash. Uttering a squeal, she flung her arms around the dog's neck. The blunt muzzle slobbered and Christen took a half step forward with a bitten-off gasp of alarm.

'Pal won't hurt her,' Guyon said, and took a swallow of wine. 'Born on the same day and litter mates ever since!'

Christen clenched her fists and restrained the impulse to pluck Emma away from the enormous dog, for both seemed delighted by the reunion and she trusted Guyon a deal more than she knew he trusted her.

'Miles told me,' he said. 'Hodierna has had this coming to her for a long time. I cannot say I shall miss her; the fire will warm the room so much better without her backside to block it.'

Christen spluttered and they shared a moment of mutual amusement before she excused herself to see that the trestles were set out for dinner. The mastiff had rolled on his belly like a pup and Emma was tickling his mottled tummy.

Guyon turned to Aude, who had just entered the hall. 'What do you make of my lord's marriage?' he asked, casting a dubious glance in Christen's direction.

Aude shook her head at him. 'She is exactly what Miles and this place need – a new broom to sweep away the cobwebs.' She touched his arm. 'Do not worry. You will not lose him just because he has taken a wife. He still needs you.'

Guyon looked at her as if she had lost her wits and, thrusting the cup into her hands, stalked off to remove his hauberk.

It began to rain and swiftly became a deluge of heavy, hard drops that drenched garments and chilled the skin to the bone. Hodierna's mule, a temperamental creature, started to fret and baulk and misbehave.

Behind Hodierna, the three men who rode escort cursed their luck at being saddled with the duty of seeing her safely to Bristol as per their lord's orders. The countryside was unsettled and lousy with marauding Welsh and English warbands, the foul weather was setting in, and the woman they were escorting was an objectionable harridan. Indeed, had they not been sworn to their lord's banner and loyal men, they would have abandoned her and turned for home.

'He wants rid of her, why would he care?' demanded the youngest of the trio, cuffing the rain off his face.

'He would care that his command had been disobeyed, Thomas,' warned their leader. Jordan was a dour serjeant in his late middle years; solid, dependable, taciturn. 'And don't say "who's to know". We would, and so would he – the moment he looked at us.'

'You reckon?' Thomas gave a cheerful grin and pushed his thick blond hair out of his eyes. 'I'd say he was too busy with his new bride to see beyond the hem of her skirts.'

'It'll wear off soon enough,' said Adam, the third man, grinning. 'Never known him to be in his hot blood for a woman longer than a month, and he's not with her now, is he?' He reached into his saddle pack for a piece of bread and a boiled egg. 'It's as much about building that new keep and expanding his territory if you ask me. I don't blame him.'

'Sir Guyon don't think much to her,' Thomas said.

'Bound not to. Master's got a new dog, a handsome bitch that knows more tricks than he does – hah, and gets more opportunity to practise them!' Adam tapped the egg on the front of his saddle to crack the shell.

'Handsome! God's arse, that English ale you've been swilling must have addled your eyesight!'

'Watch your tongue, boy, if you know what's good for you,'

warned Jordan. 'She's got hair like a Valkyrie and a nature to keep our lord guessing which way to duck for a long time yet.'

Thomas chuckled. 'Aye, you are right about him having to—' The grin dropped from his face, and he dragged on his reins and reached for his sword, shouting the alarm as several horsemen emerged from the trees in front of them.

'God's bones!'

Jordan kicked his horse up alongside the mule and turned it round by the bridle. The beast dug in its hind hooves, braying a protest, and he whacked its rump with the flat of his blade. Hodierna shrieked and flung her arms around the mule's neck as it bolted. The men spurred their horses to a fast gallop, uncaring whether Hodierna was with them or not. Protecting her against the petty outlaws and vagaries of the open road was one thing; being killed by a warband forty-strong was a different matter entirely, and without conscience they fled.

Hodierna had no breath to scream abuse at her fleeing escort, every fibre of her being caught up in her effort to remain astride the mule. Rain slapped her face and stung her eyes. Her wimple flew away like a dirty white bird. The mule's stubby, coarse mane filled her mouth.

A bare-legged warrior astride a squat Welsh pony galloped up alongside her, grabbed the bridle, and brought the mule to a rearing stand. Hodierna screamed as she was unseated and thrown, landing heavily in the mud. Hooves danced in close and she covered her head with her arms and shrieked again.

Her assailant grinned sharply and his dark eyes swiftly assessed the pack behind the saddle before returning to rake her body.

'Not worth a second thought,' said the Englishman who had ridden up alongside. 'Slit her throat and have done.' He accompanied the words with a graphic gesture.

'No!' Hodierna pleaded. 'No!'

From the woods beyond there came the sound of a cry cut short and a triumphant yell, and she knew she was on her own and about to be slaughtered. Once, five years ago when she and Felice had lived a hand-to-mouth existence on the streets of Rouen, her wits had been as sharp as the knife the Welshman was holding. Then Miles had entered their lives and blunted their instinct for survival. Kill or be killed. It was a long time since she had had to think in those desperate terms but the ability was still there. Let the English bitch go to hell in her stead.

'Wait!' she cried in halting English. 'If you kill me, you will be richer by one mule and my few poor possessions, but if you let me live, I will give you a castle.'

8

Christen watched Guyon ride away on patrol with his conroi of twelve men and as the gate closed behind the last horse she took Emma down to the undercroft to investigate the state of the supplies stored there. Paladin accompanied them, Guyon having left him behind. The dog appeared to be almost as closely attached to Emma as he was to his master and Emma had insisted that they bring him with them. 'He will save us from the monsters,' she said solemnly.

'I don't think any monsters would dare to be around such a beast!' Christen answered with a wry smile, thinking that perhaps Paladin *was* the monster. He was almost big enough for Emma to ride, and the smell of his breath was enough to make grown men back away from his greetings. Prudent folk also avoided standing near his unreliable rear end.

Milnham's undercroft was a large, barrel-vaulted store room with a low ceiling, but big enough for a man of ordinary height to stand, and within it were stored all manner of supplies. The dried stockfish was plentiful. There was not a great deal of salted meat but they were eating fresh at the moment and would not build up stores until the cold weather of late autumn. She would need to check how much salt they had in stock though. The grain store was clean. There was sufficient wine for the moment and a surplus of honey from last year. Blood puddings, flitches of bacon and a couple of hams hung from the rafters in between bunches of dried herbs, and Paladin lifted his nose towards the enticing scent.

A lean black cat slunk between some piled baskets and disappeared into the musty gloom at the end of the undercroft, but the dog took little notice of her, nor of the two half-grown kittens that followed in her wake, as if they were beneath his dignity. Christen approved of the cats, for they would control the vermin.

A pile of cowhides was heaped against the wall, but to judge from the smell emanating from them they had not been particularly well tanned and ought to be cast into the midden, although Paladin found them particularly interesting – so much so that he had to cock his leg against them.

Emma found a discarded tally stick on the floor and banged a row of vinegar barrels with it, humming to herself and then shouting, 'Red cow, white cow, red cow, white cow, bang, bang, bang!'

Christen gave her a fond smile and reached for a jar to inspect the contents, discovering that it contained some kind of fish oil. She wrinkled her nose and pulled back, and then almost jumped out of her skin, for someone was beating on the great wooden sounding board in the bailey to raise the alarm. 'Red cow, white cow' shot through Christen's mind. A moment's shock held her immobile and then she was running, snatching Emma away from her game and hastening to the hall. Paladin thundered ahead of them, uttering deep, bell-like barks.

'Rebels in the bailey!' Aude said to her briskly as they reached the hall. 'Welsh and English – dozens of them! Probably a splinter group from Eadric Cild's warband.'

A scream rose up to them on the veering wind.

'How?' Christen asked, swallowing dread. Not again, dear God, not again.

Aude shook her head. 'I don't know. I was in the chamber at my loom, heard the alarm and saw them out of the window.'

Christen turned to see Edward striding towards them, his expression grim as he buckled his sword belt over his mail shirt.

'Raise the bridge,' she told him.

'I have already given the order, my lady,' he said. 'The bastards will get no further than the outer ward, I promise you.'

Christen received the impression that she could take his words either as a comfort or a challenge. A new mistress of English blood and suspect loyalties. If Guyon le Corbeis had been organising their defence, he would have locked her up without a qualm. She wondered where he was, and if he was still alive. If he and his men had encountered a warband the size of the one currently attacking them, then she doubted his survival.

'It was Hodierna,' Edward growled. 'Came craving entrance, crying that she and her escort had been set upon by a band of raiders, and kept the men distracted and talking in the gateway while the raiders shot down the guards with arrows and overran our outer defences. She'll not betray anyone else. One of our own men returned an arrow straight through her heart.'

Christen shuddered, remembering the look Hodierna had flung at her as she departed – a silent threat but no idle one.

If the rebels controlled the outer gate, bridge and bailey, Christen knew they would not be idle. Already they would be planning how to take the keep and they would also have sent for reinforcements. Raising the bridge between keep and bailey would give the defenders a short breathing space, but unless help came swiftly, their chances were less than even.

Cursing mentally because he had no breath to spare, Guyon reined in his equally blown stallion. The destrier dropped its head and stood wheezing, flanks heaving in and out like bellows, sweat foaming along the bridle line.

'Where in the name of bloody Christ did they spring from?' The knight beside him, Etienne FitzAllen, was binding a bandage around a deep slash across the back of his hand.

Guyon shook his head and looked over his shoulder at the three men with him – wounded remnants of a solid twelve. They had been patrolling about four miles from Milnham when a large band of united English and Welsh had hit them in an ambush so well concealed and planned that four of his men were dead before he had even realised anything was amiss. There had been no chance of fighting; they had had to turn tail and run for their lives. 'They knew we were coming,' he said grimly.

'How?' asked FitzAllen, glancing around, his gaze wide and alert. 'How in God's name did they know?'

'How do you think?' Guyon growled. 'They were informed from inside the castle. I divulged my destination to no one until the breaking of fast this morning.' He thought of Christen, the wary brown eyes, the detail that she was English and the only newcomer among them – and one with good reason to hate Normans.

The others looked at him sideways and said nothing, but they were clearly absorbing the implications. Guyon glared at them. He tightened his grip on the reins and turned his stallion about.

'Alan, Hugh, ride to Ashdyke and tell my lord what has happened. Tell him I am going to find out what is happening at Milnham and I will report back to him by dusk. Etienne, come with me.' Guyon kicked his weary horse to a shambling trot, away from safety and back into the maw of danger.

At Ashdyke, Miles listened with an impassive face as a squire informed him that Guyon and Etienne had just ridden in on their exhausted mounts. A muscle ticked in his cheek. He looked down at his fists and carefully unclenched them. He dismissed the squire with a nod and walked to the gate, towards the core of what he did not want to know.

Several hours earlier, Alan le Breton and Hugh FitzRobert had arrived with news of the attack. His first impulse had been to gather every available man and ride hard for Milnham, but he had schooled himself to patience, knowing he needed more information before he acted.

A large warband raiding his lands was serious news, but no great disaster unless it was a foraging party from a much larger force, and as far as he was aware, Eadric Cild and his Welsh allies were not in the immediate vicinity. The chances of his larger manors being overrun were slight, although small homesteads would be open to pillage. But Guyon's erratic behaviour and his own gut instinct told him that something was badly wrong.

Guyon swung down from the trembling bay and almost collapsed. He tore off his helmet, grabbed the jug of spring water an attendant was holding and drank straight from the spout until he was breathless. And then he looked grimly at Miles.

'The bitch has betrayed you,' he said. 'Milnham has got a bailey full of English and Welsh rebels and if it weren't for the luck of God I'd be lying dead beside half of my men. We did not stand a chance. She knew where we were bound this morning; she knew and she told them!'

Miles stared at him blankly, not wanting to hear but not granted the mercy of deafness. He could not believe Christen would do such a thing after the rapport that had started to form between them.

'You must have been blind mad!' Guyon continued relentlessly. 'Her home burned down by FitzOsbern's mercenaries, her husband slaughtered, her brother mutilated by you, and you think she has the saintliness of heart to forgive and forget like a tame dog!'

Etienne flicked his gaze between the men and then looked at the ground as if the sight of mud was greatly interesting.

'You would do well to lower your voice,' Miles said curtly.

'You don't believe me, do you?' Guyon said harshly. 'Ask Etienne, he will bear witness.'

'I do not want to believe you,' Miles said, 'but I do not doubt the truth of what you both saw. But how could Christen have got word out to the rebels?'

'There are always ways, and always informers, even in somewhere like Milnham,' Guyon said. 'She waited for us to leave on patrol and then she summoned them, I am telling you – there is no other explanation that fits the logic.'

Miles shook his head and looked towards the setting sun – half a molten orb pooling down into banks of vermilion and charcoal. He thought of Christen fighting him, the feel and taste of her; the heavy sheaf of barley-gold hair; the melting brown eyes; the way she had arched to meet him. And then he thought of her affection towards Emma, and a maternal tie far less transient than lust of the body. He turned from the fading light and regarded the battered, cynical man slumped on the wood block. A man who had loved and protected him ever since he was a youth, a man who would die for him, but one who was not always right.

'I am going to Milnham,' he said. 'I need to know numbers, what you and Etienne saw, as much as you can remember.'

'I am coming with you,' Guyon said sharply.

'No, I need you to stay and command here. You are in no state to ride out again and neither is your warhorse. You can better serve me by remaining here. If there is a demon to face, I would rather face it alone.'

Guyon curled his lip. 'You mean you would rather evade the issue, which you cannot do if I am there to point you straight at it.'

'Sooner or later we must all look truth in the face,' Miles said pointedly.

'Meaning?' Guyon snapped.

'Meaning I will think upon what you have said and I will get to the bottom of it as soon as I can, for everyone's sake, but for now I need the details of everything you saw and heard on your reconnaissance.'

'Are you not afraid?' Aude asked as she and Christen tended to those who had been injured in the initial assault on the castle but had managed to reach the safety of the keep. 'You seem so calm.'

'I am so terrified that my mind is numb,' Christen admitted in a voice pitched low so that only Aude could hear. 'If I thought of what happened to Lyulph at Ashdyke or what they might do to Emma if they breach our defences, you would need to hold me down and silence my screams by tearing out my voice.' She placed her hand on the hilt of the small utility knife at her belt. 'I only pray that if needs must, I have the courage to use this thing. I am an English woman, married of my own free will to a Norman soldier. They will not be merciful.'

Aude stared at her, eyes widening. 'It will not come to that.'

Without answering, Christen turned and walked away from her, somehow managing to maintain her composure until she reached her chamber. Shutting the door behind her, she leaned against it, eyes closed, dry sobs racking her body.

For a brief span she indulged herself, releasing some of the pent-up tension, but then she straightened up and regained control because this would not do and it helped no one.

Emma was sound asleep in the great bed, clutching her soft toy doll. Her mother, thought Christen, must have been a beauty, for concealed within the round contours of childhood were the indications of a strong, pure bone structure, severe but delicate. Christen wondered if Felice would still be with Miles if she had survived childbirth and felt a surge of jealousy, immediately quashed. That way lay ruin, to envy a dead woman what had gone before. She placed her hand on her flat belly and wondered if she would ever conceive a living child. And then her mouth twisted at her folly because as matters stood it was unlikely that she would survive to see the morrow's dawn, let alone live long enough to become a mother.

Miles unhooked two grapnels from his saddle and from the edge of the copse, stared towards Milnham. A huge bonfire was burning in the broad horseshoe curve of the bailey, the timber structures of storage and auxiliary buildings providing the fuel. Flames shot skywards, sending jagged red tongues between the dark billows of smoke, visible above the rim of the palisade.

Miles knew these men. Nomad Welsh and rebel English, united to fight their mutual Norman foe. Once they had sufficient reinforcements they would overrun the keep and kill its inhabitants, save for those they could enslave or the ones that might prove useful to them. Everything of value would be looted, and then they would burn the place to the ground and retreat over the border, leaving a smoking ruin.

Tight-lipped, he gave one of the grapnels to Leofwin, who looped the coils of fine leather ladder over his head and diagonally to his waist. Miles turned to a slightly built Welshman who was taking one of two light coracle boats off the pack horse, normally used to fish for eels on the Wye and Severn.

'I am ready, my lord,' he said to Miles, speaking in Welsh.

'*Da*,' Miles acknowledged with a brusque nod.

He checked the knife hanging from the plain scabbard at his hip a final time. A cloud scudded across the half moon and a few drops of fitful rain struck Miles's mud-blackened face as he gave the signal.

The group slipped from the copse and made their way, crouched low, towards the motte slope. Each man wore a tunic of patched linen, grey and brown, olive and tawny, and they blended into the nocturnal landscape like moon shadows in the dark.

The first task was to use the coracles to cross the water-filled ditch before the slope to the first palisade. Four men across, two in each coracle, secured with a rope and drawn back to the outer side of the ditch, all in swift stealth until everyone was across. In the meantime, Leofwin had cast the grapnel and ladder over the palisade at the section furthest from the firelight. Miles and his men rapidly climbed the thin leather rungs, gained the walkway and moved along it left and right in stealthy, shadowed silence. It had begun to rain harder now, which was all to the good for rain made men draw up their hoods and look down.

A guard was leaning on the palisade in front of Miles, his

spear propped up against the stakes as he took a drink from a wine jug. Miles ran in, leaped upon him and severed his windpipe before he had uttered more than a grunt. Miles caught and lowered his falling body and tossed the spear over the palisade. He wiped his knife, stepped over the guard, and moved on to where the stairs led down to the timber gatehouse.

Away to his right a vixen barked twice. Miles answered the call, and paused to listen, his breathing light and tense, until a moment later the fox cried again, this time on his left, indicating accomplishment. The wall walk was theirs. Now all they had to do was deal with the guards in the gatehouse and open the doors to the rest of Miles's men.

The sun crested the horizon, red as blood. Miles wrenched his sword from the body of his opponent and, panting, wiped the blade on the man's tunic until it was clean, and then sheathed it. His wake was untidily pattered by a trail of bodies; he was spattered in blood, none of it his own, and it seemed very strange that suddenly everything was over. There was no one left to fight, and the dawn had brought both victory and annihilation. It was always like this after a battle. The fierce fight, the constant pressure, and then the moment when it all stopped. The space of transition between the last blow and the victory.

He shook himself free of the feeling – there was still much to do. He watched Leofwin drag a Welsh raider towards him, battered but still alive, and clearly of high status to judge from his fine mail shirt and the decorative work on his belt.

'The English leader's dead,' Leofwin said, 'but I thought you might want a word with this one before you send him to his maker.'

Miles frowned at Leofwin who was eyeing him sidelong and warily. The Welsh captive was frightened – terrified almost. He was very young, perhaps eighteen or nineteen years old. An age of bravado until it all went wrong. 'Why send him to his maker when he will be more useful to us alive?' Miles answered. 'His people well understand the rules of ransom and barter and he looks influential enough for someone to want to buy his life.'

Leofwin relaxed slightly. 'I only thought . . . that you might not be inclined to mercy . . .' His gaze flicked across the compound to their men who were busy searching the bodies and stripping the dead of anything useful. The bloodied corpses were then being lifted on to a cart, ready for burial in a mass grave.

Miles made an irritated sound. 'That was the heat of battle,' he said. 'And I have never fought so close to my heart before. Leave him with me and go and sort out the men.'

For a moment Leofwin hesitated, then bowed and walked away.

Miles turned to the youth. 'Your name?' he demanded in Welsh.

'Cynan ap Owain,' the young man answered, and swallowed hard.

'And, Cynan ap Owain, are you worth the trouble to keep you alive, or shall you leave here on that cart like the others who dared to presume too far on my hospitality?' Although he had sheathed his sword, he now drew his dagger from the scabbard at his back.

The youth licked his dry lips. 'My family will pay a high ransom for my return,' he croaked.

'Your family?'

'I am nephew to Prince Bleddyn; my mother is his sister.'

Miles pursed his lips, and examined the dagger blade. That information was extremely interesting. The lord Bleddyn was a petty Welsh prince, but one of the more powerful of several such, and if he chose to ally with his fellow rulers and with the rebel English instead of fighting them, he could be troublesome indeed. It raised the threat of an army rather than just bands of isolated raiders.

'The lord Bleddyn is careless to give his command to an untried pup,' Miles said scornfully, and watched the young man stiffen. 'Oh, I know you have been raiding since you were a twelve-year-old, but this is somewhat out of your depth, is it not?' He gestured at the intact fortifications of the main keep, still standing proud upon its summit.

Cynan flushed. 'It was Ingelric who said we should chance it.'

'And I assume Ingelric is one of the dead on that cart? The leader of the English?'

The youth swallowed and nodded. 'I wanted to kill the woman and have done, but Ingelric said that Eadric Cild would richly reward us if we managed to take this place.'

To kill the woman. A jolt of shock ran down Miles's spine.

'I assume your uncle knows of this venture?'

The youth looked away. 'He knows I am out raiding with Ingelric,' he said warily.

'And presumably he is a party to Eadric Cild's plans – perhaps he has had a meeting with him?'

Cynan ap Owain flushed. 'I will tell you nothing more,' he said, and pressed his lips together.

'Indeed, you have said enough for now,' Miles replied.

If Eadric was actively inciting the Welsh to join his rebellion, visiting their leaders to gain supplies and support, it was information that FitzOsbern would want to hear, and while the Earl was occupied pursuing Eadric's shadow he was less of a thorn in Miles's side. Miles relaxed his grip on the dagger, but not his vigilance, and took a single back-step. It was no use to prick this boy for further details. Such a green youth would not have been party to a war council between Eadric and Bleddyn, and if questioned about numbers would probably give a false answer anyway. Eadric would have ridden to Bleddyn with his personal guard, leaving the bulk of his army in reserve, somewhere between Wigmore and Shrewsbury.

He commanded two of his men to remove the youth to close but comfortable custody. As they led him away, Miles drew a deep breath and faced the keep and the drawbridge between the ditch and slope that had just been lowered to permit access.

Christen caught her breath and stared at Miles as he entered the hall with Leofwin, bearing a hobbling soldier between them. Miles's face was smeared with some black concoction and his blood-spattered tunic and chausses were garments the poorest peasant would have thrown in a midden. His hands were filthy, caked with dirt and blood.

'Dear God!' she gasped.

'Huw's injured,' he said shortly. 'Broke his foot as he was coming over the palisade.' He would not meet her eyes, and when she put her hand out to him he moved adroitly out of her way. 'Do what you can for him.' He laid him down on one of the pallets that had been set out for the injured down the side of the hall.

Christen looked at Leofwin in mystification, but he too avoided her gaze and followed Miles into the bedchamber and drew the curtain firmly across behind him. She stared in dismay and half contemplated going after them to ask what was wrong, but the groan from her new patient recalled her to her foremost duty.

The Welshman watched her with the wariness of a skittish horse as she drew her small knife to slit his hose and examine the damage.

'Why are you all dressed like beggars?' she asked.

'How else should we come through their lines and over the palisade?' he replied. 'How else would we get inside to open the gates to the men?'

'You came through their lines?'

'Lord Miles is one of the finest scouts beholden to King William,' he said, and there was a glint in his eyes that was almost scorn.

Christen lowered her lids and bent to her work. Something bad had happened and it concerned her, of that she was certain, but she was at a loss to know what. The Welshman's hostility was tangible and Leofwin and Miles had avoided her as if she were contagious. She wondered if her brother had been involved in the assault. Perhaps he had been killed and Miles did not want her to know.

She dealt with her patient as swiftly as possible, settled the man, and went to the bedchamber, reasoning that she had as much right to be there as the men. She was taken aback to find not just Miles and Leofwin but another dozen dark-smeared warriors. Miles was speaking but stopped abruptly when he saw her, and her conviction grew that her brother must be among the dead out there and he did not want her to know, or to intervene.

'My lady, will you arrange food and drink for us?' he said neutrally.

Christen raised her chin. 'I wish you did not deem it necessary to send me away on a pretext,' she said. 'If you do not want me to listen to your plans, then ask me to leave . . . I would rather the truth, my lord, than evasions.'

'Truth?' He raised his brows. 'We will speak of that later, but for now, we do not have time.'

She gave him a long look and went out of the door. Almost

immediately she became aware that she had gained a shadow – one of Miles's older men who might be a little slower in his reactions but still possessed keen faculties. Obviously her husband did not trust her further than he could see her and she was not going to find out anything until she spoke to him alone.

Christen was in the bedchamber with Aude when Miles finally discharged the last of his duties and sought a brief moment of respite. Everyone was still on alert lest enemy reinforcements arrived at their gates. Miles was surprised that they had not been here by dawn. Just now he was too bruised and battle-weary to care about the reasons that had caused a large raiding party to half seize his keep and then lose it for lack of support from their own allies. Whatever had happened, it had given Milnham a breathing space to regroup and shore up.

A bath tub had been prepared for him and the water was gently steaming. Christen had been leaning over it, adjusting the temperature, but now she straightened and came to him. She had taken off her wimple and pinned her braided hair on top of her head. She had removed her outer garments too and wore only her shift. The pleated linen moulded to the points of her body as she moved and, looking at her, Miles had never felt so desirous or so sick and took an involuntary back-step.

She stopped and lowered the hand she had reached to him. Turning away to the flagon on the coffer, she poured him a cup of wine and handed it to him at arm's length. 'It is not poisoned,' she said. 'Even if I wished to spike your drink with wolfsbane, there has been no opportunity so closely am I watched. What do you think I am about to do? Single-handedly slay everyone in the keep?'

'Not single-handedly,' he said, but took the cup from her and drank.

Christen paced to the window, her back to him, and folded her arms. Aude worked unobtrusively in the background, tidying away pots of salve and strips of bandage, folding, smoothing, deliberately lingering.

'Is my brother dead?' Christen asked without turning round.

Miles lowered the cup and started to undress. 'How should I know?' he said irritably. 'He was not among those in the bailey and I doubt he will come with the others. A man with only half a right hand is a liability in battle.'

'Osric is left-handed,' she replied with bitter satisfaction, 'and what you left him of his right will still grip a shield.'

'Then if he does arrive with the rest of them he can expect the same welcome his companions received.'

Miles pulled off his patchwork garments and unfastened the tie on his braies. Exhaustion had begun to wash over him in rolling waves and he could barely manage to untie the knot. His eyes were raw and gritty, and a merciless ache throbbed behind them.

'I did not betray you,' she said quietly. 'I do not know what you have been told but I give it the lie. Even for my brother's life I would not do it.'

'Nothing has been said here, at least not by anyone beholden to me, but still I do not know what to believe, and what to do with you,' Miles said wearily. 'You should know that Cynan ap Owain has implicated you in their attempt to take Milnham.'

She whipped round and stared at him in shock. 'That is a ridiculous notion! I do not even know who Cynan ap Owain is, let alone having become intimate enough to plot with him!' She took several swift steps across the room and stood before him. Stooping to his pile of discarded clothes, she drew his knife from its sheath, and he was too slow to stop her. 'If you believe I would give Emma into the hands of that rabble then you had better end it here and now.' Reversing the blade, she handed him the weapon, hilt-first, her eyes blazing with anger and tears.

Miles took it from her, and stared dully at the light gleaming on the polished metal. He had lost count of how many times he had used it today. He was utterly exhausted and almost beyond thought. If she had wanted to, she could have killed him there and then.

'If I believe you,' he said, 'then I must accept that both Guyon le Corbeis and Cynan ap Owain are lying. The Welshman I would not believe, but I trust Guyon with my life. What am I to think?'

Christen jutted her chin. 'I was in the undercroft with Emma when they struck. It was Hodierna, to whom you feel such a strong sense of duty, who distracted the guards for the time it took,' she said contemptuously.

Miles was nonplussed. Through a buzz of exhaustion he tried to remember what Guyon had told him and what ap Owain had said. *I wanted to kill the woman.*

'You said there should be truth between us, but what happens if you do not believe that truth?' She lifted her chin, dignified but with tears glistening in her eyes.

'Christen . . .' He held his hand out to her again, belatedly realising he still held the knife. She struck his gesture aside. Miles cast the knife to the floor on top of his clothes. 'I do believe you,' he said. 'I just do not understand, and I do not have the wherewithal just now even to begin trying.' He moved unsteadily to the bath tub and it was an effort to lift his leg and step into the water. As the heat lapped around him, he closed his eyes and leaned back against the head of the tub, and then it was too much effort to open his eyes again and within seconds he was asleep.

Christen bit her lip and exchanged glances with Aude. 'What

should I do?' she asked. She went to the tub and looked down at Miles.

Aude finished her last bit of folding and joined her. 'Wash him,' she said, 'and put him to bed. I doubt you will get any sense out of him for several hours. He has used up all of his reserves, and so, I think, have you. I will help you.'

Christen took a soft linen cloth and knelt at the side of the tub. Tentatively she began to clean her husband, and as she did so a feeling of tender pain grew in the pit of her belly. She realised how vulnerable he was now – just as much as herself. There were not many marks on his body, for he was swift and clever in battle, but the few bruises and contusions he did have made her pause. It took her a long time to remove the blood and grime from his hands and fingers. His face too, where he had smeared it with earth the better to hide in darkness and twilight. The cloth rasped over his stubble. She fetched a sharp knife and carefully scraped away the fledgling beard.

'Is this trust?' she said to Aude, swallowing the lump in her throat. 'Does it count if he does not know? Does it mean he trusts me not to cut his throat if he is prepared to be this exposed in my presence?'

'I suspect so,' Aude said. 'You were harsh on each other earlier. A little mending would not go amiss on either side. I am sure that even though he is asleep, he can hear us. He is like a dog that always slumbers with one ear cocked.'

Christen smiled a little at her words, although she felt tearful too. 'You are right,' she said, 'both about the mending and the harshness.'

'Come,' Aude said, practically. 'We have to stir him enough to get him out of the water before it grows cold, and dry him and put him to bed. Who knows how much grace we have until the rebels come again – if, of course, they do. Each hour that passes makes it less likely.'

Christen nodded and applied herself to practical matters, grateful to Aude for her pragmatism. Together they gently shook Miles awake, but although he responded to their commands, his eyes barely opened, and the moment he rolled into bed he fell asleep.

'We should rouse him if we come under attack again,' Aude said, 'but otherwise let him sleep.'

'Yes,' Christen said. She looked at Aude. 'Thank you. I owe you a debt for your wisdom.'

Aude embraced her and kissed her cheek. 'You owe me nothing,' she said. 'We are women and we are family, and we should stand shoulder to shoulder. I had no sisters before, but now I do.'

Miles awoke to weak grey light augmented by candle flame. Rain spattered against the shutters. When he tried to move, every bone in his body ached. Groaning softly, he lay back against the pillows. His throat was parched and his mouth so dry that his lips had stuck to his teeth.

Christen came swiftly to the bedside and asked him if he wanted a drink.

'Water,' he said hoarsely. Her expression was neutral and he was unable to gauge her mood.

She plumped the pillows, added more to support him, and brought him the water he had requested. 'You fell asleep in the bath tub,' she said. 'Aude and I had to help you to bed, but I was very tempted to drown you instead.'

He reached out, wincing as the movement twinged a pulled muscle in his arm, and then continued until he touched her face with his fingertips. 'I lose my reason where you are concerned,' he said, relieved that she did not pull away. 'Guyon said as much to me and I believe him in that – at least.'

'Excuse or accusation?' she asked.

'Apology,' he replied, and taking hold of her braid he pulled her down to him for a kiss. She resisted briefly and then yielded. He stroked her face and moved his hand to her waist, and then her hip before being brought up short by a sudden jolt of pain that made him catch his breath.

Immediately she drew back, her cheeks flaming. 'You are hurt.'

He gave her a slow smile. 'It is but a small strain,' he said. 'The part that matters has suffered no damage.'

Her lips twitched. 'Probably the only part of you that did. If I lay with you now, I would never be certain if you were groaning with pleasure or agony, and neither I hazard would you.'

'Part of the pleasure is the pain,' he argued with a mischievous grin. 'Bolt the door, and I promise not to complain.'

Sensing that she was at a disadvantage in this particular exchange, Christen changed the subject. 'You have already slept past noon. Edward has paced a hole in the floor waiting for you to rouse from sleep. Aude and I have had a difficult time keeping him out.'

'How long?' The teasing grin vanished and he threw back the covers. 'Why did you not waken me?'

'Short of exploding a barrel of pitch beneath the bed, it would have been impossible.'

Wincing at the pain from his strained muscles, he went to the clothing coffer and pulled out a clean shirt and tunic. Christen helped him to dress with quiet efficiency, and as he was fastening his hose to his braies she fetched him another cup, this time filled with wine. He finished the last tie, took the drink and looked at her.

'The Welsh . . . ?'

'There has been no sign of them. Leofwin sent out scouts to ask at the homesteads and they say the same thing, not a sighting. And no English either.'

Miles shook his head in bafflement. 'They would not turn aside with Milnham theirs for the taking.' He rubbed his brow. 'Go and bring Edward to me, and find a messenger, Rhodri by preference – you know him?'

'Yes, but—'

'And the scribe, fetch him too.'

'I don't think—'

'Oh, and see about some food. I could eat a bear!'

She gave up the unequal struggle and, throwing up her hands, went to do his bidding. This new husband of hers was a force of nature.

When she returned bearing a laden tray, he was busy preparing a message for Guyon to inform him of the situation and warning him to keep a sharp lookout for a warband of marauding Welsh and English. The scribe dealt with the first document and began a fresh page on his wax tablet as Miles dictated a second note to FitzOsbern, consigning to his care the few survivors of the raid, but excluding Cynan ap Owain. He gave FitzOsbern all the intelligence he had concerning Eadric Cild's recent dealings with the lord Bleddyn. A third and last letter went to Bleddyn himself, stating his nephew's ransom terms and requesting him to reconsider his alliance with Eadric.

'A waste of time I know,' Miles said with a shrug, 'but at least I am giving him the opportunity to think again.' He looked up at a knock on the door. 'Come!'

Edward entered, started to speak, and was jostled aside by a man almost twice his height with shoulders as wide as a hawk perch and a stride that brought him to the middle of the room within two paces.

'Gerard!' Miles sprang to his feet, his expression vacillating between pleasure and apprehension.

'Still not learned to keep your damned relatives under control, have you!' snarled his visitor, slinging a rust-streaked helm on the bed. 'I'd have thought to travel in peace in my own brother's lands, but no!'

Brother! As startled as her husband, Christen regarded this lodestar of Aude's being with astonishment. While Miles was slender and dark with the neat bones of a cat, this man was as magnificent and ruddy as a lion. His helmet-flattened hair was the colour of flame, and he had a wide mouth and full lips that were currently drawn back from a set of strong white teeth. Nothing about him suggested that he might be any sort of kin to Miles, save perhaps for a passing resemblance about the eyes.

'The area is troubled with rebellion at the moment, I agree,' Miles replied, recovering his aplomb. 'What happened?'

'Bloody Welsh and English too. We happened on a score of them wending their way straight for you here. I don't know who was more surprised, but our teeth were sharper. Got one waiting down in the bailey for you, claiming to be your kin.' He scraped his fingers through his ruddy hair and gazed around. 'God's bones, is there nothing to drink in this Godforsaken place? My throat's as parched as a priest's prick!'

Wide-eyed, astonished, Christen gave him the cup she had been about to hand to Miles. Gerard drained it in four strong swallows and then regarded her over the rim of the cup. His eyes were a vivid, clear blue. The lower lids narrowed and he turned to regard Miles.

'I was expecting them in much greater numbers,' Miles said. 'Indeed, I would have given them a sword's-edge welcome if you had not seen fit to blunder across their path and do the deed for me.'

'Hah yes, I can see you were expecting them!' Gerard thrust the cup back into Christen's hand. His gaze raked his brother's condition. 'That is why you are wearing a flimsy tunic, no armour, and drinking wine in your bedchamber at noon. Where's Guyon?'

'You're a bull at a gate,' Miles said with tolerant affection, indeed amusement. 'How can I explain everything to you in a few scant minutes? I warrant that you have yet to greet your wife!'

Gerard scowled at him. 'A bull at a gate perhaps, but wise to your dissembling tricks by now. Aude can wait for a moment, and I set no time limit on your replies.'

Miles gestured with an open hand. 'Have some more wine then.'

Gerard tossed his mud-spattered cloak on the rumpled bed and sat down on the coverlet. 'If I had any sense I'd have stayed in Normandy. This whole country is a barrel of pitch just waiting to explode. It is in my mind to send Aude back to Rouen.'

Christen handed him the refreshed cup. 'We need more wine,' she said. 'And food, I daresay.' She excused herself.

Gerard watched her to the door, appreciative eyes on the swing of her hips. 'Perhaps I need not enquire the reason for your unruly lands and your lack of armour after all,' he said, and gave the disturbed sheets a pointed look. 'Kept you long abed, has she?' He took another gulp of the wine and reached over to steal some bread and cheese from Miles's breakfast tray.

'Muster what civility remains in that thick skull of yours, Gerard, and when she returns I will formally introduce you to my wife,' Miles said.

Gerard almost choked. 'You dark Welsh bastard!' he declared, spattering crumbs. 'I do not believe it! When, and why?'

'Questions again?' Miles grinned.

'Tell me before I throttle you!' Gerard roared. 'I am in no mood for japes.'

Miles held up his hands. 'Pax, neither am I. I married her in order to secure her dead husband's lands for my own. She's an English widow with estates half a day's ride from here.'

'English?' Gerard snorted. 'God's life, little brother, you enjoy playing with fire.'

'I would not say that. Many a soldier from Normandy has married an English widow.'

Miles sought out his boots, swearing as a strained muscle complained. While he finished dressing, he told Gerard everything that had happened since the day he rode into Ashdyke and claimed it for his own.

Gerard listened with quiet and thorough attention and Miles's fondness for his brother warmed anew and deepened. Gerard had a good heart and a shrewd intelligence. He was a superb horseman, a reasonable tactician and commanded the respect and affection of his men. Aude adored him to distraction, worrying over his bovine stamina as if he possessed the frail bones of a sparrow. Miles loved Gerard as he loved very few people in the world. Gerard had been a stalwart prop to a terrified child of twelve, ripped from a life of freedom among these border hills and transported across a turbulent grey sea into a life of iron discipline and different customs, nasal French the first language rather than free-flowing Welsh. In the end Miles had adapted but at the time it had been traumatic, and Gerard the only rock amid shifting quicksand.

'Well, you have piled your trencher higher than I would dare pile mine,' Gerard said at length, puffing out his cheeks, 'but then my needs are simple and yours never have been. I am here if you have need, and I always will be.' He leaned over to strike Miles a hefty blow on the bicep that made Miles wince.

'Thank you, brother,' he said somewhat wryly. 'I know I can count on you.' He grimaced. 'FitzOsbern enjoys breathing down my neck, but for now he's muzzled by my usefulness. The Welsh can be bought with hostages and bribes, for a time at least. You said something about a relative of mine?'

Gerard finished the bread and reached to tear off another chunk. 'He was among that party of outlaws we encountered riding to join the band that had attempted your keep,' he said, waving his hand. 'He decided he would rather claim kinship than turn on the spit of my steel. I tethered him to the whipping post to await your pleasure. His companions, I am afraid, are all crows' meat.'

'I shall go and interview him in a moment,' Miles said, suspecting he knew the identity of this particular relative and deciding that he could afford to let him stew a short while longer.

'What does Guyon think of your marital status?' Gerard enquired, amusement dancing in his eyes.

Miles shrugged. 'He will grow accustomed,' he said.

'Aha, your old warhorse doesn't approve of the match?' Gerard gave Miles a broad grin.

'You know what he's like,' Miles said with a shrug. 'Muttering dire warnings into his beard and glowering like a thunderstorm.'

'Apt to be a trifle possessive of his last fledgling,' Gerard said with a sympathetic nod. 'Where is he?' he repeated. 'I would have expected him to be stuck to you like your shadow.'

'At Ashdyke,' Miles said, and looked round as the door opened and Christen returned bearing a platter of bread and cold meat. Aude followed her with a brimming flagon. Gerard abandoned what he had been about to say and jumped to his feet, his expression brightening. His wife set down the flagon on the chest, and put her hands on her hips.

'So I can wait for a moment indeed,' she said, eyes sparking.

Gerard's gaze flashed from Aude to Christen, who jutted her chin.

'Don't cross swords with her,' Miles warned, chuckling. 'You'll only lose.' He moved to attack the new food, purloining Gerard's portion in revenge for Gerard stealing his breakfast.

'You know best how to deal with the English,' Gerard retorted, and going to Christen, grabbed her by the shoulders and gave her a resounding, less than brotherly kiss on the lips. 'Welcome, sister,' he saluted. 'If you ignore my lacks, then I will ignore yours and we should rub along together very well.'

Christen staggered as he released her from the bear-grip. Her mouth was numb, but she did her best to smile at him. 'I am sure that will be the case,' she said. He reminded her a little of Guyon, but without the underlying resentment.

She had been irritated at his casual dismissal of Aude, who plainly worshipped him, but he rectified this now as he turned to his wife, gently drew her to him and, cupping her face, kissed her tenderly, murmuring something against her ear that caused her to blush and smile like a bride.

Christen looked beyond them to Miles. 'Edward said he would wait for you in the hall.' She raised her eyebrows meaningfully.

Miles glanced at the entwined couple, raised his own brows in reply and headed for the door. 'I'll see him now,' he said. 'And I have my reprobate kinsman to deal with too. I can wait a little longer for other stories.' Gerard would have told him if the news was immediate, and clearly he was preoccupied now with Aude. She might not be the reason he was here but she was the honey on his bread. First and foremost, Gerard was a soldier, and even while he was prepared to wait, Gerard's presence here gave Miles cause for worry.

9

Siorl ap Gruffydd squinted up at his nephew. One eye was almost swollen shut and resembled a ripe purple plum, and the other was not in much better case. 'Don't recognise me, do you?' he said, curling a bloody lip.

Miles straightened from severing the Welshman's bonds and sheathed his knife. 'Your own sister would not recognise you at the moment, Uncle,' he retorted. 'At your age you should have the sense to cosset your old bones by the hearth, not risk them scouring the borders causing trouble.'

'Less of the old; you always were a disrespectful whelp.' His uncle spat out a mouthful of bloody saliva. A front tooth was not long missing.

'Old enough to get caught and well thrashed,' Miles answered scathingly, and pulled his mother's twin brother to his feet.

Siorl ap Gruffydd staggered, regained his balance and pushed away from Miles as if his touch was poison. 'How was I to know that hulking whoreson was going to cross our path?' He rubbed the livid welts on his wrists.

'You always taught me that surprise was the principal element of victory.'

'Yes, well, that was too much of a surprise. At first I took him for your devil-spawned father returning from the gates of hell to grieve me anew. I would put nothing past your sire even if he is rotting in his grave.' Siorl crossed himself in a protective gesture.

Miles concealed a grin behind his hand. Gerard bore a strong resemblance to their father and Siorl had hated him from the moment he had set eyes upon him, and had made no effort to hide it. The feeling had been mutual.

'Serves you right for trespassing. If you had stayed at home you would not be in this predicament now, would you?'

Siorl curled his lip and spat again, ejecting a chip of tooth. 'Nothing to do with being bested in a fight. My horse bolted and threw me against a tree.'

Miles was tempted to comment on the state of his uncle's horsemanship, but decided it would be rubbing salt into an already sore wound, and while he did not mind puncturing Siorl's sense of worth, he would not take it too far. Without commenting on the matter, he drew Siorl over to a cooking fire and told the servant tending it to go and bring some cider.

'I doubt you'll want to eat, given the state of your mouth,' he said, eyeing his uncle's split lip.

'No.' Siorl regarded Miles warily. 'What are you going to do with me?'

'You tell me,' Miles said, hands on hips.

Siorl said slyly, 'We are blood kin. I taught you to live off the land where a *saison* would have starved. I taught you stealth and to track like a wolf.'

'So you did,' Miles said, folding his arms. 'And you seek to claim that debt from me. As I recall, it was at my grandfather's command that you undertook my training.'

The servant returned with a horn of cider. Siorl took a cautious but thirsty swallow from the less damaged side of his mouth. 'I admit I was loath to teach anything to a son of a Norman lecher, but since I had no choice I did the best I could with you. You owe me that.'

Miles's brows shot up at such skewed presumption. 'I owe you nothing. Were it not for my grandfather's keen eye on you and the fact that you needed his goodwill, you would have kicked me away like a stray dog.'

Siorl shrugged and sat on the ground, suddenly looking old and weary beneath his bravado. 'For your mother's sake then.'

Miles snorted. He had been wondering how long it would take Siorl to apply that particular goad. 'You and she were never that close. You did not come when she died. I doubt her soul will grieve long whatever I do with you.' He crouched to his uncle's level. 'Just what were you doing on my lands?'

Siorl gave him a bloody smile. 'I had heard they were yours no longer. Seems I was mistaken.'

'A green boy and an undisciplined rabble are no opposition,' Miles replied with contempt.

'Perhaps, but the full hosts of Bleddyn and Eadric Cild would be more than you could chew up and spit out!' Siorl retorted, his voice thickening with anger. 'Do not be so swift to scorn your opposition. Were it not for being busy elsewhere they would have been down on you before this morning's dawn and your remains would now be scattered to the four winds.'

'Busy elsewhere?' Miles stared at his uncle and felt a prickle of unease.

Siorl dropped his gaze. 'I will say no more,' he growled, and attended to his horn of cider. 'Even if you cut off my hands you will not get me to speak. You will find out soon enough.'

'Dear me,' said Miles. 'Who's been filling your ears with tall tales? A fingerless Englishman perchance?'

Siorl flicked him a disdainful look. 'You're clever, nephew, but not clever enough.'

'What were you doing on my lands?' Miles reiterated. 'Alerting the troops to the prospect of a greater prize than Milnham?'

Siorl said nothing.

Miles rose to his feet and gingerly stretched. 'Which is it this time? Hereford? I think not. Too tough a nut to crack these days. Worcester? Shrewsbury?' Eadric's camp would be within striking distance of all three places but Miles suspected he would be closest to Shrewsbury, and he had not missed the flicker of tension in Siorl's cheek muscle when he mentioned the place. 'I would rather that William FitzOsbern hazard the odds,' he said thoughtfully. Seeing the head groom crossing the bailey, he called to him to bring a saddled pack horse. 'Eadric and Bleddyn are fools,' he said as the groom departed on his errand. 'To play chase across the border is one thing. To challenge the likes of FitzOsbern and Roger de Montgomery of Shrewsbury on their own ground is a different kettle of fish.'

'Yes, bad fish!' Siorl spat. 'And they will finish their lives in a cess pit! It is not only Eadric Cild and Bleddyn who will bring you Normans down. It is Edwin and Morcar of Mercia. It is the sons of Harold Godwinson who will avenge their father's death. It is the King of Norway, and Hereward Leofricson in the Fens. You cannot stand against so many enemies.'

'That depends,' Miles said brusquely. 'All of those you name are certainly fearsome in their own right, but each one has his own separate dreams of power and is unlikely to share it with others. I agree that they might see Normandy as the common enemy, but uniting against that common enemy is another matter entirely. William the Bastard is harder in battle than any of those you have mentioned.'

'Go to hell,' Siorl said, tossing the empty horn on the ground.

'I warrant you will precede me there,' Miles replied, exasperated but unruffled. His uncle had told him what he wanted to know, although it was nothing that surprised him.

The groom returned, leading a bay pack pony. Miles took the rope rein and dismissed him. 'Here,' he said, handing the bridle to his uncle. 'Take the beast and your life and get out of here. And should you happen on the lord Bleddyn, tell him I have his stray gosling cooped up safely if he cares to come and fetch him.'

Siorl snatched the bridle from Miles's hand. The pony jibbed and sidled as he pulled himself across its back, grimacing at the pain from his injuries. There were no stirrups, just a stuffed sack for a saddle.

'I shall remember your hospitality,' Siorl said, turning his stocky little mount towards the gates. 'Perhaps one day very soon I will return the favour when your Norman pride lies bleeding beneath our spears.'

'Dreams warm the heart, Uncle,' Miles said with a sarcastic smile.

Siorl lashed the reins on the pony's neck and kicked its sides with his heels, setting it to an indignant canter.

The smile dropped from Miles's face and he went to find a messenger.

Gerard bit into a roasted chicken thigh, chewed vigorously and swallowed. 'Shrewsbury?' he said. 'Hah! Roger de Montgomery will be running around like a scalded cat.'

Miles waved away the youth waiting to replenish his cup. 'It is no cause for mirth. The English still hold Chester. It only needs Stafford or Shrewsbury to fall and all the northern and middle marches will be theirs. We are not so firmly entrenched in this land that we can afford to lean back and laugh.'

'I wasn't laughing,' Gerard said, 'or at least not at the situation. Christ knows, there is little enough reason for rejoicing these days unless you happen to be English.' He took another bite and washed it down with a swallow of wine.

Miles looked at his brother, noting his tension, the tightness at his eye corners and the determined way he was champing his food with more than usual concentration. 'Where do you see the trouble coming from first?' he asked, thinking of his earlier conversation with Siorl.

Gerard shrugged his broad shoulders. 'Who can say? I would need to read minds to answer that one. But the Danes have got a fleet at sea off the north coast and the people there are more Dane than English. If that fleet lands they will receive a brave welcome, and it's likely that King Harold's sons are on the move in Ireland and may link up with them – although none of them are of the calibre of their father. It doesn't stop them being troublesome though.' Gerard wiped his fingers on a napkin and lifted his cup.

Miles grimaced. 'It is fortunate there is no one of King William's ability to unite all these ants' nests.' He pushed aside his own empty dish. 'What I do want to know is what are you doing here if the country is set to erupt into rebellion? Why aren't you with the King?'

Gerard picked up another portion of chicken. 'I am in the still before a storm that may yet blow over, I hope,' he said. 'I have not seen my wife since before Easter and the King granted me leave to visit you in the Marches.' He spat a shard of bone into the rushes. 'Oh, and he wants me to bring you with me when I return.'

'What for?' Miles demanded brusquely, feeling a cold hand squeeze his gut. He had no taste for returning to King William's service just yet.

'He's short of good scouts,' Gerard said. 'Aubrey FitzSimon lost his brains to an English axe at York last month.'

Miles crossed himself and said the obligatory words for the repose of FitzSimon's soul. 'What about his Welshman?'

'Prys? Got himself knifed in a quarrel over a game of dice. He always had as much sense as a headless chicken once he'd had a drink. Now he's as dead as one too.'

'There is more than enough to keep me occupied here,' Miles said, frowning.

Gerard tossed the chicken bone on to his platter and wiped his hands. 'That may be so, but when has that stood in the way of our seigneur? There are not many such as you, trained to both warhorse and stealth. You are valuable to him, brother, too valuable to spare.'

Miles glanced at Christen and Aude. They had fallen silent and it was obvious from their expressions that they had heard at least the hindmost part of the conversation.

Quickly, but too late, Gerard changed the subject. 'The King also has a commission for you to fulfil to the benefit of your coffers.'

'Giving with one hand what he strips with the other?' Miles said cynically.

'He wants a horse for his youngest, Prince Henry.'

Miles snorted. 'The boy's not yet two years old. What is he asking me to look for – a Hibernian pony?'

'No, for when he is older,' Gerard said. 'The King says that if he is introduced to the horse now they will be well acquainted by the time the lad is six or seven. The King trusts you to find a good beast among your stud herd – although if I were him I'd be asking you to find him decent warhorses, not a child's palfrey.'

Miles grunted and leaned back in his chair to gaze round the hall which was occupied by a medley of Normans, English and Welsh, eating in companionship – at least for the moment. He thought of what Siorl had said, astride his circling pony in the compound. Norman pride bleeding beneath rebel spears. What a hair-thin line they all trod. He did not want to leave his territory and ride with the King again. Something within him had changed of late. He wanted to settle and have peace. To nurture, tend and till. Much of his feeling was bound up in what had happened at Ashdyke when he had chased the rebels as far as the settlement and in the midst of fire and destruction had discovered Christen. Like a blow striking the iron on an anvil, that moment had altered him for ever. He wanted to stay here with his wife and come to know who she was. He wanted to live to be an old man and die in his bed and know that he had run a good race.

Christen put down her distaff. She had been spinning wool for the last hour and the narrow, weighted stick was now clad in a chunky coat fashioned from many layers of fine off-white thread.

'I have never seen anyone with such nimble fingers,' Aude said enviously. 'You have spun twice as much as me and your work is far finer than anything I can do.'

Christen blushed a little at the praise, but accepted it as her due. She had a particular skill for the craft. Wool and flax both turned quickly to strong, fine thread under her fingers. 'I enjoy it,' she said. 'And your own work is very good.'

'Ha, you are kind,' Aude said, 'but I know my limitations.'

Christen rose to stretch, and then stooped to little Emma who had been emulating the women with her own little spindle and a fluff of teased fleece, but having grown bored was now playing with her soft doll. Her hair, neatly plaited over one shoulder and tied with a blue ribbon, was the colour of autumn beech leaves.

'Come,' she said. 'Let us leave the spinning for a little while and go for a walk and see if we can find your father.'

Emma happily jumped to her feet, tucked her doll under one arm and trustingly took Christen's hand.

They discovered Miles in the stables examining a small horse and discussing its merits with Godwin the head groom. Alerted by Emma's high-pitched happy chatter, the men turned. The groom bowed and touched his forehead. Miles smiled a greeting and came around the animal to join them.

He lifted Emma in his arms and kissed her cheek. 'We'll soon have you riding a horse, eh?'

Emma wrinkled her nose at him and giggled. 'And Alina,' she said, waggling her doll from side to side. 'She can ride!'

Miles rolled his eyes. 'Yes, and Alina,' he said.

Christen looked at the animal Miles had been examining with his groom. Although not large it was perfectly proportioned with a hide that gleamed like a polished carnelian.

'For Prince Henry?' she said.

'Indeed.' Miles turned to fondle the horse's soft muzzle. There was a hint of regret in his voice; he was loath to part with this colt but had nothing else of the same age and stature to offer to the King who was an excellent judge of horseflesh and would know the difference between merely good and superb.

Emma put out her little hand and from the safety of her father's arms patted the whorled star marking on the pony's forehead.

'Hah, I shall have to find a mount for you soon enough, madam,' he said, and set her down as she wriggled against him. An upturned bucket had caught her eye and she skipped off to sit down on it with her doll, talking away to it, telling it an involved story.

'How long before you must go?' Christen asked.

Miles ran his hand down the bay's sturdy forelegs. 'A month, perhaps, if I can eke out the time. No more than that.'

The pony nudged her, seeking an offering. 'But what about the building at Ashdyke?' she asked, frowning. 'What about FitzOsbern? And this recent raid too. Can you not send a message to the King that you cannot go?'

Miles gave a humourless laugh. 'No one refuses the King or tells him that something is impossible – if they want to live.' He stood straight. 'Time and again he has won with the odds stacked so high against him that only a madman would wager in his favour. Duke of Normandy and King of England by his own iron will. If I refused him, he would destroy me. FitzOsbern is nothing compared to the King.'

A cold lump settled in the pit of Christen's belly. She had had this same conversation with Lyulph before he rode away at the command of King Harold to repulse the Norwegians at Stamford. He had returned to her from his service – oh yes, he had returned, but borne on a litter, his leg bandaged and festering and his life spirit quenched.

'How long will you be gone?'

He shrugged. 'I do not know. The King will campaign throughout the winter if he must, and he will expect the same of his men.'

Christen dropped her gaze so he would not see her fear, but they were standing too close for him to be deceived.

'You cannot turn it aside,' he said. 'William owns my allegiance and my oath of service.'

'As Harold owned Lyulph's! I watched him die by inches for three years until the Earl of Hereford's henchmen cut him to pieces. It will break me if I have to endure that horror again!'

'You have the strength to endure whatever happens. This much I already know about you. If not for me, if not for yourself, then for Emma. I know how much she means to you already. Another woman may have borne her, but you have already become her mother.'

They both looked at the little girl, playing with her doll and banging her palms on the surface of the bucket like a drum. Sensing their scrutiny, she looked up at them and smiled.

Christen swallowed and bit her lip. Miles took her by the shoulders and looked into her eyes. 'I will return to you as swiftly as I can, but should I go down in battle my death will be outright. You will not be chained to a living corpse, I promise you that.'

Christen blinked, breaking the demanding eye contact. 'I am afraid,' she said, and pressed her head against his shoulder. 'I am afraid that in the end all that will be left of me is a pillar hewn from the rock of enduring without the ability to feel, because I shall have been forced to lock all feeling away. It is all very well for you to say that I will not be chained to a living corpse, but if you do not return, what happens then? How safe will any of us be?'

He stroked her spine. 'I have to go,' he said. 'I have no choice and so we both must deal with the parting. If I do not return, then I trust to your resourcefulness. Seek the aid of the Church. Guyon will be remaining behind, and whatever your past differences, he is a rock you can lean on, I promise you. I know this is difficult . . .'

She nodded and pushed away to look up at him. 'Yes,' she said. 'I know you are right. I cannot hide in a corner and wish all this to go away, because God helps those who help themselves.'

'We still have a little time before I have to leave,' he said. 'We can make plans and safeguards.'

Emma came and pushed between them and looked up at Christen, her blue eyes wide with concern. 'Why are you crying, Mama?' she asked.

Christen forced a smile, wiped her eyes, and crouched to the child's level. 'See, I am not crying now,' she said. 'I had a sad feeling, but then I looked at you and I was happy again. You make me happy; you always will.' She stood up and took Emma's hand. 'Come, your aunt Aude will be wondering where we are, and I have some spinning to finish, but I will tell you a story while I spin. A tale you have not heard before about a lady who could spin straw into gold.'

Emma's face lit up.

Christen looked at Miles. 'We shall see you later in the hall,' she said. 'Not too much later I hope.'

'No, I will not be long,' he said, and he too made an effort to smile. 'You both make me happy too, and always will.'

10

Manor of Ashdyke, Welsh Marches

Guyon listened to the dripping of the rain. Steady and relentless, it had been falling since dawn and the sky was a low, leaden grey, filled with more to come. He examined the edge of his sword for flaws and lovingly honed out a nick in the edge along a whetstone. The rebels had attempted to take Milnham and Miles had sent a message warning him that they might attempt Ashdyke too. He hoped that they did for he would relish a good, fierce battle to clear the air. Everything clean and set in terms that he understood and could deal with – no subtle fencing with words. It had been almost a month since the attempt on Milnham and Guyon was still trying to come to terms with the fact that he had been wrong about Christen's betrayal. He felt guilty and foolish, and resentful of the situation in which he found himself. Christen wasn't to blame, and yet a part of him still felt as if it was her fault.

'Messire Miles is here,' announced Alan de Barfleur, one of

the garrison serjeants, squelching into the now just about liveable hall to give the news. 'I thought you would want to know.' He gestured over his shoulder in the direction of the gate.

Guyon jerked to his feet. 'At last! But why did he not send word in advance?' he asked out of irritation.

Alan shrugged. 'Safer, perhaps,' he said, avoiding Guyon's gaze.

Guyon grasped his newly sharpened sword by the hilt and, muttering under his breath, strode out into the downpour to greet Miles.

The sight of him helping Christen to the ground stopped Guyon like a hammer blow. Tightening his fist around the sword hilt, he halted for a moment, before putting his head down and continuing forward. Miles tensed his jaw and set a protective arm around Christen's waist.

'Here comes trouble,' Gerard said in a loud voice as he dismounted from his grey stallion, addressing his comment to Guyon. 'He looks like a bull intent on charging down trespassers, doesn't he?'

Guyon stopped again and glared at Gerard. They were of a similar height and breadth. 'You give me no reason not to,' he retorted.

Gerard let out a snort of ironic laughter. 'As ever.'

Christen cast her gaze heavenwards in exasperation and came over to lay her hand on Guyon's muscle-corded arm above the bare sword. 'Please,' she said. 'Matters cannot remain as they are, and I do not wish to come between you and your lord.' She lowered her voice so that it was for him alone and spoke briskly lest her fear of him overcome her courage. 'Thus far I have no reason to like you. You have made it clear that you do not trust me, but for the sake of these lands and everyone, including Miles, we must come to an understanding. It is against his better judgement that I am here now, and he cannot afford to be torn two ways. There is too much at stake. We should be allies.'

Guyon jutted his jaw. 'I owe you an apology for thinking that it was you who betrayed Milnham to the rebels,' he growled. 'I fully own my mistake, But even so, you will not wheedle your way inside my armour, the way you have wheedled yourself inside my lord's.'

Christen let out a hard breath. 'A truce will suffice. Miles needs you. There is room for us both, and the better so, even if our paths seldom cross.' She removed her hand from his arm. 'I have to see to unpacking the baggage, and I have a little girl to care for who means all to me – as does her father. And we need to be out of this downpour.'

Christen turned back and held out her hand to Emma, who had just been lifted out of the baggage cart by Wulfhild. Emma ran to Christen, embraced her hips, and looked round at Guyon.

'Paladin,' she said. 'Where's Paladin?'

A bemused Guyon gestured towards the hall. 'Hiding inside,' he said. 'You know he doesn't like rain.'

At table in Ashdyke's new makeshift hall, Guyon was oddly silent, eating and drinking much less than usual, and contributing nothing to the conversation around the table He knew he had committed a grave injustice in condemning Christen to Miles. She had done all she could to prevent Milnham from falling into rebel hands and had tended the injured with compassion and diligence.

He hunched his shoulders like a moulting hawk and stared into his cup. He knew he should be more gracious toward her, but resentful pride caused the words to stick in his throat. He glanced at her circumspectly but there was nothing in her expression or manner to suggest that she was gloating, or intent on exacting revenge. Having changed into warm, dry garments, she was wearing her hair in the Norman fashion and her braids showed below the hem of her veil in two glossy ash-blonde plaits. She might not be beautiful in the conventional sense, he thought, but she had presence, and there was a new, slumberous knowledge in her doe-brown eyes. She possessed a quiet, understated power that would only develop with time.

Was he jealous? Guyon shied away from the thought. He disliked the process of self-examination. He was a simple man and enjoyed a simple life without undercurrents. Eat, sleep, war and wench. 'I am made of coarse bread,' he muttered under his breath. It was beyond him to live with all these romantic ideals. A cup was a cup no matter how much you embellished it.

He almost choked as Gerard clapped him heartily on the back. 'Stop moping, you old warhorse!' he said cheerfully.

'Can't I drink my wine in peace without you bedevilling me?' Guyon growled.

'Can't bear to see the last of us fly the nest, can you?' Gerard grinned, topping up his own cup and sitting down on the bench at Guyon's side.

Guyon glared at him. 'Wine always did addle your imagination,' he said sourly.

Gerard eyed him keenly. 'At least I have one,' he retorted. He folded his arms on the trestle and leaned forward on them. 'Ever since my father employed you, you've had younglings to train to arms. Six boys, one after the other. You were always needed. And then after our mother died he married the Welsh woman, and just as we grew out of your care, Miles arrived and you had a new youngster to train. But what happens to an old warhorse when he is no longer required to serve? Turned out to grass perhaps?'

Guyon gathered himself to lash out at his tormentor who had just baldly stated a truth he would not admit, but Gerard seized his wrist in a young man's grip of steel. 'Listen, you fool: if you bide your time and make your peace with Miles's wife, you may have another generation to raise and train.'

Guyon regarded him through narrowed eyes, but Gerard's blue gaze was wide and candid, lacking all mockery.

'Don't be so stubborn. You jeopardise your own future.'

He released him, and Guyon shrugged away and returned to hunching over his wine. His mood, however, had lightened. The notion of training Miles's sons in their first feats of arms had not occurred to him before, and now he contemplated it thoughtfully.

As a youth, Miles had been a very different prospect when compared to his brood of boisterous golden brothers. Slight and dark, without their breadth, but twice their speed in tight corners, and a lively intelligence. Even when at rest, the lad's mind had been working, turning like the cogs in a mill wheel to grind the grain. Likely a child of his fathered on this woman would be neither too hulking to dodge behind a shield nor too slight to turn the blade of a Danish axe. Unless of course the woman was barren or birthed only daughters. He scowled at the thought and drained his cup. As the youth stepped forward to refill it he refused with an impatient wave of his hand and, thrusting himself away from the board, stalked outside to relieve himself.

'You should not torment him,' Aude remonstrated, nudging her husband.

'Guyon wears a blindfold unless someone snatches it away,' Gerard replied with an unrepentant shrug. 'When we were children we were always doing it, but as men we are too often blindfolded ourselves, and we lose the ability and the candour.

I might tease him, but in truth I love the old bastard here.' He clenched his fist under his heart. 'I want him to be content with his lot, and if that involves telling him some home truths, then so be it.'

Miles eyed his brother keenly. More than any of them, Gerard understood Guyon. In some ways their natures were alike, different facets of the same gem. Gerard was the louder, more ebullient version, and with a younger man's flexibility. He was less hidebound than Guyon and open to change, but they had a similar way of viewing the world, especially when it came to military matters, and they both regarded Miles as someone requiring their tuition and wisdom.

'Wherein lies the remedy then?' Miles asked. 'Am I to be constantly flaying him with my tongue in order to have the best out of him?'

'Just the occasional prick of the spur should suffice,' Gerard answered with a smile. 'Work him hard and keep him occupied until you have sons enough to snatch his blindfold. The moment he thinks he has been put out to grass is the moment you will lose him.' He took another swallow of his wine. 'He's getting older, I admit, but not yet too old.'

There was a small wine spill on the board and Miles traced a pattern in it with his fingertip. 'You preach a fine homily, Gerard, but how in God's name am I to convince Guyon's imagination?'

'What imagination?' Gerard scoffed, and then shook his head. 'Do not worry, brother. I have already done the sowing for you. The rest is left to your lady to fill the cradle.'

Miles raised his brows and glanced at Christen, who was staring at the tablecloth and blushing. He smiled, remembering one or two highly satisfying recent encounters between them. 'It is in hand,' he said. 'I—'

He did not complete the rest of the sentence, but stared in dismay. Guyon, returning to the hall from his piss, had stepped aside to admit the Earl of Hereford and two knights of his bodyguard.

Immediately Christen was on her feet, her expression filled with anger and revulsion. Miles rose too, and grasped her hand in firm warning. 'Gently, my love,' he murmured. 'We must greet the Earl of Hereford as an honoured guest, although I suspect this is not a social visit.' He made a peremptory gesture that sent servants scurrying to set more places at the high table.

FitzOsbern stripped his riding gauntlets as he mounted the steps to the dais, and then tossed them on the trestle. Of heavy leather, they still looked as if they were occupied by a pair of hands. His men went left and right and sat down.

Miles made a perfunctory obeisance. 'This is indeed a surprise, sire,' he said, 'but you are very welcome to join our meal?'

The Earl shook his head but accepted the cup of wine that Aude poured and presented to him. 'I do not have the time to think of my stomach,' he said curtly.

Miles reseated himself, pulling Christen down with him.

'I was out of Hereford when your messenger arrived, and he did not catch up with me until yesterday evening,' FitzOsbern said. 'It is a great pity he was not timelier.' He drank, put his cup down and splayed his huge hands on the board. 'The city of York has fallen to the Danes. There is a Danish fleet in the Humber and the locals have welcomed it with joy and risen up against us. The King is bound north to put an end to this impudence once and for all. You and Gerard are summoned with all haste.'

'York has fallen?' Gerard exchanged looks with Miles.

'And Stafford and Shrewsbury. Bleddyn and Eadric Cild have

burned the latter to the ground. I am bound there now to relieve the garrison while the castle still holds. Exeter is in turmoil, and Somerset has risen up. The sons of Harold Godwinson have landed from Ireland and are wreaking havoc. The King is already riding to Stafford to deal with that uprising himself, and then across to York, to put that one down.' FitzOsbern bared his teeth. 'I could use you myself, but the King has prior claim, and I know which of us you would rather serve.'

Miles grimaced. Neither for the moment. 'Where shall I find him?'

'Chasing Danes in Holderness, and he wants you with him now – sooner than now,' FitzOsbern said, and finished his wine.

'The Devil's arse,' muttered Gerard, palming his face.

'Precisely. And we are like to be up it unless we can bring these rebellions under control.' His gaze roved the board and fixed hawk-like on Christen, who sat white-faced on the edge of the bench. 'Lock her up while you are gone and have her watched. The English renege on their promises.'

Christen trembled under his scrutiny, and had to look down so that she would not reveal the blaze of hatred in her eyes.

'I will deal with my wife as she deserves and as I see fit,' Miles replied neutrally, and turned to Christen. 'You may leave,' he said. 'Take Aude with you; these matters are no concern of women.' He reached beneath the trestle to press her knee.

Christen swallowed bile and rose to her feet. Aude at her side, she curtseyed deeply and left the hall. Behind her she heard FitzOsbern remarking to Miles that she ought not to be permitted the dangerous privilege of an eating knife at her belt.

Once in the safety of her chamber, Christen drew the small antler-hilted dagger of which FitzOsbern had spoken and eyed the blade. She imagined thrusting it into the Earl of Hereford's body. And then she cast it away from her and covered her face with her hands.

Aude stooped to retrieve it and returned it to Christen. 'Yes,' she said, 'I feel the same way. The sooner that man leaves here the better, but the hard tidings he brings will remain when he has gone.'

'Yes indeed,' Christen said. A feeling of cold dread had begun to creep through her from her core, from the buried things she had kept to herself and not spoken about because she had thought she might never have to do so. But FitzOsbern's news had changed all that.

'Is something wrong?' Aude asked with concern. 'Other than FitzOsbern?'

Christen sheathed the little knife. She had had it since she was a child and her name was engraved along the centre of the blade. 'I cannot tell you,' she said, 'because I need to tell Miles first – something I should have told him before now. And it concerns FitzOsbern's news.'

Aude looked at Christen with worried eyes. Her expression held a mingling of both sympathy and suspicion. 'You do weave a tangled web,' she said.

'It is not treasonous,' Christen replied, 'but it is a family matter and one I ought to have cleared up at the outset. It is just that the time has never been right.'

Aude clucked her tongue against the roof of her mouth in exasperation, but gave Christen a swift peck on the cheek. 'Whatever it is, I wish you well, and I will pray for a good outcome.'

Christen thanked her. She was going to need every prayer she could garner.

*

FitzOsbern finished his wine and started to pull on his gauntlets. 'I mean what I said about watching your English wife,' he said. 'She could be dangerous.'

Guyon stood up from the trestle. 'I have not always seen matters the same way as the lady Christen,' he growled, dark eyes filled with challenge, 'but I say to you that she is as loyal and true as the King's own wife. I have doubted her in the past of my own folly, and I have been proved wrong. And when I am wrong, I say so.'

'That is as may be,' retorted the Earl, 'but it does no harm to remain on your guard, because people, women especially, are fickle, even the ones you trust in good faith. Look what happened to Samson in the Bible when he trusted Delilah.'

'My wife is not like that,' Miles said. 'As my marshal says, I would trust her with my life – with my child's life. She is everything I could desire.'

'Well, take leave of such desire,' the Earl snapped as they left the hall for the stables. 'It will be a long, hard winter before you see it again. Your mind needs to be clear for your work, not fettered by a woman's wiles.'

'I hazard my mind is less fettered than yours, sire,' Miles said as they went outside. It was still raining – a light but persistent drizzle.

FitzOsbern cast him a fierce stare. 'Pray that your clever tongue does not outstrip your usefulness,' he warned.

His horse was brought out from shelter and the rug removed from over the saddle. Seizing the reins, FitzOsbern mounted the stallion.

'Make haste,' FitzOsbern barked at Miles. 'The King awaits your service. You should be on the road within the hour. There's still enough daylight left to make a start. You can get to Hereford by nightfall.'

Miles made the customary obeisance, exaggerating it slightly, and held it while the Earl turned the stallion and spurred away through the open gate and on to the puddle-blotted Hereford road.

Christen glanced up from her sewing as Miles entered the room. The rain reflected the firelight, making topaz droplets sparkle in his hair and twinkle on his cloak. He sat down on the bed and, uttering a heavy sigh, rubbed his eyes.

'I am sorry about FitzOsbern,' he said. 'I do not want to leave, but I must.'

She nodded and stitched without speaking until she reached the end of her thread. If she lost him in battle, FitzOsbern would claim Ashdyke and Milnham for his own and either do away with her or give her to one of his men. Airing her fears might ease her burden but would only add to the heavy one she was about to lay on him, and the next moments were not going to be easy.

'There is a matter on my mind of much greater weight than the behaviour of the Earl of Hereford,' she said, biting her lip.

'Oh?' He gave her a sharp look.

'It concerns my grandfather.'

Frowning, Miles folded his arms. 'I thought that saving your brother, you were without living kin.'

'It wasn't necessary to mention it before.'

Miles snorted. 'Just as it was not important that I mentioned Emma to you? How well I remember your response to that!'

Heat burned Christen's face but she held her ground. 'That was different. She is a child of your loins, given house-room under your roof. I have not seen my grandsire since I married Lyulph. For all I know he may be dead, but if he is not and his life is in danger, then I owe him my duty.'

'And why should his life be endangered?'

'He lives in Staffordshire, in the north of the county . . . he is thegn of a manor there called Oxley.'

'I see, and just what would you have me do?'

'Keep the wolves from his door as you kept them from mine. You have the King's favour. Surely it will not be too difficult to give my grandsire your protection.'

Miles shook his head. 'If the King's ire falls on Staffordshire, I can tell you from experience that there is nothing anyone can do.' He went to examine his shield which was leaning up against the wall and checked the straps for signs of wear. All of the military kit would need to be gone over and prepared for a battle campaign. Once his heart would have leaped in anticipation, but now he was aware of a dragging feeling of reluctance. 'I am useful to the King, but not part of his inner circle.'

'But he needs you badly, or else he would not have sent such urgent word by FitzOsbern.'

He raised his brows. 'Not so badly that he would grant me whatever I wanted for the asking.'

Christen put her sewing aside and faced him. 'If you do not want to agree to it, forget the words were ever spoken.'

Miles rubbed his palm over his face. 'No, but I want to know much more before I step into the arena.'

Christen folded her arms, protecting herself. 'He is Wulfric, lord of Oxley, and he is my mother's sire,' she said. 'If death has not claimed him, then he will enter his sixty-fifth winter this Martinmas.'

'Not a deal to choose between him and Lyulph in age then,' Miles observed. The candle fluttered on its pricket from a draught blowing under one of the shutters and the sound of rain spattered against the wood. It was mid-afternoon already. Hardly the time to be setting out on a campaign, but when the King commanded, a wise man obeyed.

'There were ten years between them and it was one of the reasons he cut all ties after my marriage. When I was a child, my grandfather doted upon me. He would buy me ribbons and trinkets from the fairs and I was his cosseted pet. Apparently I was the living image of my grandmother who had been the love and joy of his life. Osric resembled my father's side and my grandsire related to him as another male of the line. When my parents died, my grandfather thought that my wardship should be given to him and the right of my marriage to a man of his choosing. He offered money for that right, but King Edward preferred to give me in marriage to Lyulph as a reward for services rendered. I was fifteen years old and dutiful and it was not possible to disobey the King's wishes.'

'And your grandfather objected because you belonged to him and he felt he should have had the right to say who you should wed?'

She nodded. 'He was angry. His will had been thwarted. He said that the King was meddling and that it was a family matter, but because my father was a tenant in chief to the King, my marriage was indeed within the royal gift. My grandsire refused to bless the match – he said Lyulph was not good enough for me, and he severed all ties. I have not seen him since. A few times I sent messages, but he never replied. If he still lives, he may not welcome an intervention, but I still need to try and keep him safe for the sake of my conscience. We are estranged now, but we are kin and we were close once.'

Miles pondered what she had said. An old man, as prickly as a thorn thicket with pride and probably as dangerous as the wild boars that habitually dwelt in such places. No, not an old man, he corrected himself. At three score and five, some men were ready for the grave, but others still had mettle in them. His own maternal grandfather had led a warband and taken active joy in the fighting until his seventieth winter.

'Do you know if he fought on Hastings field with King Harold? Was he capable?'

'I know that he sent men to Stamford and to Senlac but my brother led them, being the heir, and for that he was dispossessed of my father's lands which had come to him the year before. A vassal of Montgomery's holds my father's lands now, but I am not so foolish as to believe you can do anything about that particular situation.'

'No,' Miles agreed wryly. 'Did your grandfather submit after the great battle?'

'For the sake of the village, I heard so. Osric turned rebel and fled into Wales to join Eadric Cild's warband. That is as much as I know.'

Miles sighed, and rumpled his hair. 'I might be able to help him given more than my fair share of fortune and the King's goodwill, but your brother is a serious obstacle in my path. Eadric and his allies are wreaking havoc between Shrewsbury and Chester. It is very possible that Osric may head for Oxley as he headed for Ashdyke, and to similar effect. King William in a rage makes FitzOsbern look like a saint. If Oxley is discovered succouring rebels, William will wipe it from the face of the earth.'

Christen looked at him in dismayed alarm. 'Knowing Osric it is exactly what he will do. You have to stop him.'

He grimaced. 'I could indeed go to Oxley and warn your grandfather of his peril, which he may well choose to ignore because he is more likely to take Osric's part than mine and blood is thicker than water.' He rubbed his chin. 'I could track down your brother, tie a millstone round his feckless neck and throw him in the nearest river – which I am sorely tempted to do. Or I suppose I could go directly to the King.'

'But you just said that when he is in a rage he makes FitzOsbern look like a saint!' Christen stared at him in bafflement. 'Where would be the use in that?'

He shook his head. 'Come, help me arm,' he said, and went to the clothing pole and took down his quilted under-tunic from the coffer. Having worked his way into the garment with Christen pulling and tugging it into place, he paused before donning his mail shirt. 'I would not go to William with this tale as it stands,' he said.

'But if you lied to him and he found out, he would flay you alive. I have heard enough about him to know that much.'

'I do not intend to lie. I value my own skin too much to chance it, and I owe King William my loyalty too. Whatever my doubts, I knelt to him and swore to be his man.'

'Then what are you going to do?' she demanded. 'This is not some Twelfth Night guessing game!'

Miles caught her hands in his and lifted them to his lips. 'Indeed,' he said, 'and Gerard would have rightly throttled me by now. I am going to ask him to give me Oxley to hold for him.'

Christen wondered how she had ever dared to think she could match wits with this man. 'You are what?'

He shrugged his way into his hauberk – a steel mesh comprised of thousands of steel rings riveted together and falling to the knee in a sinuous layer of protection. It had cost his father sufficient to complain only half in jest that Miles had better not grow any taller or wider unless he was prepared to go into lifelong debt with the Jews, and that if he broke any links or left it to get rusty he could pay for the repairs and maintenance himself.

'Any place that does not swear loyalty will either be razed to the ground or brought ruthlessly to heel. I have ridden and foraged with King William's army and I know what happens. I will ask him to give me Oxley to deal with as I see fit, since my wife has family connections.'

He flexed his arm within the mesh casing, making sure he had sufficient ease of movement.

'And if my grandfather should still be alive and offer you resistance?' Christen asked, feeling sick.

'I shall cross that bridge when I come to it; I need to do a great deal of thinking between here and Stafford and hone the rough edges until they are smooth.'

'Smooth enough to slip your feet from under you,' she said with a shiver. 'Do not overreach yourself.'

Miles passed his sword belt around his waist and latched the buckle. Then attached the scabbarded sword itself and tied the thongs. 'Would you rather I rode directly to Oxley to confront your grandsire, or set out to track down your brother?' he demanded. 'At least this way the King's wrath will be deflected and I can try and do something about saving your grandfather and his village – if he is still alive. If he is not, then Oxley will still come to you anyway, and to our heirs, his great grandchildren. Osric will never inherit. I can tell you that for a certainty. His only course is exile or death.'

'I don't know!' Christen spread her arms. 'If you asked me my own name I would not know it at the moment. Probably you are right, and I have the suspicion you will go your own way regardless.'

Miles drew her against him and held her in a light embrace so that she was not bruised against the glittering mesh of his armour. 'I swear I will keep faith. Fret if you must, but do not drive yourself to distraction. I promise I will do my best for your grandfather and for Oxley.'

His lips were as fierce as his hands were gentle and she responded to him with a desperation born of the need to believe and the knowledge that she might never see him again.

Behind them came the sound of a raucously cleared throat, followed by the gentle clack of the curtain rings. Miles glanced over his shoulder and met the sympathetic regard of his brother.

'The horses are saddled and the men waiting,' Gerard said. 'Christ, but it's foul weather for riding. I tell you, the wilds of the north are no substitute for the warmth and comfort offered here.'

'Then do not go,' Christen said, a desolate note in her voice.

'I'd rather my flesh clothed my hide than a whipping post,' Gerard said wryly. He gave Christen a strained smile. 'We'll be back before you know it, and dripping with booty to adorn you and Aude like queens!'

'The booty of the English, dyed in their blood?' Christen said bitterly.

Catching Miles's look of exasperation, Gerard muttered an excuse and left the room.

'Will it be like that, Miles?' Christen whispered.

'Do you really want me to answer?'

She stared at him, clad in his mail shirt as she had first seen him, that same hardness of steel pointing up the differences between them. A Norman invader and an English widow. But she had married him, dwelt with him, fought with him and then laughed, taken his child into her love, and begun to discover the complex, often tender man beneath that protective netted surface. It was all as nothing. She could not read his eyes – or perhaps she read them all too well.

'No,' she said. 'I do not think that I do.'

Miles took her in his arms again, and after a brief hesitation she clung to him, but felt only the bite of steel beneath his cloak.

'God keep you, my lord,' she whispered as he released her from the kiss.

'Rather God help me,' he replied grimly, and drew the curtain aside to enter the main room where those who were riding with him were gathered around the hearth drinking cups of hot broth to sustain them on the road.

Christen donned her own thick cloak and a pair of stout boots and went into the hall, not to join Miles, who was already occupied among the men, but to find Aude so that they could each draw comfort from the other as their men rode away to war.

11

Stafford Castle, November 1069

Miles slid from the grey's back and stood in the almost ankle-deep sludge of Stafford Castle's bailey. A bitter wind drove his sodden cloak against his back and whipped the stallion's tail between his mired hocks. A groom came running from the shelter of the stable building to take the reins and Miles handed Cloud into the man's care.

The rain, which had held off for the last hour of their journey, began again, fine in the wind as wet mist, a rain to penetrate the bones until they would never be warm again. He removed his helm and absently touched a sore spot where his coif had chafed his skin. He commanded Leofwin to take the supplies they had foraged to the master marshal.

The pack horses squelched away in Leofwin's wake. The light was fading fast although it was barely mid-afternoon, and torches glimmered in the main keep. Miles turned in the opposite direction towards one of the ramshackle cooking sheds set up on the edge of the bailey palisade. A bulky Flemish woman with two stringy brown plaits was tending the huge iron cooking pot suspended over the flames. Standing back to wipe her forehead on her rolled-back sleeve, she looked at Miles.

'What you brought me this time?' she demanded in a heavy Flemish accent.

Miles extended his hands to the heat from the fire and the bubbling rich stew. The smell of the food teased his nostrils and at the same time made him feel sick. 'Enough to keep your cauldron simmering,' he said shortly and sat down on the bench at the side of the cooking pot. He tried not to see the bewildered, frightened country people from whom the supplies to feed the Norman army had been taken, but his mind still filled with the vision of the homes burning beneath the bleak November sky, and he could still hear the wails of women and children, and the angry despair of the men.

Will it be like that? Christen had asked him with reproach in her eyes, and he thought he would not be able to meet her gaze ever again.

'Nothing to match yesterday I'll warrant, sire,' said the woman with a chuckle, not in the least deterred by his abruptness. 'Never seen so many sheep at one time.'

Miles grunted. He and Leofwin, ahead of the main foraging party, had come across a large herd of black-faced sheep guarded only by an old man and his grandson. As a sop to his conscience and with the thought of Christen's damning gaze on him, Miles had left them a dozen ewes in lamb and their tup, and driven the remainder back to the castle to feed the troops.

'Might as well have a share in your labour,' she added as he said nothing, and ladled a generous portion of mutton stew into a bowl and gave it to him.

Miles took it automatically. Greasy chunks of meat floated

amid a broth of onions, sage and barley. He thanked her and moved away as two men arrived dripping and cold from guard duty.

Cupping his hands around the bowl, he raised it to his lips and took a sip. Outside the awning the rain pelted down, filling the hollows in the churned-up mud of the bailey floor. A boy ran across the ward, torch in hand, and disappeared over the bridge and into the keep. Another foraging party rode in with a cow and bellowing calf, a pack horse in tow laden with sacks of flour and strings of onions. The men swore roughly in Flemish, cursing the foul English weather, but their manner was jovial.

The woman at the cauldron shrieked a greeting and coarse banter in Flemish ensued that Miles only half understood. In the midst of the repartee, the leader of the troop, Lukas, recognised Miles and, handing his mount to a companion, came to purloin a bowl of stew. The woman blushed and batted her sparse eyelashes at him. He slapped her good-naturedly on the rump, gestured his guffawing men away and sat down beside Miles on the bench.

'Stinking weather,' he commented by way of greeting, and took a noisy gulp of the broth. 'Is this your mutton?'

Miles murmured assent.

'The marshal didn't believe his eyes when he saw all those sheep bleating around the bailey. I thought his eyes were going to pop out of his skull!' He took another slurp of the broth and considered Miles with shrewd eyes. 'You don't look too happy about it – but then this rain is enough to draggle anyone's tail feathers.'

Miles shook his head and wished the Fleming would go away.

'Nothing to do with having an English wife then?' Lukas grinned and elbowed Miles in the ribs. 'Your men and mine exchange tales at the campfire. I hear she has a temper and a way between the sheets to match?'

'It is nothing of that,' Miles said evenly, although his own temper was on edge and he was irritated that his men thought his life with Christen fair game for campfire gossip. 'If you must pry, I am surfeited with pursuing pathetic peasants across the mire in order to take away their food.' Thrusting his half-empty bowl into the astonished mercenary's hand, he rose to his feet and stalked from the shed into the murky drizzle.

Across the bailey, the stables bustled with activity as other foraging parties returned from their day scouring the countryside. Miles entered the building and dismissed the harassed lad who had been attending Cloud. 'Leave him,' he said. 'Attend elsewhere before the King has a rebellion here among his own soldiers.' He took the grey's halter and stroked the soft grey muzzle.

'Sire.' The lad ducked under Cloud's neck and went to deal with a Breton knight's horse that was kicking and stamping.

Cloud snuffled Miles's hair and face, and butted him, seeking food. Miles pushed him away and balled up a wisp of hay to finish rubbing him down. 'Give over, you walking dog's dinner,' he said as Cloud lipped the back of his neck. The stallion's coat had grown thick and coarse for winter, the smoky dappling shrouded in white hair so deep that it was almost a pelt. Mud caked him to the belly but there was no sense in tackling that until it had dried and could be dealt with using a curry comb.

Miles lifted Cloud's hooves, each one in turn, to check that the shoes were still securely nailed and that the frogs were clean. A stone in the off hind needed the attention of his dagger and, straddling the hoof, shoulder pressed to the stallion's rump, he dug the obstruction free. Suddenly the horse flinched and plunged, and as the stone came loose Miles lost his balance and was flung against the partition, his breath driven from his lungs. Wheezing, he struggled to his feet and stooped over for a moment while he recovered his breath and controlled the pain. Then he took a closer look at the horse. Cloud was trained for battle and mettlesome, but he was amiable and playful with Miles, never skittish. Gently examining the stallion, Miles stopped abruptly as he saw the narrow red gash scored down Cloud's haunch under the heavy winter coat, and disappearing into the thick mud. It was not a serious wound, but sufficient to cause sharp discomfort if pressed upon as he had just done. Thinking back over the last few hours, Miles realised it must have been inflicted by the burly giant with the pitchfork who had almost run him through on the tines before Leofwin's axe had cloven the man from crown to chin.

Still short of breath, Miles gentled the horse, speaking in a soothing murmur, stroking his neck and face. The grey whickered and butted him again, and Miles fed him an apple he had been saving for himself, although he took a bite before giving the remainder to his horse. Glancing along Cloud's powerful dappled body to the wound, he admitted to himself that his heart had ceased to take joy in battle campaigns, and had he not given his oath to serve the King in return for his lands he would have packed his baggage and returned to the Marches.

He and Gerard had joined the King at Lindsay, pursuing the Danes through the marshy reaches of Holderness. Miles had taken to the chase with alacrity, for the enemy were foreigners like themselves, mostly adventurers out for their own gain, and there had been no tenderness of conscience to hinder the pursuit. He had used his scouting skills to track them down, and then attacked without warning, using the power of the horseback charge if the land permitted, the stealth of a long knife in the dark if it did not. Neither he nor Gerard lost a single man.

Their sole casualty had been a horse that foundered in the marsh and was easily replaced from the booty they seized from the fleeing Danes.

Defeated but unwilling to concede the fight, their quarry retired across the Humber which was inaccessible to the Norman host because they had no ships in those waters to give chase. William had glowered savagely across the estuary at his enemy, and broken westwards instead, first to Nottingham to gather more troops and to assess the situation throughout England as intelligence reports came in, and then, confident that the other areas of rebellion were at least being contained for the time being, he had struck out for Staffordshire, to wreak his revenge on the rebels there.

Thus far Miles had neither had the time nor opportunity to speak to William about Oxley. At Nottingham, where he might have done so, the King had sent him on a reconnaissance of the roads to the north that would lead them into Staffordshire, and by the time he returned, William was occupied elsewhere and his report had been made instead to one of the King's adjutants.

It had not mattered in Lindsay when their quarry was Danish, or in Nottingham for that matter, but here in Stafford, with the ravaging going forth in ever-widening circles from the castle, it had become a matter of urgency. He had requested to see the King that morning before he had ridden out, but God alone knew when such a request would be granted, if at all.

He thought of the village they had raided that afternoon – Fletesbroc its name. They had instructions to brook no resistance. If the people refused to give up their goods and chattels to supply the Norman army, their homes were to be torched and the ringleaders killed. The livelihood of the entire village was to be destroyed so that those who remained would be too busy struggling to survive to think of raising rebellion, and even if they did, there would be no one of sufficient stature to do so. William of Normandy was determined to starve the people of northern England into submission.

Miles gazed at his hand where it lay on his stallion's rough hide and imagined it gripping a clotted sword. And then he thought of Christen. Nausea swept over him and he stumbled to a corner of the stall and was sick far beyond the mutton stew he had just eaten.

Entering the stable in search of Miles, Gerard discovered him grey and retching at the back of Cloud's stall. Gerard's generous mouth hardened into a thin line. He remembered when Miles had first come to Normandy, to the family castle outside Rouen. The strangeness of it all to a hill-bred boy of twelve; the malicious teasing and scorn from the oldest boys, who were not at ease with Miles's slight build and strange lilting accent. Miles had borne it well, too well, with an impassive face and blank eyes, but more than once Gerard had come across him like this in the privy or a corner of the ward.

'Save it for later,' he said, bracing a muscular arm across Miles's shoulder. 'The King wants to see you. I have just had the order from his usher. Best make haste.'

Another shudder rippled through Miles. 'Tell him to go to hell,' he gulped.

'Tell him yourself!' Gerard snapped. 'I have no wish to lose my hide repeating a remark made by you.'

Miles steadied himself against Gerard's bulk and stood straight. 'I cannot go,' he said hoarsely, his voice filled with dark loathing. 'Gerard, I cannot go. It is beyond me.'

Gerard gave him a swift, hard shake. 'You must, you have no choice.'

Miles ran his hand along Cloud's powerful neck, digging his

fingers into the thick silver coat. 'I should not have married an English wife and given her care of my heart and conscience. I doubt I will ever be able to look her in the face again.'

'I don't see . . .' Gerard started to protest, and then shrugged. 'You will certainly not be able to look her in the face again if you do not go to the King now and ask him for Oxley,' he said instead. 'This is your only chance.'

Miles tightened his fingers in Cloud's winter coat, making the stallion stamp and sidle. God in heaven, was that the blood price? Oxley? 'I wish I had died on Hastings field,' he said to Gerard, and walked out of the stable into the pouring rain.

'What kept you?' demanded William, Duke of Normandy and King of those parts of England that would accept him. He was thickset, verging on the corpulent, but powerful and muscular too; the size of his belly, swelling beneath his heavy scarlet robe, was no obstacle to his physical vigour. His dark hair was receding from his brow, and threaded with silver where it was cropped above his ears.

Miles advanced and bent the knee at William's chair. 'Your pardon, sire,' he replied woodenly. 'My stallion was wounded during a skirmish today and I was tending to him when I received your summons.'

William raked him with a piercing stare and gestured for him to rise. 'Nothing serious? We need to keep as many horses sound as we can.'

'No, sire, a gash from a pitchfork and a flesh wound. It did not go deep.' Miles swallowed. A torch sputtered in its sconce and flared up at an impurity, and Miles jumped.

William bade him sit on a bench at the side of his chair, and beckoned a youth to give Miles a cup of wine. 'They will not have the wherewithal to raise their hands to beg when I have done with them, let alone pitchforks,' he said icily. 'You will make a wider circuit tomorrow, Miles. Take what will be useful to us and torch the rest. I will send fire through this land like the tail of the comet that predicted the death of Harold the Usurper. By fire and sword, the English shall acknowledge me as their king if they will not have it any other way.'

Miles was silent, although William plainly took his downcast eyes for deference.

One of the other men in the room, a high-ranking lord named Robert de Tosny, turned from warming his hands at the brazier. 'I heard a rumour that you have an English wife, le Gallois?' he said. 'This must be a long, cold way from your marriage bed.'

William looked sharply at Miles. Robert de Tosny was FitzOsbern's brother-in-law and the information so casually dropped could be no less than true. 'What do you say to this?'

De Tosny grinned like a fox and arched a sardonic brow at Miles, challenging him to extricate himself.

'It is indeed true,' Miles answered with a deliberately untroubled shrug. 'And it is also stale. I dispatched a copy of the contract to the King on the very day of the wedding and lodged another with the monks in Hereford.'

'Well, I have certainly not seen it,' William growled, 'and it should have been called to my attention by my clerks. What right do you have to take a wife without my permission?'

De Tosny looked smug.

'The right of conquest, sire?' Miles retorted, and then compressed his lips before he said something even more imprudent to his king.

The uncomfortable moment stretched out while everything hung in the balance, but eventually William's scowl lightened and his thin lips twitched in what might have been the beginnings of a smile. 'Likely one of my officials decided that the marriage of a minor half-Welsh vassal paled to insignificance in the light cast by the flames of rebellion,' he said, 'and probably he was right, unless your bride happens to be Eadgyth Swan-neck.'

'Not a patch on Harold's former mistress,' de Tosny intervened again, 'but generously dowered withal from what I heard.'

'She would have been better dowered if your brother-by-marriage had not been so eager to send in his minions to destroy her lands,' Miles retorted.

De Tosny arched his brows and, looking superior, said nothing. William shifted in his chair, which was on the small side for his muscular bulk.

'I had not looked for the complication of your marriage,' he said. 'An English woman you say?'

'Yes, sire, Christen of Ashdyke. Her husband fought against the Norwegians at Stamford and was too badly injured to fight us at Hastings. He performed homage for his lands to your officials, but he died in a dispute between the Earl of Hereford's men and his wife's brother, a dispute not of his making.'

William rubbed his jaw. 'I suspect you are being lean with the details here for a deliberate reason,' he said. 'But I will leave that for the moment. What I want to know is do you trust this new wife of yours?'

'I do not doubt her loyalty,' Miles said.

De Tosny snorted. 'Women do not know the meaning of the word! Likely she has already taken one of your English serfs into her bed and when you return she will claim the brat she spawns as yours and laugh behind your back!'

De Tosny never knew how it happened, only that suddenly he was locked in an excruciating wrestler's grip, and that his face was being rammed down towards the glowing lumps of charcoal in the brazier.

'Beg pardon now,' Miles snarled, 'before I brand a new smile on your face!'

'You addle-witted Welsh whoreson, let me go!'

De Tosny writhed, trying to break the impossible hold. Miles responded by tightening his grip and inching de Tosny's face closer to the glowing coals.

The King leaned forward. 'Let him go, Miles – so that he may apologise also to me. Plain speaking I value; unfounded gutter-smirching I will not tolerate.'

Miles reluctantly slackened his grip and stepped back. His victim pushed away from him, red-faced and furious, and, straightening his tunic, turned to the King. 'If I have offended, then I crave your pardon, sire,' he said, although his pinched expression revealed how much it was costing him to do so.

William jerked his head and said curtly, 'Go and bring me your brother, I want a word with him.'

De Tosny bowed, and rubbing his abused throat, threw another dagger glance at Miles and left the room. Background conversation which had ceased during the exchange began again, stilted at first, but gradually gathering a natural volume.

'So, Miles,' said William, leaning back again and stretching out his legs. 'Tell me about this sudden marriage of yours, and this English woman who is such a paragon that you would brand de Tosny's face for the kind of remark you would usually pass over with a shrug. You have given me the bare bones of the tale, but now I want the full story, and I will know if you do not give it to me.'

Miles returned to his wine and took a long drink. Unleashing his temper upon Robert de Tosny had settled him down, and he was able to give William what he wanted with rational neutrality.

The King listened, watching Miles through half-closed eyes

and pinching his stubble-dark chin. In another vassal the appropriating of Ashdyke would have been purely for personal gain, but Miles's motives were clearly more complex, and while William considered Miles le Gallois to be one of his most valuable scouts, he was not without his difficult side. It was a matter of balancing one against the other, and just now he was not so certain of which way the scales were weighted.

'There is another matter connected with Ashdyke, sire, a boon I would ask of you,' Miles ventured when he had finished.

'Name it then,' William said. 'Let us see just how far your impudence will go. I suppose I owe you for my son's horse – it is a fine animal.'

Miles squared his shoulders and drew a deep breath. 'My wife's grandsire, if he still lives, holds land in this county – the chief part being a village named Oxley. Rather than see it wasted if he should prove hostile, I ask you to grant it to me. I do not know the size of the holding, but I am given to believe that it is not large – or at least not large enough to interest any of your senior lords.'

William pursed his lips and gave Miles an evaluating look. 'Everything has its price, le Gallois.'

'Yes, sire, I know from experience that it is so.'

'Then in return for the granting you the favour of the right to this land, I expect you to remain in my service at your own expense until Candlemas. From Stafford, we are striking up to York and then through the mountains to sweep the English out of Chester. I will have sore need of your talents.' He gave Miles a hard stare and clenched his large fists on the arms of his chair. 'You have your choice. I cannot constrain you beyond Christmas, but if you go, be sure that you will lose the Staffordshire holding to the torch, and the other Marcher land you have acquired will be given to the Earl of Hereford.'

Miles stared at William, his sovereign lord, and strove to remain calm. He had his answer. Oxley was indeed the blood price. There was no mercy in William's face, for he had sought and found Miles's weak spot, and Miles understood that in this moment William was setting such hard terms upon him as a test, as a punishment, and as a warning to stay within the bounds of his service.

Swallowing bile, Miles forced himself to kneel before his king and set his hands between William's thick, powerful ones to do homage for the new lands, selling himself into bondage for the duration of the harsh winter campaign.

William gave him the kiss of peace, and, the deed complete, grunted with satisfaction. 'Good,' he said. 'Hold to your bargain, and I shall hold to mine.'

Miles bowed from William's presence, walked away to a solitary corner, and was sick.

12

Oxley, north Staffordshire

Miles guided Cloud through the oak and beech trees that formed Oxley's northernmost boundary. On the edge of winter, most of the leaves now carpeted the ground, but the ragged tail ends were still fluttering from the branches. Distantly a wolf howled in the fading light and was answered by at least two companions. The stallion threw up his head and snorted, eyes rolling. Miles gentled his ears and spoke softly to him in Welsh.

Leofwin eased his buttocks in the saddle and stared round, tense and on guard, his sword loose in the scabbard, ready to be drawn on the instant.

The sharp wind whipped leaves through the air, one striking Miles's face like a clammy small hand. It had taken most of the day to reach this deserted north corner of Staffordshire. Sleet had blown into their faces for much of the journey, sometimes turning to icy rain. Just now the sky was clear, but the wind in their faces was as keen as the blade of a filleting knife.

Miles parted his lips in a humourless smile. If Guyon rather than Leofwin had been guarding his back he would long since have been treated to a lecture on the inadvisability of taking on a Godforsaken place like this, miles from the beaten track, surrounded by a forested wilderness, populated by deer and wolves and the occasional surly English peasant, its only commendation that of a hunting preserve. Oxley, the blood price – a handful of nothing. Miles chuckled, causing Leofwin to stare at him askance.

'Never make a bargain with a king or a woman, for you will regret it,' he told his bemused knight. 'The deals struck are seldom worth a bean and you'll pay your soul in recompense.'

'My lord?'

'Ah, nothing,' Miles said, shaking his head as they began the descent to a tree-lined ford. 'The wanderings of a fevered—' He reined Cloud to a sudden stand and leaned over the stallion's tossing neck to examine the muddy ground.

'What is it?' Leofwin held up his hand to halt the nine men riding behind.

Miles dismounted to scrutinise more closely the churned mud and a heap of greenish horse droppings mulched among them. Then he rose from his crouch to study the tangled bramble bushes at the margins of the ford. 'About twelve horses to create this much disturbance,' he said, 'some shod, some not. Either the lord of Oxley is a renowned dealer in horseflesh or there is another reason for a group to have come through here recently.' He remounted Cloud and threaded his left arm through his shield straps.

'A dozen?' said Leofwin. 'We are evenly matched then should they prove to be rebels or hostile.'

Miles shook his head. 'Not quite. I would say there are at least another five on foot, and well armed. See the marks of hafts in the mud where they have rested their spears and axes while waiting to cross after the mounted ones? And if they have access to shod horseflesh, they will have equal access to good weapons.'

'Christ's wounds,' muttered Leofwin, glancing behind at the men who had not heard Miles's quietly spoken words but who had guessed from his actions that something was afoot. 'Do we carry on?' Again, his gaze flicked around their vicinity, filled with tension.

'Oh yes, we carry on,' Miles answered, 'but with caution until we know their exact numbers and capabilities.'

He grasped the reins and urged Cloud down to the swirling brown water. Even though the place was a ford, the crossing was not especially shallow after all the rainfall. The swift flow foamed around Cloud's hocks and rose in the middle of the stream to tug and suck at shoulders, belly and haunch. Cold as the high ground from which it came, it numbed the men's legs and thighs even in the short time they were in the water.

Once across, Miles again dismounted to check the churned hoof- and footprints before gathering his men together and explaining the situation and his plan to deal with it. Once decided, he turned to remount. 'Leofwin, come with me, the rest of you take shelter in the trees and muzzle your horses. We need to be as silent as possible.' He nodded to a sturdy Norman soldier on a stocky chestnut. 'Etienne, you have the command in my absence. I hold you responsible. The usual signals for advance or retreat.'

'Yes, my lord. What ab—'

The knight turned his head towards the boggy track leading to the village, following Miles's gaze which was already nailed there. The sound of a querulous male voice came to them, punctuated by the agitated sobs of a woman, and the wails of a distressed infant. It was too late to retreat into the trees. Miles quickly remounted and drew his sword.

A man appeared around the bend in the track and advanced on them out of the gloom. He was making heavy going of pushing a handcart laden with belongings for he was scrawny and approaching old age. Silver straggles of hair wisped from the edge of his woollen cap. He wore a short tunic of russet cloth, patched in several places, and topped by a moth-eaten cloak. A little behind him ran a woman, a generation younger, wearing a gown of the same russet cloth and a matted sheepskin cloak. Upon her back was a baby of about nine months old, bundled in a shawl that was knotted around her shoulders.

The man's head was down into the wind as he struggled to drag the cart down to the ford, although God alone knew how he expected to cross, and it was the woman who saw them first. She slithered to a stop, her eyes growing wide, and let out a great, square-mouthed wail. The baby howled even louder. The man raised his head, followed her stare and slowly let his handcart subside into the mud. A look of total despair crumpled his face and he sank to his knees, weeping beside his precariously balanced possessions.

Miles and Leofwin exchanged glances. The woman turned and began to stumble back the way she had come, sobbing and screaming. Miles kicked Cloud forward. The stallion's hooves flung up clods of mud, spattering the old man as Miles trotted past him to turn the woman about before she could raise the alarm in the village, although their presence at the ford and in such desperate straits suggested that perhaps it was already too late.

She fell to her knees, begging him in English to spare her life and that of the infant screaming on her back.

'Get up,' Miles replied curtly. 'You are not going to die.'

She covered her head with her hands and rocked to and fro, oblivious in her terror of what he was saying. He looked down at her, thinking of how he had first seen Christen rushing to the defence of her brother, neglectful of her own life.

'Get up,' he repeated sharply. 'I give you my word that you will not be harmed. Why are you fleeing the village?'

Her response was another wail, and Cloud plunged sideways, ears flickering, forelegs dancing a drum beat. Miles swore, turned the jibbing stallion in a half circle and trotted him back to the old man who had regained his feet and was staring numbly into the murky November twilight.

'Why are you running?' Miles demanded to know. 'Had you knowledge of our coming?'

The man shook his head, teeth chattering, and his gaze darted to Miles's band on their warhorses. 'No, lord,' he stuttered in a cracking voice, his body shuddering as much from cold as from fear.

'God's love, give him a horse blanket!' Miles snapped to Leofwin, and then: 'I am seeking Wulfric, lord of Oxley. I mean him no harm; he is my kin.'

The old man caught the blanket Leofwin threw to him and looked first at the coarse, thick fabric clutched in his knotty fingers, then back at Miles. 'Lord Wulfric ain't lord no longer,' he said, baring a mouth of worn yellow stumps. 'Not since this afternoon. Me and Freda – we saw our chance and fled with the bairn. They killed her husband, see, and used her for their sport; it is no wonder the lass is wandering in her wits.' His gaze circled their group again and he crossed himself. 'Norman or English,' he spat, suddenly vehement, 'what does it matter, you are all the same. Go on, finish me and my girl and have done!' He threw down the blanket and tore open the frayed neck of his tunic to bare his skeletal breast.

Miles ignored the defiant, dramatic gesture and stared along the track, eyes narrowing. 'So, are you saying you are fleeing from the English? That they have taken the manor?'

The old man gave a jerky nod. 'Yes. Came on us like a pack of wolves. What I say – you are all the same.'

'Lord Wulfric, is he dead?'

'As good as. They cut him down when he tried to stop them, the bastards. Ride on, go and finish what they have begun, but be quick about it. There isn't much of Oxley left to plunder.'

'How far to the village?'

'About five furlongs.' He closed his tunic, staring at Miles in bewilderment, plainly wondering why he was not dead.

'Where are they now?'

'When we ran, they were all in the hall, God rot them, sorting their plunder and swilling Lord Wulfric's ale.'

'Not for long,' Miles said grimly. 'Tonight they will sleep sightless in the midden. What is your name?'

'Golding, my lord.'

'So, Golding, go and comfort your daughter and return to your home if it still stands. You'll not cross the ford anyway in this spate, and you would not survive the soaking.'

The old man gaped at him.

'In Christ's name, either wrap yourself in that blanket or give it back; I'll not see it wasted in the mud.' He reined Cloud around and prepared to ride on with his men for a couple more furlongs.

'Lord Wulfric doesn't have any Norman kin,' Golding said, folding the blanket around his shoulders.

'He does now,' Miles replied.

It was full dark when Miles led his men to take on the English rebels who were roistering in Oxley's hall. There were fourteen in all, mostly English but with a couple of Welshmen and a Dane among their ranks. Eleven were carousing within and three were outside on guard duty but they were busy emptying Oxley's cellars and none were sober.

Miles and his men crouched behind the palisade and waited with the patience of stalking predators. Some of the stakes were rotten and a couple missing altogether, showing that the place had been neglected for several years, probably well before the great battles at Stamford and Hastings.

Through the gap, Miles could see the well housing and the guard lounging against it taking hearty swigs from a drinking horn. The sound of shouts and raucous laughter spilled from the hall and then a ripe belch as a reveller staggered outside to urinate against the manor's daub and wattle wall. A woman screamed unseen in the shadows. Moments later, a raider lurched into the torchlight, pushing his genitals back into his breeches. 'Your turn next!' he hailed the guard by the well, and cupped his crotch to emphasise the point, before tottering back inside the hall.

Chuckling, the guard raised the horn to finish his drink, discovered only dregs, and tossed it across the garth before wiping his face and shambling over to the wall to relieve his own bladder.

Miles signalled to Leofwin, slipped inside the compound through the gap and moved across the garth on cat-silent feet. A knife flashed and blood covered Miles's hand in a hot flood as his victim buckled to the ground and twitched in his death throes. Miles stepped over him, uttered the tawny owl's cry and was answered by Leofwin, who had dealt with the guard he had targeted. Miles pivoted and made his way in swift stealth to deal with the third one.

*

Wulfric of Oxley moved his hands over the old sable cloak that covered his body, remembering how his father had given it to him as a wedding gift when he married Aelfreda. A covering for two to share in the warm darkness. He felt that darkness pulling at him now, and Aelfreda was there waiting in his peripheral vision, young like a maiden, her silver hair loose to her waist and her lips parted in a soft, welcoming smile.

Light flickered painfully against his lids, intruding on the beauty of his vision and returning him to the squalid reality of the serf's hut where they had borne him to bleed his life away through the spear wound in his side. Opening his eyes, he saw a string of blood puddings and a flitch of smoked bacon hanging from the roof beam. The raiders hadn't yet found those. One of the hall servants, Bonde, was holding a lighted brand close to his face, and as he squinted away from the intrusive light he heard Bonde's wife, Gythe, murmur to her husband that he was still alive but hadn't they better fetch the priest.

'Father Eadgar has gone,' Bonde muttered from the side of his mouth. 'Took the plate and ran for the woods like all the others with any sense. It is only fools like us that are left for the sport of those nithings in the hall.'

'Hush,' the woman said, 'he will hear. He is not beyond that yet.'

Bonde mumbled something and the glare of the brand mercifully dipped away from Wulfric's eyes as its bearer retreated to hunch before the embers in the hearth.

'Drink this, my lord,' said Gythe, gently lifting Wulfric's head and touching his lips with the rim of a wooden beaker. 'It will ease your thirst.'

He turned aside and the bitter liquid spilled into his beard. 'Go,' he whispered. 'You can do nothing more for me. Your husband is right. You should take to the woods and save yourselves while you still have time.'

Gythe chewed her lower lip and shook her head in distress. All her life she had served in the hall, and she could not change the habit now.

Once more Wulfric closed his eyes, seeking the elusive darkness. Sixty-five years he had seen out in this place and were it not for this wound would probably have seen out another ten, for his health was robust, his body that of a man still remembering his prime. Ironic that it should be an English spear that brought him to his death when all around his countrymen were falling prey to Norman brutality.

They had come shortly after noon, a well-armed but badly disciplined splinter mob from the Welsh, English and Danes that had sacked Shrewsbury and Stafford and were now fleeing from the wrath of FitzOsbern and William the Bastard, and finding shelter where they could.

Wulfric's first emotions at the sight of them had been of angry fear and anticipation, the latter quickly disappointed as he realised that his grandson Osric was not among their company.

Under different circumstances he might have given this particular warband food and supplies and sent them on their way, but with the Normans too close for comfort he had made the mistake of hesitating, and when they had threatened him rather than negotiate, he had lost his temper and ordered them to leave. The result was that they now occupied his hall and all it provided, while he lay in a serf's hut, wounded by a spear, his life slowly trickling away through the hole in his side.

A spasm twisted his face. The Normans would come now anyway and raze Oxley for succouring English rebels. He had thrown away his life for nothing, for a moment of weakness and the making of a wrong decision. He was not surprised, because his life had been a litany of such decisions compounded by ill fortune.

He thought of his beloved Aelfreda, and for a moment she was there again in the shadows, holding out her hand, encouraging him to take it, but he couldn't, not yet. His time was close at hand, but he still had breath in his body.

Aelfreda had gone ahead long ago. She had died in childbed in her thirtieth winter. Their daughter Saea had made a good marriage to a wealthy Shropshire thegn, Burwald Trigson, but he and his son-in-law had never been more than tepidly cordial. The children had brightened his life for a time. Osric irrepressibly mischievous, a handful, and Christen so much like Aelfreda with her thick, barley-blonde hair that it broke his heart.

The boy had grown up feckless and selfish; the girl had been wasted on marriage to an old man, becoming a staid matron when she was barely fifteen. His behaviour at the time had been unforgivable he knew, but so had the blow of her union with Lyulph, King Edward's huscarl, a man of prowess, rewarded for his service with Christen's hand in marriage, but so much older than her, and of lower status. Wulfric had often contemplated mending the rift, but his pride had kept him rooted here in his own darkness, too fettered to make the move, and now it was too late.

A sudden draught blew smoke over the bed ledge in the hut where he lay, wrapped in the sable cloak, and he started to choke and splutter. Gythe was quickly at his side, admonishing her husband to close the door.

'Hush, woman!' Bonde said urgently, gesticulating back at her, his head and shoulders thrust out of the doorway. 'Something is happening at the hall. Listen.'

She came to his side.

'Fighting, do you hear it?'

She nodded.

Wulfric's teeth chattered. Distantly, almost as if it was a part of his dark dream, he heard the shouts of men, the language English and alarmed, and then the sound of a sword blade sliding off iron.

Bonde hastily ducked back indoors. 'It's the Normans,' he said, wild-eyed. 'We are surely finished now!'

Horses pounded past at a canter and a terse command was shouted in French, followed by a thud and a scream. Gythe pressed the end of her wimple over her face and sat down on a stool, whimpering and rocking.

Wulfric gathered his flagging strength and by a supreme effort of will slid his legs over the side of the bed shelf and pushed himself to his feet. Every breath he took burned his lungs and his vision was brown and blurred at the edges. He felt hot blood sliding down from his waist. Hunched over, clutching the wall for support, he staggered to the door.

A Norman soldier was bent over one of the rebels who was sprawled in the road. Another knight, mounted, held his companion's roan horse by the bridle. The rebel's battleaxe lay in the mud beside him, its blade smirched with mire. The Norman picked it up, hefted it with a remark to his companion and then strapped it to his saddle and remounted the roan. Lances couched, the two men reined about towards the hall.

Once they were sufficiently distant, Bonde hurried from the dwelling to examine the dead man lying in the road. He was a ruddy-bearded warrior, his temple crushed in by one of the horses. He wore a decorated silver bracelet and a good fur-lined cloak, both of which Bonde grabbed, all the time glancing around in fear.

Wulfric groaned and slid down the door post to the ground, clutching his wound. Gythe cried out to Bonde as he returned with his spoils and between them they bore the lord of Oxley back to the bed bench and laid him down, covering him again with the sable cloak.

'Go,' Wulfric panted. 'I order you to go. If you stay, like me and that bastard out there, you will die.'

Exchanging looks of mutual agreement, Gythe and Bonde gathered their belongings into a bundle and prepared to run. They could do nothing more for their lord.

'God bless you and God take you to His bosom and keep you,' Gythe said, tears running down her face as she set a jug of water near Wulfric's arm, and half a loaf.

Wulfric said nothing, and closed his eyes.

Moments later, Gythe and Bonde slipped from their dwelling and headed for the woods with their three goats and the five silver pennies dug up from under the hearth stone that was all their fortune, leaving Wulfric to his sable cloak and his dying dreams.

Miles wiped his sword blade clean on the body of the dead man at his feet, sheathed the weapon, and stepped over the bench at the high table to stand at the head of the hall. The place was a shambles of upturned benches, broken jugs, spilled food, strewn loot and dead rebels. They had not stood a chance. Sated with food and three parts drunk, secure in the knowledge that no Normans would be this far abroad in the Staffordshire wilds on a bitter night like this, they had been lulled into a false sense of security and had paid with their lives.

Tight-lipped, Miles stalked down the hall he had just made his by a combination of stealth and ferocity. He stepped over another body and advanced upon the servants who were huddled together in a corner like a brood of hens confronted by a starving fox.

'You and you,' he commanded, pointing at two youths. 'Find a cart, pick up the dead, and deliver them to the church. They are God's responsibility now. The rest of you put the trestles against the wall and set the place to rights as best you may.' He looked round. 'Where is your lord? I am given to understand that he has been wounded.'

They stared at him numbly, for they had just seen him burst into the hall and kill the rebel leader as he sat at meat in their lord Wulfric's chair.

'Set aside your fear,' Miles said in fluent English, 'the killing is finished. Where is your lord? I need to speak with him, and I swear that I mean him no harm.'

After a long pause, a fair-haired boy on the edge of adolescence stepped forward. His mother made to jerk him back into anonymity by the scruff but it was too late. 'He is down in the village, sire,' he said, and sleeved a drip from his nose. 'Gythe and Bonde are tending him.'

'Take me to him,' Miles said, and gestured with an open hand to make the command less peremptory.

The lad nodded, glanced at his agitated mother and then back to Miles, a glint in his eyes that Miles read as being a taste for adventure and the opportunity to seem important, even for a moment.

On the short journey to the village, Miles took the boy up on Cloud's saddle and learned everything that had happened in the hall after the raiders arrived in the village. His young guide was eager to tell him everything. 'Lord Wulfric told them they could take some fodder for themselves and their horses but then they must leave because it was too dangerous for him to harbour them.'

Miles listened and thought that this was almost a repeat of the situation he had come across with Christen and Lyulph.

Perhaps it happened regularly. Certainly, people were afraid of marauders whatever their affiliation.

'They called him a Norman lick-arse and a traitor to his blood,' the boy continued. 'Lord Wulfric shouted at them to be gone, and drew his sword, but then a fight started and Lord Wulfric was wounded by a spear. Our men could not stand against theirs. Some were killed and the rest ran away into the woods.' His voice tailed off.

'What's your name, lad?'

'Eric, sire, Eric son of Brixi, but my father's dead and Mam's a widow.'

'Did your father die in battle?' Miles enquired.

Eric shook his head. 'Cut himself on a scythe last harvest and his wound festered. I'm the man of the house now. There's no one left for Mam to remarry.'

'And a fine job you are doing,' Miles said. 'It must be difficult.'

Eric shrugged. 'Why do you speak English so well if you are a Norman?'

'Because I am only half Norman and I was born in this land when King Edward sat on the throne. My mother was Welsh, but I had an English nurse.' He smiled at the boy. 'I am a mongrel if you will.'

The boy grinned back and then turned in the saddle. 'Here we are, this is Gythe's cottage.'

Miles consigned the lad's name to his memory as he handed him down from Cloud's back. He clung like an ape for a moment, and then his feet found the ground and he let go, his face bright with exultation. Miles thought that he might find employment for him in his retinue. There was always room for someone with confidence and a quick mind.

Miles dismounted and tied the reins to a pear tree standing outside the cottage. 'Look after him,' he said, patting both horse and boy. He pushed open the door of woven withies, ducked his head and entered the dwelling.

He stood blinking in the darkness. The central fire gave off a little light but it was almost out and he had to use his other senses to gather information. He could feel the still-warm hearth near his boots and smell the pungent aroma of cooked onions, which told him that the occupants had but recently departed. A hearth stone was loose under his foot, from which he assumed that whoever had lived here had dug up their money before they fled. He moved lightly around the hearth then paused to listen, holding his breath to concentrate upon the scarce thread of sound mewing within the darkest shadows in the corner along the partition wall.

'My lord Wulfric?' he said softly.

He heard a groan and another breath indrawn. Miles, his eyesight growing accustomed, made out the dim shape of a pallet upon a low bed ledge. Squatting to the fire, he found a branch of kindling beside it and coaxed a flame. The room flared with tawny light and danced with gigantic black shadows. Holding the torch on high, he trod softly across the floor to the pallet. The flamelight wavered, throwing up to him in skull-like relief the features of the old man lying there, his body covered by a sable-skin cloak.

'My lord Wulfric?' Miles said again. He crouched at the bedside.

The old man's bushy brows twitched together in distress. 'Leave me alone for pity's sake,' he croaked. 'And take that cursed torch away. Let me die in peace or else do what you must and end it, if that is what you are here to do.'

'I am not here to kill you, my lord,' Miles said.

He found a small candle lamp and kindled it from the torch before dropping the latter in the hearth. The light between the shadows lightened to a dull golden-brown. Returning to the pallet, he gently lifted the sables.

'No!' The old man snatched the cloak away from him with desperate strength, but not before Miles had seen the extensive staining on the linen bandage between rib and hip.

'Lie still,' he soothed as Wulfric struggled.

'It is a mortal wound, I cannot be helped. You should go away.' Wulfric closed his eyes from the glint of mail and the intent young face leaning over his.

'And so I would, but I have come a long way to see you. I am here because of your granddaughter Christen of Ashdyke. She is safe and in good health and sends you her love and duty.'

Wulfric's eyelids flickered. 'Christen,' he whispered, licking parched lips. 'But you are a Norman – if I am not mistaken. You speak English, but with the accent of a foreigner.'

Looking at the sheen on Wulfric's face and the pallor, Miles knew he had very little time left, and certainly none for detailed explanation. 'Lyulph died during a raid on Ashdyke and Christen married me of her own will. I promised her I would keep you and Oxley safe if I could. For you, my lord, I come too late, but I will do my best for the village and its people. King William will not reave it while it is in my keeping.'

Wulfric stared at Miles, narrowing his eyes, struggling to focus. 'Christen . . . It was not right that she married Lyulph. A young maid and an old man . . . They said I was jealous, and perhaps I was, but not in the way they meant.'

'She remembers you in her heart.'

'She was a good girl – your wife now, you say?'

'In haste to save Ashdyke from the Earl of Hereford,' Miles admitted, 'but neither of us regrets the decision. I would ask you as a last act of charity and forgiveness to give us your blessing.'

'Forgiveness for whom?' The travesty of a smile crossed Wulfric's pain-ravaged features. 'Come closer that I may see your eyes.'

Miles did so. Wulfric's gaze, suddenly as clean as a sharpened blade, examined him, stripping him to the soul. The silence stretched out. Miles let the old man pare him beyond bone. If there were stains on his conscience, his love for Christen was not one of them.

'You are a Norman,' Wulfric said again, and licked his dry lips.

'My father was Norman, but settled here in the time of King Edward. My mother was Welsh. I was born here and I had an English wet nurse.'

'So you stand in a triangle,' Wulfric said. 'A part of each, but which do you choose?'

'I choose to blend,' Miles said. 'For there can be no other way to eventual peace.'

'You will not find it easy,' Wulfric said. 'You know I would fight you if I had the strength to do so.'

Miles said nothing, and there was a deep silence between them as Christen's grandfather summoned the strength to continue.

'Even so, my instinct tells me that you are honourable, and in the circumstances I will have to settle for that.' He reached out a shaking hand to place it for an instant on Miles's cropped black curls. 'My blessing on your marriage, may it be long and fruitful. In token, I have something I wish you to give to my granddaughter . . . Here, stitched into the pelt . . . It was my wife Aelfreda's and her mother's before that . . . Use your knife . . .' Urgency filled Wulfric's breathless voice.

Miles drew the dagger from his belt, grasped the sables where Wulfric indicated, and found the small pouch, also of sable, with something round and hard raising its centre.

'Quickly!' Wulfric panted.

Miles slit the stitching along the top and pulled out a piece of soft, folded leather. Unfolding it, he discovered a circular cloak brooch of intricate delicacy. Gold and garnets worked in the shape of a sinuous wolf chasing its own tail. It glinted in his hand, the limbs flickering as if alive in the shifting flame.

'Swear you will give it to her.'

'I swear,' Miles said. 'On my soul I swear.'

'Almost forty summers it has lain against my breast ever since she died . . . great waste . . . Bury me in this pelt . . . I will sleep easier for it.' He gazed beyond Miles at something only he could see. 'Aelfreda . . . yes, yes, I will come now. You have been patient, and now all is done.' Wulfric smiled as the light went from his eyes.

Miles leaned over Christen's grandfather to close his lids and let him dream. Gently he drew the sable furs up to the old man's chin. The brooch in his hand had warmed from the contact with his skin and Miles studied it again, admiring the workmanship with half his mind while pondering the interwoven follies, as intricate as the tooling on the brooch, that had brought Christen's grandfather to end his life in this squalid hut with a stranger at his side, his past filled with regrets, and he prayed for the wisdom to avoid the trap of such follies himself. A wolf chasing its own tail.

Carefully he pinned the brooch to the inside of his own cloak and eased to his feet. His knife still lay on the sable fur and he bent to retrieve it.

Behind him, the door flung open and a wild wind gusted into the room. 'You stinking Norman whoreson!' Osric roared, and leaped upon him, taking the advantage of surprise to throw Miles to the floor, and in an instant the ice of a blade was against his throat and Miles knew it was his turn to die. Dead he would have been were it not for the boy Eric, who ran into the hut and flung himself upon Osric so that the knife slipped and grated against the bunched links of Miles's mail coif.

Uttering a roar, Osric heaved Eric off and slammed him into the hut wall as if dealing with a rat. Miles groped for his knife, closed his fingers on it, and flashed to his feet.

'You murdering bastard!' Osric's voice was a raw sob. 'I had almost come to believe that Christen was right, that I was a fool to keep on fighting and that I should make my peace, but God help me, when I see what you and your kind have done, I will kill you all until the rivers run red with Norman blood!'

'Your grandfather died at English hands, not mine!' Miles answered, breathing hard. 'I had no cause to wish him ill.'

'Liar! He stood in your way, and you murdered him!'

Osric sprang again. Miles ducked beneath the wild assault, twisted, and thrust out his foot to trip Osric and send him sprawling against the edge of the embers. And then he was on top of him, and this time the knife edged Osric's windpipe.

'Go on, do it!' goaded Osric. 'Why should one more corpse trouble your conscience?'

'It wouldn't,' Miles panted, 'and I would probably be doing the English cause a great service if I did, but for your sister's sake and for my promise to her, I will spare your life.'

He took his knee from the small of Osric's back and, standing up, sheathed his knife, having first confiscated Osric's weapon.

On his hands and knees, Osric crawled over to the bed niche to look upon his grandsire's body. An English wound, so le Gallois claimed, but Osric did not believe him. The Normans were ravaging all of Staffordshire, and despite his disclaimer, the man watching him with such wary contempt had every cause to wish the old man dead. He raised the coverlet and gazed at the blood-saturated bandages. Bitterness flooded Osric's soul and overflowed. He replaced the covering and kissed his grandfather's cooling cheek. Then, without warning, he whirled, seizing a branch of kindling as he did so, and struck out at Miles. Miles dived hard to one side, avoiding that blow, but struck his head on the edge of the jug shelf as he fell. Osric hit Miles again to make sure he stayed down and then, panting, stared at his brother-by-marriage, still and bleeding at his feet. 'You bastard,' he said, his upper lip curled back from his teeth. He stooped to retrieve his weapon and, taking the knife from Miles's belt, stood over him, deliberating.

A faint noise spun him round, to see the boy backing along the wall towards the open door. Osric advanced on him, knife in hand, and made a sudden grab. He succeeded in grasping the boy's sleeve, but Eric tore free and ran out into the night shrieking for help at the top of his lungs. Osric heard questioning voices in nasal French and the thud of hooves on the track quickening to a canter.

Cursing, he ducked out of the hovel, untied Miles's grey from the pear tree and vaulted into the saddle. Cloud plunged and circled, unsettled by the unfamiliar weight on his back and the jerk on the bit.

'Come up, you bloody lump of crows' meat!' Osric snarled.

'Hola!' shouted a Norman knight, pounding towards him through the murky gloom. 'My lord?'

Osric clapped his heels to the grey's sides as hard as he could and the stallion took off in an erratic, bucking gallop away from the Normans.

Etienne FitzAllen reined in his own mount and chewed his lip. The river mist was swiftly thickening into full fog, and pursuit of a grey horse through grey cloud over strange terrain was at best time-consuming and at worst fruitless. Still, it was his lord's stallion . . . but in that case where was his lord? Etienne dismounted, picked the sobbing English boy off the ground and shook him.

'Where is my lord?'

The boy did not understand the rapid French, but the knight's meaning was plain and Eric pointed to the hut. Drawing his sword, Etienne pushed him aside.

The hut door hung on a single precarious hinge. Faint light from outside and the sullen flicker of a tallow lamp illuminated the interior.

'Oh Christ,' he muttered, eyes straining in the shadows. 'Oh Christ in heaven.'

Miles became aware of sounds in the room, the soft jink of mail as someone paced the floor, the whispering of women, the whimper of a dog, and the sudden irascible bark of his brother's voice as the animal's wagging tail swept a goblet from the table and it broke on the floor.

'Get that mangy hound out of here!' Gerard snapped in garbled English.

A boy's voice replied. Eric, Miles thought, and wondered why he should know the name when he knew very little else apart from the fact that his skull felt as if the entire baggage train of an army was marching over it with iron-shod cart wheels.

His suffering groan brought Gerard to his bedside, although Miles felt rather than saw him, for his lids appeared to be weighed down with lead ingots.

'Miles, thank God!' Gerard said, his tone filled with relief and anxiety. 'Can you hear me?'

'Stop bellowing, you oaf, you'll blow my head off,' Miles muttered through clenched teeth.

'If it weren't so solid you would be dead!' Gerard retorted.

'A full day and a half you have lain here witless. Leofwin sent for me because he did not know if you were going to live.'

'Go away.'

'Look at me, damn you, and I will!'

Swallowing the urge to vomit, Miles forced open his lids. Gerard's worried gaze met his own. He was wearing his hauberk, and freckles of mud spattered his florid face. Glancing beyond him, Miles saw Leofwin and Etienne with the same expressions on their faces. 'Holy Virgin,' he groaned. 'Someone cut off my head and bring me a new one that does not hurt. What happened?'

'You were stupid enough to go without a helm, that's what,' Gerard said, blustering angrily to offset his concern. 'Always the same. I can remember our father and Guyon both tanning your backside for that particular sin. Well, you have certainly learned the hard way this time.'

'Stop lecturing me, and stop shouting.' Miles closed his eyes again and swallowed.

Gerard inhaled to scold further, but Miles turned his head on the pillow, and the sight of the swollen blue bruise on his temple and the clotted wound disappearing into his hair stopped Gerard short. 'God's blood, you Welsh half breed, I wish I did not love you,' he growled.

'That's the problem with stray dogs,' Miles mumbled. 'Give them house-room and before you know it they've torn out your heart.'

Gerard snorted. 'The only tearing has been of my hair, and by my own hand in response to your folly. If it weren't for that English lad crying the alarm to Etienne, you'd be dead and buried by now instead of nursing a cracked skull.'

'Eric?'

Gerard pounced. 'Hah, so you do remember?'

'No . . . At least I don't think . . . God's bones, my brains are falling out.'

'I'll get one of the women to bring you a tisane.'

Gerard strode to the curtain and spoke briskly to one of the women. When he returned, Miles was gingerly feeling the extent of his injury.

'What happened?' he asked again.

'According to the lad, you were attacked by a stray English rebel whom you missed when you took Oxley. He bested you in the brawl, took your knife, and was about to finish you off when he saw the boy and went after him instead to silence him. Etienne heard the lad's cries and saw him run into the lane, but by that time the rebel had taken Cloud and escaped into the fog. We've had search parties out after him, but he has disappeared without trace, and our best tracker is laid up and out of his wits.'

Miles frowned. Something important hovered just beyond his reach, something he knew he ought to remember about his attacker, but that knowledge too was lost in the fog.

'Etienne thought at first you were dead. When you could not be roused, Leofwin sent for me.' Gerard set his hands to his hips. 'Better be on your feet fast, Miles. I do not make a tender nursemaid.'

Miles ignored the jibe, lunging through a field of wool to recall what had happened in the moments before he was struck down. The boy. Eric. He had left Eric standing with Cloud outside the hut. It had been dark inside and he had kindled a brand at the hearth and found an old man dying on the bed bench at the side. His eyes flew open.

'My cloak,' he said with urgency. 'Gerard, where is my cloak?'

'Not as fast as that!' Gerard answered, holding up his hands. 'Jesting aside, you need time to recover.'

Miles started to shake his head but swiftly desisted as pain shot through his skull. 'My cloak, give it to me. There is something I need to do.'

Gerard went to the chest and picked up the folded garment which was covered in splashes of mud and dung and clinging stems of straw from the hovel floor. He eyed Miles dubiously. 'You are not going anywhere,' he reiterated. 'Even if I have to hold you down and sit on you.'

Miles ignored Gerard's blustering. 'Help me sit up,' he said.

Gerard shook his head, but leaned over Miles and as gently as a mother with an infant lifted him up and plumped the pillows behind him, adding an extra couple. 'You have gone green,' he said. 'Do you need to puke?'

Miles swallowed a surge of nausea. 'No,' he said. 'Just give me the cloak.'

'Looks more like a peasant's rag to me,' Gerard remarked. 'I hope your wife is as proficient with a needle as she is at overseeing the rest of your household.'

Miles ignored him and felt around the top edge of the cloak until he found his own silver and garnet cloak pin.

'Whatever it is, let me do it; you will never manage,' Gerard said.

Miles continued to pretend he was deaf. The effort of movement was making him sicker by the second but he was determined not to yield. Reversing the cloak, he exposed the soft squirrel lining. Nestled deep within the fur, clipped through pelt and wool, the wolf brooch glimmered, its red eyes almost alive and filling his vision.

'This is the last thing I remember,' he said. 'Christen's grandfather gave me this for her and he blessed our union. The rest I do not know, except that it is important that I should.'

Gerard leaned over to look at the brooch couched in its fur

setting and edged with light. 'Perhaps he told you the whereabouts of more of this stuff,' he suggested. 'It is rich enough to have come out of a king's burial.'

'I do not think so,' Miles said thoughtfully. 'The colour of gold would not dwell so strongly in my mind, even while no man is immune to treasure. *Anwyl Crist*! I wish I could remember.' He clutched his head. His skull felt as though a thunderstorm was rumbling around inside it.

A serving woman arrived, bearing a cup of honey and wine in which an opiate had been mixed.

'Here,' said Gerard, taking the cup from the woman's hands. 'This will ease your pain and help you sleep. You must not overtax yourself.'

'Your fault,' Miles said weakly. He managed to drink a third of the draught, spilling as much as he swallowed. 'You should have gone away when I told you.'

'Ungrateful wretch,' Gerard said gruffly. 'I am certainly going now. You sleep, and I will see you later.'

Miles made no reply, aware that if he so much as opened his mouth, he would succumb to his nausea.

Gerard stood for a moment longer, regarding him and gnawing his lip, and then shrugged his shoulders heavily inside his mail and left the room to begin organising the shambles that was Oxley.

Although he had narrowly escaped death, Miles was young and strong, and mended quickly. Within a week he was on his feet and acquainting himself with Oxley and its occupants and discovering how his predecessor had ruled the place, its uses and customs, and within a fortnight he was back in the saddle despite Gerard's comment that he would break his head for good if he should suddenly become dizzy and fall off.

'I am not a babe to be wrapped in swaddling,' Miles said with irritated humour as he left his chestnut remount in Eric's care and, blowing on his cold hands, crunched across the frost-silvered garth into Oxley's timber hall. 'If I am to rejoin the King by next week, I need to be fit to ride. You know the distance he covers in a day.' He watched the smoke twirl from the long firebox towards the louvres in the roof.

Gerard wiped a drip from the end of his nose. 'He's not covering that distance just now, so the messenger said yesterday. He's bogged down on the banks of the Aire and no decent fording place after all this rain.' He gave Miles a nudge. 'Weren't you listening, or had your wits gone wandering again?'

'I heard him as plainly as you did,' Miles retorted, advancing to the firebox to stand before the heat from the coals. 'The King is bogged down because he needs the likes of me to find him a fording place.'

A youth was basting a row of pigeons on a spit. Gerard eyed the glistening bodies hungrily. 'Changed your mind, haven't you,' he said as he took a long, two-pronged implement from the fire tools, stuck it in a pigeon and slid it off the iron bar. 'Last time you were employed doing William's work, I caught you vomiting up your guts and saying you could go no further. Has that knock on the head restored your senses?'

Miles shook his head. 'Armed men I will fight at my lord's command. If he is bound for York to clear out the English and Danes then honour binds me to go there with him, but let others perform the raids and chevauché.'

Gerard swore as the hot pigeon scalded his fingers. 'You are mad. You know William. He will lay waste as he marches until not a living thing remains. Better to go home with your wound as good reason and not stir from your hearth.'

'I cannot.' Miles shivered, chilled to his bones despite the warmth from the firebox. 'I gave my oath to serve until Candlemas day, and if I do not fulfil my promise, he will take Ashdyke and Oxley and bestow them elsewhere. You know what he thinks of oath breakers.'

Gerard bit into the pigeon and wiped clear a spurt of fat from his cheek. He acknowledged that Miles was probably right. Once an oath was given to the King it was sacred. There was never any option to retreat. Harold Godwinson had forsworn his promise to aid William to the throne and had taken the crown for himself, and now Harold's body lay in broken pieces in an unmarked grave, its location a secret so that it could not become a focus of worship and miracles for the English rebel cause.

'You have always taken too much on your shoulders,' he said around his mouthful of meat. 'I am only glad I have no such burdens – well, except from keeping you alive of course.'

Miles gave a humourless smile of acknowledgement. 'Does it never concern you that you have no lands of your own?'

Gerard shrugged. 'When you are the youngest of six sons, you know it's little more than a dream. You expect to make your living by the sword and at another man's hearth.'

'But do you never desire somewhere to put down roots? I know when I go home to Milnham it is mine, every stick and stone and hide of land.'

'I have never given it a thought,' Gerard answered, tossing the pigeon remains to an attentive hound and preparing to dismiss the subject as easily.

'What about Aude?'

Gerard grimaced and rubbed the back of his neck – a habit Miles had acquired. 'I suppose she feels the lack sometimes,' he said with a shrug. 'I know being the wife of an itinerant soldier is not easy and many knights in my position do not marry, but she is content with your Christen at Milnham and we have the rents from the house in Rouen too and that brings in extra income.'

'But if the King should offer you a fief?'

Gerard's eyes narrowed in suspicion. 'Just what are you plotting?'

Miles gave him a nonchalant look. 'It occurred to me that it might be useful to have a row of strongholds along the March, protecting each other. Ashdyke and Milnham to form the lower section, Oxley and perhaps a like number of your own spreading towards Chester.'

Gerard stared at him in astonishment. 'Just how long has this notion been brewing in that head of yours?' His tone was not altogether amenable.

'Since we rode the demesne this morning. That scarp overlooking the river would be an ideal site for a watch tower. You can see clean across to Wales and for miles in all directions.'

'Your mind is like the machinery inside a mill, indeed more than that, for it is always grinding and never stops.' Gerard shook his head, laughing even while he frowned. 'There's me pitying you because I thought when you bid me stop during our ride that your strength was flagging, and all the time you were hatching plots!'

'Laying, not hatching,' Miles corrected with a grin. 'Whatever happens I am going to build a keep on that escarpment. Whether or not your own towers answer mine with a watchfire is up to your ambition. It's a time for men like us to build, Gerard.'

'Hah, and what do I do?' Gerard snorted. 'March up to William and ask him to grant me a fief just like that? "Sire, my brother desires you to give me land on the Welsh border so that in the future our family will become a powerful threat"?'

'Don't be an ass,' Miles said with exasperated affection. 'Even if you were given a fistful of honours, we would hardly outrank the likes of FitzOsbern and Montgomery, would we?'

'I am content with my life as it is,' Gerard growled. 'Leave me alone.' He slanted Miles another look. 'A few weeks ago you were swearing that all you wanted to do was go home and cover your head with a blanket and never emerge, and now look at you – filled to the brim with ambition and building empires!'

'It is a matter of balance,' Miles replied. 'And surely it is better to think of building than destroying.'

'Just don't overreach yourself – or me by proxy,' Gerard said, and shrugging his broad shoulders as if to shake off an irritation, he stalked off down the hall.

Miles watched him and contained his smile. The egg had been laid. Now all that was needed was for Gerard to sit on it until he accepted it as his own offspring.

13

Milnham-on-Wye, December 1069

Christen knelt in front of the oak clothing chest in Milnham's top chamber and sorted through the folded bales of cloth, searching for fabric to make a new tunic for Miles to add to her baggage. She was going to spend the days of the Christmas feast at Ashdyke as its lady, and occupy the chair at the head of the table, in honour of Lyulph, establishing her own position and presiding over the seasonal manor court.

A length of wool in a deep woad-blue caught her eye. The moths had attacked one corner, but otherwise it was intact. Embellished with embroidery, it would be suitable for both father and daughter. She took the piece from the chest and delved further, finding a decent length of tawny-gold tabby, woven with lozenges, and brought it out to set beside the blue.

An icy draught made her shiver, despite the warmth from the brazier and the thick layers of clothing she wore. Leaving the chest, Christen went to the shutters to see if she could make them more secure. Opening one side to pull it in again tight, she saw that it was snowing. Slow white flakes twirled from a leaden sky by the million, but there was no wind. It was a hushed falling, like feathers from heaven. For a short while she stood rapt, watching them, but at last pulled the shutters fast and secured the catch firmly, and then, rubbing her arms, sought the warmth at the brazier. The red heart glowed like a dragon's eye, but she was still cold.

The bitter weather had come early and the Norman clergy in Hereford had declared that it was retribution on folk for daring to oppose the anointed king, and they had cast censorious eyes towards the north where the rebellion was the most intense.

Christen had received a letter from Miles before the autumn rains had swollen the rivers and impeded messengers. Penned by a scribe in Nottingham, Miles had informed her that he was well and that the invading Danes had been flushed from Holderness and chased across the Humber. The tone had been almost cheerful, and had given her cause for misgiving because warfare was no game for the victims. She was still coming to know Miles, but she had a suspicion that the tone and content masked a situation darker and more turbulent than he was reporting to her.

A few weeks ago, tidings had arrived of what the King was doing in Staffordshire. They had come in the form of a bedraggled, half-starved family of five from a place called Fletesbroc. They had appeared at Milnham's gates one wet evening, travel-weary, hungry and cast down. There was a blacksmith, his wife and three children and they claimed that Miles had sent them to settle at Milnham because their own village had been torched by the Normans. Since Milnham needed a blacksmith, and such craftsmen were always of use, Christen had found him a dwelling in the village and set him on at the keep. Her maternal instincts outraged by the sight of the thin, blue-faced children, she had taken the entire family under her wing and seen them fed, clothed and settled. At first she had refused to believe the smith when he told her that Miles was responsible for torching Fletesbroc, accusing him of lying, but the expression on his wife's face and that of his eldest daughter stopped her short. She stared truth in the face and found it so unpalatable that she could not face it, but nevertheless was forced to do so. The blacksmith had shrugged, saying bleakly that Fletesbroc was fortunate. Miles had not made a thorough search to discover if they had hidden their livestock and foodstuffs from him. Other places had suffered far more grievously at the hands of the Flemings with all the young men of fighting age put to death and every source of food either burned or taken to supply the Norman troops.

'We are the lucky ones,' he said, picking up the five-year-old as she whimpered around his legs. 'When the snows come it will be a white hell up there, and William of Normandy has not yet begun. Your lord told me such, when he offered me his mercy.' There was an ironic twist to his lips when he said the word. 'There will be no mercy for anyone dwelling north of the Humber this winter-tide.'

Christen shivered again, unable to rid herself of the ice permeating her bones. She had asked Miles in her innocence if the Normans would reave and plunder and he had asked her in return if she really desired such knowledge.

There had been no word from him since the arrival of these fugitives from starvation, and Christmas was fast approaching. Sometimes it was possible to believe that she was not married at all – half the reason she had sought out the bales of cloth. Sewing a tunic for Miles would prove to her that the waking dream was solid reality, that she had a husband who, God willing, would be home and whole before the spring grass greened the slopes. But prayers were not always answered. Spring would come too late for many whose bones would bleach beneath the snows of a Norman-haunted winter, perhaps the people of Oxley among them. And this man, to whom she was married, and for whom she had already developed deep and complex feelings, was part of that destructive army. Sometimes she wondered what Lyulph would have thought, and would hastily turn her mind to other matters.

This morning she had had to let out the belt on which her household keys were hung by two notches. Aude had watched her and had asked with a raised brow if there was something she should know. Christen had shaken her head, for her flux had come as usual every month since her marriage, albeit with no more than a few spots and for no more than a day. Her health was good, although sometimes she was tired, but otherwise she felt well. It would be a blessing if she had quickened, for she would not be so taken up with brooding upon what was happening in the north.

Emma was a bright handful, but caring for her only took up so much of her energy and when the child was tucked in bed the long hours of the night were dark and lonely. She had Aude to keep her company, but Aude was Norman and sympathetic to the cause for which her husband fought. Aude was also inured by twelve years as a soldier's wife to the long absences and fraught waiting. If it preyed on her mind, she did not show it.

Christen turned from the fire, and taking the tawny wool went down to the bustling hall to seek out the woman from Fletesbroc. She was sitting near the hearth, weaving a basket, a watchful eye on her older children, girls of seven and five, roughing and tumbling among the rushes. Emma dashed in between and around them, shrieking with delight. One braid had tumbled loose and thick, coppery strands streamed down her back; her cheeks were flushed and her eyes alight. The baby crawled away from her mother towards the playing children and the woman, whose name was Wenfled, left her work to pursue and scoop her up. Suddenly becoming aware of Christen, she bobbed a tense curtsey.

Christen smiled. 'It is good to see them at play,' she said. 'They are at an age when they can drop their cares for a game of chase.'

'Indeed, my lady,' Wenfled said. 'I wish I was that age now.'

Christen bit her lip and presented her with the folded tawny cloth. 'I have no need of this,' she said, 'but I thought you could put it to good use.'

The woman gave her a reserved look and then accepted it with dignity, placing it beside her. 'Indeed I can,' she said, 'and I thank you.'

'It is the least I could do,' Christen said. 'I hope you will settle here and make a new life.'

Wenfled inclined her head. 'I hope so too, my lady.'

'May I?' She held out her arms, and the woman took the baby and gave her to Christen.

'Her name is Freda,' she said.

Christen chucked the infant beneath the chin, and admired her bright blue eyes and rosy cheeks. 'She is beautiful.'

'Yes,' said Wenfled, 'but I worry for her and my other daughters in such uncertain times.' She tilted her head a little to one side and regarded Christen. 'You married a Norman lord,' she said curiously. 'Does it not bother you?'

Christen kissed the baby's curls. 'Yes, of course it does,' she said, 'but it is about surviving, and among all of us there are good and honourable people, be they Norman, English or Welsh. It was my own brother's rashness that led to me being made a widow, and it was my Norman husband who saved me from the mercenaries of William FitzOsbern. We do what we must – and we pray for grace.'

A soldier entered, flicking snow from his mantle, a huge fawn mastiff trotting at his side. He crossed to the hearth and extended his hands to the heat. Emma deserted her playmates with a shriek of 'Paladin!' and rushed to the dog to fling her arms around his heavy neck. Paladin wagged his tail so hard that his rear end almost became his front. Christen returned the baby to Wenfled and went to Guyon.

'I did not think you would come with this snow threatening to engulf us,' she said, and directed a servant to bring him wine.

'It will hold off for another day yet.' Guyon took the cup when it came and drained it in three swallows. 'The men are ready to journey when you are.'

Her lips twitched. A truce, but only just. She was well aware of his discomfort at escorting her to Ashdyke to celebrate the Christmas festivities and preside over the manor court. Still, they had dealt well enough together thus far and not come to argument or blows. Cynan ap Owain had been ransomed back to his family for ten marks and a promise not to raid Miles's territory, the negotiations conducted between Guyon and Miles's uncle, Siorl ap Gruffydd, who had been captured during the raid on Milnham and subsequently released by Miles. Guyon said he was a rogue who needed watching, but since he was kin could probably be trusted in this case not to bend the rules too far.

Guyon looked round the hall. 'The new blacksmith,' he said. 'Is he settling in well?'

'He works hard, and so does his wife,' Christen replied. 'They are still very frightened after what happened to them – you will turn her into a marrow jelly if you continue to glare at her like that. I remember when you first did it to me.'

He shot her a keen glance, but then a reluctant smile tugged at his mouth corners and he stroked his moustache to conceal it. 'I had good reason at the time,' he said, 'but a man can change his mind.'

He stooped to speak to Emma, who immediately flung herself into his arms like a puppy and delivered a smacking kiss to the tip of his beaky nose.

'And perhaps I have learned that your bark is sometimes worse than your bite,' Christen said.

Guyon raised his brows. 'Only sometimes,' he said.

Smiling, Christen went to fetch her thick outdoor mantle and made her farewells to Aude who was remaining behind as chatelaine in her absence.

'If we are not snowed in, I shall see you again in January,' Christen said, kissing Aude's cheek and feeling a warm glow of affection for her. It was true what she had said to Wenfled about goodness and honour being particular to a person and she cherished Aude's honesty and plain-speaking. 'I shall miss you.'

'And I you,' Aude said warmly. 'Take care and God speed your journey.'

Christen's pied mare was not enthusiastic about leaving her stall in the raw cold of a December day, and made the fact known to all by kicking and snapping. Christen, a doubtful horsewoman at the best of times, was almost unseated. Biting her lip and clinging to the saddle, she rode out of Milnham, jogging like a sack of straw, while Guyon valiantly forbore to comment and pressed his lips together.

The village, as they rode along its outskirts before swinging on to the road that would take them to Ashdyke, was busy with people bringing their fuel and livestock close to their hearths under the lowering threat of snow. A man in a thick quilted tunic saluted them as they rode past. A wolf spear was clenched in his mitten-clad fist.

Guyon grunted. 'Now's the time the wolves come down to the villages,' he said. 'Reckon we'll see a pack or two this winter. Their pelts are warm, but God's life they stink.'

'Those in the north will feed well, both the four-legged and the two-legged,' Christen said grimly as they passed the last croft and its midden to trot across the scrubby common grazing where the villagers' goats and sheep were tugging at the short tufts of grass, overlooked by two shepherds and their fearsome curly-coated dogs.

'You should count yourself fortunate, my lady, that you run with the pack as a wolf's mate,' Guyon answered.

Christen narrowed her eyes at him. 'Fortunate,' she said, and nodded. 'Indeed, you do well to remind me just how fortunate I am.'

Guyon returned her look, but she held him fast with her own stare, and he was the first to retreat.

They rode through a wooded area bordering the road, the branches stark black in the pale winter light. Desultory snowflakes floated through the trees like pale moths. Their horses' hooves thudded with a muted, hollow sound over a carpet of moss and mulched leaves. Now and again the click of metal against horn sounded from a mount with a loose shoe.

In front of them a wood pigeon took sudden flight, the beat of its wings an eerie echo in the tunnelled silence. Guyon glanced up, frowning. A flicker of silver movement among the trunks to his right caught his eye and he reached to his sword. And suddenly the wood was alive with men, whooping and calling, surging from the trees and on to the road. Some were on foot and wore plain Welsh garb, but others, coming straight towards them, were mounted and wearing mail. In the instant before

Guyon raised his shield to ward off the blow aimed at his head, he met the eyes of his attacker, and recognised with shock Christen's brother. Guyon thrust outward with his shield, controlled his stallion with his thighs and completed the act of drawing his sword. Somewhere a woman was screaming – Christen's maid, he thought at the back of his mind, but his immediate concentration was on his adversary. He dug in his spurs and forced his horse forward against Osric's grey. The horse did not give ground, but reared, and struck out with pawing forehooves, and even as Guyon brought his blade down to bite Osric's shield, he recognised Cloud and was stunned.

A snarling tawny streak leaped between the two men and Paladin took the blow intended for his master. The dog's dying howl mingled with Guyon's roar of anguish. He launched a blow at Osric and might have reached him had not one of the Welshmen used his long knife to run in and hamstring the chestnut, sending both man and horse crashing to the ground. Guyon cried out as the stallion rolled on him and his shin bone snapped with an audible crack.

Christen's panicked mare, refusing all commands from the bit, bucked until she unseated Christen, and thundered back the way she had come as if there was a firedrake on her heels.

Christen lay winded and shocked by the fall, but Emma's frantic screams roused her to act. A Welsh reaver had dragged Wulfhild down from her mule and had her spread-eagled on the ground, intent on rape, while Emma watched, huge-eyed with terror. Without pause for thought, Christen drew her belt knife – the one that William FitzOsbern had told Miles not to let her carry – and lunged.

The Welshman died without knowing he had been stabbed, as more by accident than skill she succeeded in severing a vital blood vessel. Blood fountained and saturated Wulfhild's gown.

Frantic with revulsion, Wulfhild heaved the dying man aside and scrambled to her feet. Christen threw the knife aside and enfolded Emma in her arms, hiding the child's face in her bosom, trying to soothe her.

'My lady!'

Wulfhild's scream of warning came too late and Christen turned, only to be spun to the ground by a blow from a warrior's fist. Emma's screams hit top note again.

'You carrion crow, would you kill your own?' Wulfhild shouted at him in English.

'A Norman's whore – she'll get what she deserves!' the warrior retorted, knife ready in his hand. 'Here's one who won't spawn a devil's brat!'

Wulfhild leaped at him and he fisted her down. Christen struggled to her knees, hampered by the folds of her garments, and pushed Emma behind her.

'Hold, Goldwin!' bellowed Osric from the saddle of the plunging grey. 'She is mine to deal with!'

Christen stared up at her brother in horrified, furious shock. 'Osric! What have you done? What treachery is this?'

'I would bid you ask that misbegotten Norman husband of yours were he still alive!' Osric snarled.

The soldier called Goldwin spat on the ground at her feet, shoved the knife back in its sheath and joined his comrades who were stripping the dead of their armour and weapons.

Osric turned and took the reins of the captured horse Hrothgar was holding. 'Mount up, Christen,' he commanded. 'I am taking you into Wales.'

'I'll not go anywhere with you,' she hissed. 'I call you *nithing*!' She shot a look of furious contempt at Hrothgar. 'And you too!'

Hrothgar flinched. Osric reddened to the roots of his hair at the insult, unswallowable to an Englishman. 'You have no choice. On a saddle or tied across one, I don't care. Do as I say.'

'There's one here still alive, shall I slit his throat?'

Osric reined about and rode over to Guyon whom they had dragged out from beneath the body of his chestnut stallion. He lay on the ground, grey with pain and sweating. Blood oozed sluggishly from his broken leg.

'Why are you riding my lord's horse?' Guyon demanded in mangled English, as if he were the victor, and not about to be dispatched by the hard-eyed man staring down at him.

'My horse,' Osric corrected with a sneer. 'Le Gallois lies dead in a peasant's hut by my hand in revenge for the murder of my grandsire and the people of Oxley.'

'That's a lie,' Guyon wheezed. 'The likes of you would never better my lord in a fight and he wanted Oxley whole for my lady's sake. He had no cause to destroy it.'

The Welshman who stood behind Guyon jerked back his head, pricked his knife to Guyon's throat and looked at Osric, awaiting his command.

Osric shook his head. 'No,' he said. 'An eye for an eye and a hand for a hand, I think. Lop off his right one so that even if his leg heals, he may never wield a sword again.'

'No!' screamed Christen, struggling to her feet and running to Osric's stirrup. 'You cannot!'

'Watch me.' He bared his teeth.

Christen launched herself at him but Hrothgar dismounted, seized hold of her and dragged her away. Cloud reared, fore-hooves pawing. Osric struggled to control him. Heedless with rage and grief, Christen would have gone for him again, but Hrothgar held her fast and he was too strong for her. Another warrior came to help him and between them they tied a halter around her upper body and forced her on to the spare horse.

Osric finally succeeded in controlling Cloud, pulling the reins in hard until the stallion's head was curved deeply into his chest.

'Off!' he snarled.

A sword chopped down across Guyon's wrist, severing bone and tendon. A short, harshly bitten cry was all the satisfaction they had of him before he fainted and the Welshman kicked him away.

'What about the maid?' asked Hrothgar. 'And the child?'

'Leave them, they will hinder us.' Osric cast them an indifferent look. 'They can thank God on their prayer bones that I choose to be merciful.'

Wulfhild ran over to Guyon and tried to staunch the bleeding with one of his leg bindings.

'Mama!' sobbed Emma. 'Mama, *je suis effrayée*!'

The little girl's French was not lost on Osric, neither language nor meaning.

'Whose is the brat?' he demanded of Wulfhild.

'A servant's child, no more,' Wulfhild replied quickly. 'Lady Christen has taken her to serve in her chamber, that is all.'

'Look at her eyes, I'd know her siring anywhere.' Hrothgar leaned down to scoop the little girl across his saddle and, pulling back her coppery hair, turned her to face Osric.

Osric's good hand twitched towards his sword hilt.

'In God's name, she is only three years old!' Wulfhild cried in horror, her fingers sheeted in Guyon's blood.

Hrothgar reined his mount away from Osric. 'No,' he croaked. 'No, my lord, do not do it.'

Osric took a deep, shuddering breath. 'Very well, bring her then,' he said, and shrugged. 'The Welsh can have her for a slave. Head over the Wye at the ford. I'll meet you there when we have torched the village.'

Hrothgar nodded and reined his horse towards Wales, with

Christen's horse on a lead rein and Christen herself parcelled up like a piece of game.

'Christen, it was for your own good,' Osric said impatiently, as if to a wearisome child. 'Why are you being so unreasonable?'

'Unreasonable?' Christen cried. 'Mary Mother of God! You say that to me after all you have done?'

She looked away from him and around the smoky hall that belonged to Cynan ap Owain, who was now a Welsh leader following the demise of his father from the sweating sickness. The only light came from sputtering rush dips, for the shutters were all tightly closed against the howling blizzard outside.

The central fire was being banked for the night and people were arranging their beds around it. Emma slept in twitching exhaustion at Christen's side, now and then whimpering as dreams crept too close towards reality.

'If you had seen Oxley deserted and him standing over our grandsire with a knife in his hand—'

'I do not believe you,' she said flatly. 'Miles would not—'

'I am not a liar!' Osric bristled. 'I know what I saw. I left Eadric Cild's warband to make my way to Oxley and ensure our grandfather was safe and I found him with your husband standing over him with a knife in his hand.'

'It is true, my lady,' said Hrothgar. 'Oxley was plundered, and the lord Wulfric murdered. I saw with my own eyes.'

Christen stared at Hrothgar. His expression was candid and truthful, bearing witness. 'No,' she said with a swallow. 'It will break me. I do not want to know any more. Why didn't you let that man of yours kill me when he desired?'

Osric looked at her in bewilderment. 'You are my sister,' he said.

'And blood has a duty to blood?' she scoffed. 'Oh yes, but I can see the people of Milnham running from their burning homes. You are no better than the Norman wolves who reave our land – worse, for at Milnham there was peace, and Miles was born and bred there before ever the trouble started. Now you have left the door open for FitzOsbern to swallow Ashdyke, Milnham and Oxley in one great gulp. Indeed, your blood can be proud of you this day!'

Osric's eyes blazed. 'What do you know of duty to blood when you kennel like a heated bitch with a Norman murderer!'

He lifted his hand to strike her, but Hrothgar restrained him. Christen flinched away, weeping, her spirit close to breaking.

Osric turned aside with a sound of revulsion and Christen covered her face with her hands.

'Here's a cheerful gathering for one who has raided so successfully,' mocked Cynan ap Owain, appearing like a cat out of the smoky gloom, a cup of mead in his hand.

'My sister harbours affection for what we burned,' Osric answered, glaring at Christen in disgust. 'And reviles me for taking my just revenge.'

'What *you* burned. I had no part in the matter except to grant you shelter from the storm,' Cynan retorted.

He looked at Christen with both interest and sympathy. His time as a closely guarded but well-treated hostage had afforded him a glimpse of her in the domestic sphere, overseeing the household, making sure that everything ran as smoothly as the thread she miraculously spun from her distaff of raw wool. She had been the obvious delight of her lord, and her eyes had sparkled when she looked in his direction. Small wonder she detested her brother for kicking away the supports of her life as if they were so much rotten wood.

Cynan had been home a fortnight when his father had sickened and died, and the full responsibility for the welfare of his people had devolved upon his shoulders, forcing him to come to a new maturity. He looked now from the huddled woman to Osric, knowing he would be glad to see the back of the man. He was dangerous company having so recently come from raiding a village that Cynan's people had sworn to leave well alone, and there was a touch of madness about him.

'She is in no fit state to follow the other women when you return to Eadric,' he said, finishing the mead. 'And the child will find it hard because of her Norman blood.'

'Why should it matter to me?' Osric said with a shrug.

'It may not matter to you, but it does to me. The girl is kin through her grandmother to Siorl ap Gruffydd and he may wish to give them room in his hall. Have you thought that your sister might slip away and betray you to the Normans if you take her with you to Eadric? She seems to have sufficient reason.'

Osric opened his mouth to deny that Christen would do such a thing, but Cynan was right. Six months ago he would have trusted her, but no more. She had become a millstone round his neck and neither cajolery nor a beating could command her obedience. 'So, what do you suggest in your wisdom that I do?' he half sneered.

Cynan raised his brows at Osric's tone, but responded equably, 'That you leave her with us until spring. I will send a rider to Siorl to tell him she is here . . . I am sure we can all come to an amicable arrangement.'

14

Chester, February 1070

Gerard peered dolefully into the stew as it started to bubble. Three strips of dried meat, half a mouldy onion and a handful of barley hardly constituted fighting rations for a man of his size, but it was all they had unless he slaughtered his horse, and he had no intention of walking the rest of the way across the Pennines to Chester.

Sleety rain stung the fire and pricked his face with icy needles. The boy Eric returned from tending the horses, his hood pulled up over his ears and his hands tucked into his armpits for warmth. Hunkering down in front of the flames, he sneezed and wiped his sleeve across his nose.

Gerard stared into the flames, oblivious of the shivering English boy opposite him, and wondered if spring would ever come again. Phlegmatic, stoical, hardened to war, Gerard was so sick of this particular campaign that had it not been for his sword oath to William and his own self-respect he would have deserted the army weeks ago and headed down to Milnham and the solace of his wife's arms.

He watched two men struggling to erect a shelter of hides while the biting north wind played havoc with their efforts. They had fought their way across the River Aire and ploughed on to York, burning and harrying as they rode, depending on scouts such as Miles to find their way through stark and treacherous landscapes. They had seen heavy fighting in Holderness, the Danes having re-crossed the Humber to celebrate the winter feast with their kinsmen of Lindsay. Bloody and bitter. Gerard looked down at a recently healed slash across the back of his hand where an opponent's knife had caught him and sent his sword spinning awry. Fortunately for him the man had worn no helm and he had clubbed him down with his shield.

They had beaten the Danes back across the Humber but still lacked the sea power to pursue them over the estuary and William had turned once more for York, meeting little resistance along the way. Those capable of fleeing had done so. Those who had stayed were either dead or scattered, and the English and their allies had abandoned York to its grim Norman master.

William had celebrated Christmas there, sending to Winchester for the regalia and wearing it through the twelve days as a stark reminder to the few remaining English that he was anointed king of the land and that rebellion against him was self-imposed destruction.

From York in the new year the dregs of his army had swept out to do their worst, devastating and harrying the land so that not a living soul remained and the crows and wolves fattened themselves on carrion. The northern earls in rebellion, Gospatric and Waltheof, surrendered. Only Chester remained free and defiant.

William had marched his army across the bleak Pennines

towards the city, a journey of such horrendous privation and difficulty that even the most stalwart had baulked. Contemptuous of their weakness, William had bidden his army either to follow him or fall back – without wages or reward if the latter – and he had ploughed on, leading from the front, turning back to chivvy the stragglers. Tireless, ruthless, tyrannical. His approach had succeeded and the men had rallied, but they were grim.

Gerard rubbed his jaw. Miles had not been among the dissenters. Hill-bred, he knew what to expect, and while the men in their mail floundered or drowned in the marshy valley bottoms or slithered up and down soggy slopes, buffeted by crosswinds, their destriers casting shoes and going lame, Miles had ridden in relative comfort, wearing his motley scouting gear, his hauberk rolled up in a deer hide bundle behind his saddle, his mount a hardy native pony, well able to survive on the poorest diet and with twice the stamina of the destriers. He was in his element, and it was sweet revenge for all the taunts he had endured during an adolescence adrift among mailed knights on elegant warhorses.

In the distance a wolf howled. Eric turned sharply towards the sound, eyes straining in the darkness, his fingers tightening around a branch of kindling he had foraged. Another wolf joined in, and the sound keened through Gerard's blood like a frozen knife. He set his hand to his sword and stood up, staring in the direction of the horse lines where their mounts were jibbing and snorting. His scalp prickled. Silence. He turned back to the fire and almost leaped out of his skin to see Miles crouched there, warming his hands.

'Christ on the cross, what do you mean sneaking up on us like that!' he rebuked, shouting because he had been terrified. 'I might have spitted you on my blade!'

'You wouldn't,' Miles retorted with amusement. 'My knife

would have found your throat before you'd even cleared your scabbard. You're a sitting target for the Welsh if they were of a mind to take you. Here, stop scowling at me like that and put this in the pot.' He held out a limp body dressed in white winter fur.

'God's bones, hare!' Gerard's mouth watered. 'For that I will not only cease scowling, I will caper a jig round the fire!'

'There is no need to conduct such antics,' Miles said with a laugh. 'Belike the fire would go out. Here, give it back; I'll skin it.'

Gerard watched Miles work with dextrous speed and acknowledged that his brother possessed skills vital to the survival of the Norman army, and to the stomach of one member in particular. He adroitly jointed the hare and dropped the pieces into the pot.

'How did you catch him?'

'It wasn't easy,' Miles said. 'I had to separate him from the English messenger who was carrying him for his own supper and he wasn't keen to give him up.' He patted the knife at his belt. 'I made it look like a Welsh job.'

Gerard eyed him askance. 'What do you mean English messenger? How far away was this?'

'Five or six miles.' He fed a branch on to the flames. 'Just outside Chester.'

'We are that close?' Gerard rumpled his hair. 'Thank Christ for that. My arms are already twice their length from pulling my horse out of mud holes and forcing him to go where he baulks.'

'You may not thank Christ when you face their axes,' Miles said with a quelling glance, throwing into the pot a handful of dried herbs taken from a small box in his pouch.

'Bad?'

'King Harold's common-law wife and sons are in the city. It's the last rallying point.'

'Then the rumours are true?' Gerard put a couple more branches under the fire.

'The Englishman who so obligingly donated your dinner was also helpful enough to tell me that the lady Eadgyth is summoning all the loyal English to Chester to make a stand.' Miles raised sombre eyes to his brother. 'It's fighting talk, Gerard. Mingled with fear I grant you, but they have turned at bay with bared teeth. It is going to be bloody.'

'Nothing new in that,' Gerard said with a shrug, trying for nonchalance and not quite succeeding.

'No,' Miles agreed. 'It might as well be Stafford, or York, or Durham.'

'At least this time we can go home when it's over.'

'You haven't got a home over here,' Miles needled, giving him a half smile.

'If the King offers me a fief, then I will take it, but I am not going to crawl at his feet begging for crumbs. I am content as I am.'

'He owes you an earldom, let alone a fief,' Miles said with a knowing look. 'If you had not dragged him out of that snowdrift and brought him back to the vanguard when he lost the path, then every rebel Englishman in the country would be rejoicing.'

'You should have been a mercenary,' Gerard said with a scowl. 'It was nothing. He wasn't lost. Just needed a piece of rope and a tug.'

'Just reward for just effort expended. And do not prate to me of price. I am paying mine now for the privilege of owning Oxley.' Miles picked up a stick and stirred the stew, expression controlled but the movement of his hand jerky.

They had been too long at war, Gerard thought. Punch-drunk

and reeling from battle to battle through lands charred and starving, or through wilds like this where no sane man would dream of venturing in the depths of winter unless that man was William the Bastard.

'You need a distraction, something to give you ease – like that wench in York,' he said. 'That's what you need.'

Miles ceased stirring. His vision filled with the image of a young woman, generously endowed and eager to share. He looked at his brother and then laughed. 'I thought she was going to smother me!'

'Granted she was a little . . .' Gerard cupped his hands and extended his arms.

'A little! It was like fu—'

He broke off as Eric returned to the fire with some more kindling and poked his nose over the cauldron from which an appetising meaty aroma was starting to rise.

'A whale,' Miles finished, laughing again, the tension easing from him. 'You have a deal to answer for.' He sobered. 'It's always good after long abstinence, but I want my wife, Gerard. I want to lie in my own bed, in my own keep, on my own lands, with Christen at my side. I want to stay there for a month and do nothing but sleep, eat decent food and make love . . . although perhaps not in that order. If my wife will have me back.' He smiled at Eric and tousled the boy's hair, as if he spoke in jest, but in truth he was apprehensive.

How much Christen knew about this northern campaign he did not know. The vile weather and his constantly changing position had separated them from regular communication. Home was a dream that haunted him in half-remembered snatches. Sometimes he would wake in a cold sweat of panic, wondering if such a place really existed, wondering if he had only imagined the woman with the wide brown eyes and silver-blonde hair, and wondering if that woman would welcome him with open arms or yield him the scorn of her turned back when he gave her the deeds of Oxley drowned in English blood.

'Why should she not?' Gerard asked, folding his arms inside his cloak.

Miles shook his head and stood up, knowing Gerard would not understand, and not sure that he understood himself. They had lived under the shadow of dark clouds for so long that an imminent clear sky was impossible to imagine.

'I'll leave you to cooking duty,' he said instead. 'The King needs my report, and now I have filled the pot and warmed my bones, I must be about my duties again. I will see you later when that hare is cooked.'

Gerard narrowed his eyes. Leofwin spoke to him, and he turned to reply. When he looked round again, the place by the fire was empty, and the wild night growled around them like a wolf, gusting the fire under the cauldron.

15

Miles ducked beneath the swinging blade of the battleaxe, jabbed the boss of his shield into the English warrior's face, and as his opponent recoiled, struck at his throat. The blade was blunt from a day of hard use and Miles had to lean into it to feel it bite through. The axeman buckled into the red-stained mud and died in the late grey afternoon with purple clouds banking in the west.

Miles caught the bridle of a plunging loose destrier, untangled the foot of its dead rider from the stirrup and scrambled into the saddle. His own chestnut had gone down beneath English axes during the dawn assault on the city's defences.

He spurred his new mount towards a cluster of English blocking the road leading to St Olaf's and their lady Eadgyth, hand-fasted wife of the former King Harold. She and her son had left it too late to flee the city for the safety of Wales, and just as the huscarls had surrounded Harold to the last bitter blow, so these Englishmen now defended Harold's uncrowned queen. The city walls might have been betrayed by a handful of burghers, frightened for their livelihood, but Eadgyth's huscarls were a loyal core who would not give an inch of ground while they lived.

Another English warrior blocked Miles's path, battleaxe swinging – a huscarl in full mail and nasal-bar helm, the mirror of Miles's own garb, but he was almost twice Miles's weight and head and shoulders taller, and wild with rage.

Miles's newly acquired mount went down beneath the slicing blade. He rolled out from under the stallion's death throes and wove and dodged for his life. The round shield hastily seized from the corpse of a footsoldier after he had lost his own was no protection against the cleaving power of an English axe, and Miles could only evade and duck, waiting for his opponent to make a mistake or begin to tire.

Miles had the advantage of swift, light youth whereas the English warrior was an older man, his beard salted with grey. Yet therein lay the danger of long experience, of weight and strength and burning purpose.

The axe bit the ground hard by Miles's leg. He streaked beneath the other's guard, but was thrust backwards by a vicious kick and again the axe blade swooped to take him. He was swifter but felt the killing wind of the notched steel graze his cheek as he rolled. He could hear his opponent's harsh breathing, could see the gaps in the mottled teeth as his mouth gaped wide to draw more air into starving lungs.

Miles launched himself before his opponent could resume the striking position, but slithered in a greasy patch of spilled blood and entrails, and sprawled helpless upon his back, knowing it was the end. He was about to be split open from stem to stern. The descending axe crashed down to earth beside his skull and the huscarl toppled and fell across him, the side of his face stoved in by the mace whose handle occupied Gerard's fist.

'God you're a liability!' his brother panted, curbing his stallion. 'Where's Leofwin, for Christ's sweet sake?'

'Gone. I lost him in the press.'

Gerard extended a blood-spattered hand. 'Come up behind me, you'll not last a minute in this broil without a horse.'

'Ware!' Miles bellowed.

Gerard's upflung shield caught the blow from the battleaxe. Gerard swung the mace hard and guided his stallion with his knees, making it pivot and rear. The mace lashed and descended again in tandem with the stallion's forehooves, and as the huscarl went down, Miles finished him.

Panting, Gerard held out his arm again and this time Miles caught it and leaped up behind him. Gerard turned the destrier, and in the brief lull, regrouped the men. About a third of them had become separated when the English had driven a wedge into their ranks but they had not possessed sufficient numbers to make good. Soldiers, English and Norman, sprawled in the streets, fallen in common endeavour on different sides of the divide.

Miles caught another loose horse, a brown stallion with a white star, reins trailing and saddle blood-streaked. He recognised the horse, for he had bred the animal himself and bartered him last year to Hamo FitzWarren in exchange for service. The young man now lay face down, hacked and dead with companions and adversaries alike. Miles patted the brown's shaggy neck and spoke to him in a firm, level voice, until the stallion's eyes ceased to show a rolling white rim. Having exchanged his foot-soldier's round shield for Hamo's kite one, he mounted the horse. Hamo had no use for his equipment now.

Grimly they fought on, and with equal determination the

English resisted. The fighting changed, becoming a lethal game of hide and seek, of ambush and attack, and death among gutted and burning houses and gardens. Come nightfall it continued by the lurid light from the burning dwellings. Bitter and bloody, as Miles had known it would be. The sky was a hazy red and the stench of burning tainted every breath he took.

Just before dawn, near the wharves, they caught the lady Eadgyth and her youngest son Ulf attempting to escape in a coracle, the pair of them disguised as nuns. The last huscarls fought savagely, vainly, to prevent their lady's capture and died as they had died on Senlac Field at Hastings, around their king.

The mort was blown around the city and finally the ashes of Chester belonged to the Normans.

Miles heard the horn and hung his head, his sword arm throbbing all the way to his shoulder, his whole body trembling with refusal and fatigue. He was spent, could go no further. A noise to the left caused him to turn, weapon shakily raised. The sound resolved itself in a slithering clatter as the last man he had killed relinquished hold of his sword and the hilt struck the ground.

Miles looked dully at the steel, reflecting fire and blood, and was assailed by a surge of cold sweat and nausea. The declaration of victory meant nothing to him for the moment except that he did not have to wield his blade again. Further than that he was utterly numb.

'Miles?'

He swallowed and opened his eyes. Gerard rode up beside him, with Leofwin behind, his face bloody from a sword cut to his cheek. Nearby, flames roared and a wayward gush of sparks shot skywards as a burning house collapsed on itself. Miles wiped his sword and sheathed it.

'It's over,' Gerard said.

Miles nodded, too tired for elation, and too sick. 'Yes,' he said, thinking it would never be over.

Through the smoke, a beautiful dawn was gilding the sky.

In the hall of the house that King William had commandeered, Miles gave his name and was admitted into the smoky warmth. Drifting gauzy layers of blue and gold hazed the air, meaty cooking smells wafting with them. Nigel de Burcy, one of William's aides, made a jocular remark to him about the victory and slapped his arm. Miles forced out an appropriate response, and made his way slowly up the hall towards the King, who sat at a trestle table on the dais with various battle captains and several scribes. Miles recognised among them a messenger of FitzOsbern's and wondered what news he brought from the Marches. Perhaps there was trouble in Hereford. Miles's general irritation at being summoned was joined by a prickle of anxiety.

The King looked up from his deliberations and fixed his gaze on Miles. His usually clear grey eyes were blood-shot and heavy and his jaw sported a plantation of dark auburn stubble.

'You sent for me, sire?' Miles knelt with difficulty. Bowing his head, he noticed the dried blood still caked beneath his fingernails.

'Get up,' William said, and as Miles stumbled stiffly to his feet, he thrust a weather-stained piece of parchment at him. 'My cousin the Earl of Hereford appears to believe you are dead,' he said curtly. 'And so do your wife and constable according to the contents of this letter.'

Miles stared at the flowing phrases penned by FitzOsbern's scribe in dark oak-gall ink and for a moment his mind was a white blank of exhaustion. He shook his head mutely and applied himself to the document again, taking each word with slow care as he had done as a child of seven, struggling to learn his letters at Father Urien's knee. His father had insisted that Miles learn to read as it was another skill and could be acquired by using an hour a day that would otherwise be spent in play or getting into mischief.

FitzOsbern wished to know if there was any truth in the rumours that Miles was dead. The Earl had sent a troop to Milnham to investigate and had been greeted by the sight of the villagers sorting through the charred remnants of their homes, and at the keep itself had found a badly injured Guyon le Corbeis sick with wound fever. Le Corbeis said he had learned of Miles's death from Miles's rebel brother-in-law, who claimed to have personally killed him. Guyon had reason to believe his tale because Osric had been riding Cloud and another man, Hrothgar, had confirmed that the story was true and Miles was indeed dead.

Osric and his raiding party had vanished into the teeth of the worst snowstorm of the winter, taking Christen and Emma with them, first cutting off Guyon's right hand in revenge for Miles's action at Ashdyke. Le Corbeis, the message reported, had also suffered a broken leg during the assault. In the circumstances, the Earl had felt it his God-given duty to take control of Ashdyke, Milnham and their villages until more was known.

Miles swallowed bile. Christen . . . Osric had Christen and Emma. Dear Christ in heaven. His memory blazed a sudden trail of colour across his brain, short and bright as a blow to the back of the skull, and he had to lean against a nearby trestle table for support. A peasant's hut. Darkness and torchlight and the wild, grief-contorted face of Christen's brother, a knife in his hand.

'You have my leave to depart immediately and deal with this matter,' William said brusquely. 'You have served me well and

I have no more need of you for the moment. Return home and sort out your lands – and your wife. I will have a scribe draw up a document for the estate in Stafford, and also charters confirming your tenure of the Hereford estates lest anyone should doubt your right to them.' It was the nearest the King would come to admitting in public that FitzOsbern, excellent warrior and kin though he might be, was a tenacious mastiff, and once he acquired land it was nigh impossible to prise his jaws apart and make him disgorge it.

'Sire,' Miles acknowledged, although his mind was numb with disbelief. Christen and Emma seized by Osric, Guyon sorely wounded, and William FitzOsbern in command of his lands. The ground had turned to quicksand beneath him.

'What are you waiting for?' William said when he did not move.

Miles drew himself together, enough to make his obeisance and to back from William's presence, although he felt as though he was drowning.

He stumbled back to his tent and sat down on an empty stool as his legs gave way.

Gerard was immediately at his side. 'What's wrong?' He shouted at Eric to bring wine.

'FitzOsbern has Milnham,' Miles said, 'and Osric has Christen and Emma. Apparently I am dead.'

'What? Don't talk such rot. Your wits are addled.'

'They must be,' Miles said. He took the wine that Eric brought and drank a mouthful, although he felt sick. 'Read this,' he said, and handed the letter to Gerard. 'I remember what happened at Oxley now. It was Osric who struck me down.'

Gerard turned the letter to the light and squinted, lips moving laboriously as he read the words. 'Christ, what a mess,' he said.

'The King has given me leave to go and deal with this,' Miles replied. 'I'll ride out as soon as I have packed my baggage.'

'I will go and ask the King for leave and come with you,' Gerard said, his jaw grimly set. 'And do not say you can do it alone, because you are going to need someone to take Guyon's place once you have the lands back from FitzOsbern.'

Miles took another drink of wine and looked up at his brother. 'I was going to say nothing of the sort. I was going to say that I need you for that very task, and that you have always been a rock to me when my feet are in quicksand.'

'Hah!' Gerard said, and slapped Miles's shoulder so vigorously that wine slopped over the rim of his cup. 'I have my uses.'

Miles gave him a bleak look. 'I am going to find them, Gerard,' he said. 'I am going to find Christen and Emma, or die in the attempt.'

'No, little brother,' Gerard said, 'you are going to succeed.'

16

Hereford Castle

William FitzOsbern regarded his unexpected visitor with an outward show of calm and an inner ripple of disappointed exasperation. His wife being indisposed with a severe cold, it fell to his youngest daughter Alicia to bring wine and play hostess to their unwelcome guest. She kept her deep blue eyes modestly lowered and her manner was self-effacing.

'As you can see, sire,' Miles said, his tone curt, 'the rumours about my demise were unfounded and you have no reason to keep your men on my lands. I have the King's writ confirming me in possession.' He showed FitzOsbern the document validated by the royal seal.

Alicia withdrew, dark braids swinging. Miles glanced once her way and then back to FitzOsbern. There was a tight knot at his core. Over the past days as he rode south, the quicksand had solidified and become as hard as granite. His focus, his existence, was all bent on getting Christen and his daughter back from Osric.

'What else was I to do?' FitzOsbern growled. 'The lands had to be defended from the Welsh and from Eadric's warbands. I could not ignore the rumours of your death and wait and see until spring. It would have been the height of folly to ignore the rumours of your death, especially as there were good grounds for believing it to be true. I acted as any man of military sense would do, and I wrote to the King for confirmation of the tale.'

'Having first occupied Ashdyke and Milnham.'

'It appeared that you were dead without heirs to lay claim and those places had to be ruled and defended, especially given the condition of your marshal. That you would expect me to do otherwise leads me to wonder about your own soundness of mind.'

Miles tasted the wine, found it sour, and set it down on the trestle. FitzOsbern's daughter was watching him circumspectly, her red woollen gown a splash of colour against the limewashed wall.

'I take your point,' Miles said curtly, 'but I ask you to withdraw your men forthwith.'

'It shall be done,' FitzOsbern said with an open-handed gesture. He wished heartily that some English rebel had had the wit and fortune to cleave Miles down the middle with his battleaxe. As it was, he would now have to return Miles's lands. It was not worth risking the royal ire over them and there were always other fish to fry. Besides, there was still one way of keeping this particular one dangling on his hook.

'Daughter, fetch the scribe, and send a boy to find Waleran for me,' he commanded.

She curtseyed and left to do his bidding.

'Alicia is a good girl and strives to please,' FitzOsbern said, and flicked Miles a sly glance. 'Her mother will miss her when she leaves to be married.'

'You have contracted your daughter to wed then?' Miles asked politely, making a strong effort not to let his impatience show.

'Not precisely, but I have hopes. More wine?'

Miles shook his head. 'Thank you, sire, but as soon as the scribe has written your order, I shall be on my way.'

The Earl shrugged and refilled his own cup. 'Maurice of Ravenstow, Montgomery's bastard, has asked for her, but I would be willing to offer her to you as a token of goodwill. Her dowry is not large but there are some useful lands to the east of yours that I would cede to your firstborn son.'

His words jolted through Miles and tightened the knot in his belly. 'Interesting though it would be to have you call me son,' he replied expressionlessly, 'bigamy is greatly frowned upon by the Church and I already have a wife, as you know, sire.'

'Bigamy? Oh, the English woman.' FitzOsbern waved a war-scarred hand. 'Holy Mother Church will grant you an annulment for desertion. That is easily accomplished. A little coin to grease the wheels and you will be free. My girl is a far more fitting mate for you.'

Miles kept his expression impassive. 'Christen was abducted against her will,' he said. 'I do not call that desertion.'

'Whatever the reason for her loss, there is no profit to be had out of her now,' FitzOsbern replied, eyeing Miles with sidelong surprise and a slight curl to his lips. 'You have the lands. What does it matter?'

Miles swallowed and turned away, fingers digging into his palms. Only a witless fool would make an enemy of William FitzOsbern.

The Earl finished his wine in a long gulp. 'She disappeared with those raiders into the teeth of a blizzard. Belike she is dead.'

'As I was dead?' Miles snapped before he could bite down on the words.

'Do not be an ass, Miles,' warned the Earl. 'I am offering you Alicia to wife – a blood-bond with the earldom itself. You stand need to cast thorns in your own path.'

Miles stood straight, once more his own master. 'I am sensible of the honour you do me, my lord. Indeed, were I free, I would accept.'

'You are free, you fool!'

'Not so, my lord. I need at least to discover what happened to my wife – and to my daughter.'

'Your daughter? Oh, you mean the child whelped in Rouen? Why bother? Like as not she's not yours anyway, these whores are all the same.' He drew his brows together in a deep frown. 'No need to look at me like that. I know she might have been useful for making a marriage alliance, particularly with the Welsh. Bastardy does not bother their codes of bloodline.'

Miles feigned an indifference he was far from feeling. 'She is still my property,' he said.

Unaccustomed to being challenged, FitzOsbern narrowed his eyes. 'So what are you going to do?' he enquired with sarcasm. 'Comb all of Wales until you find them?'

'Yes.'

'You truly are mad!'

'If I find Eadric Cild, then I will find Christen's brother, and if I find her brother, then she will not be far away.'

FitzOsbern rubbed his jaw. 'My troops and Montgomery's will be going into Wales any day now to mop up Eadric's blood – once we have spilled it for him. If your wife is among the camp followers, you had better forget her now and take Alicia for your bride. You know what happens to the women who follow an army, when that army is defeated.'

Miles stared at him, cold prickles running up and down his spine.

'I tell you this now,' said FitzOsbern, 'so that you do not accuse me later of deliberately scheming to rid you of what is to me an encumbrance. Perhaps she is not with the English wives and whores who follow Eadric. Perhaps her brother fled to Ireland. Most likely they all perished in that foul blizzard. But whatever their story, you are wasting your time.'

Fortunately for Miles, who was about to leap at the Earl's throat, Alicia FitzOsbern returned with a scribe. Miles clenched his fists tightly around his belt. He was not wearing his sword, which had been taken at the door, and it was a good thing, for he thought he would have drawn it upon FitzOsbern. He knew this man. The campaign would be conducted with ruthless skill, and as a minor side-line to stop his Flemings from becoming bored between the more serious battle campaigns. He would unleash them on the rebel camp followers without a qualm, and Miles had seen what had happened in the north.

'I will find her, or I will find out her fate,' he said with burning intensity.

FitzOsbern was the first to look away, snapping a brusque command to the scribe to set up his lectern.

The necessary documents having been obtained from FitzOsbern, Miles was in the main hall, gathering his men for the ride to Milnham, when Alicia FitzOsbern approached him.

'My lady,' he said as she halted several feet away – outside of the range of his fist, he noted, and clearly a precaution of long habit.

Colour flushed her cheeks as she lifted her gaze to his and he realised she was less dominated by her father than her manner in his presence had initially suggested.

'I know my father for what he is,' she said, her tone low and sweet so that it would not carry beyond the space in which they stood to speak. 'My stepmother is dying and he berates her for being lazy when she can barely rise from her bed.' She drew a deep breath. 'If I could escape from here I would. When he broached the idea of this marriage, I wanted to dance with joy. I have heard it is not your way to ill-treat a woman on a whim or to take out your temper on her . . . no, hear me out, I pray you.' She reached across to put her hand on his sleeve as he began to turn away. 'I want to tell you that although it is my dearest wish to leave my father's roof and be wed to a man who will not abuse me for his own failings, I will not be a party to my father's schemes. I would rather be cast out in nothing but my chemise.'

'Fine sentiments, my lady,' Miles said without warmth.

'And true ones. He has beaten me into defiance, not submission. I know you must hate me because I am his daughter, but I truly wish you well and I hope you find your wife and child.'

Looking at her, Miles was suddenly reminded of the flowers that bloomed upon granite crags without soil to support them. 'No,' he answered in a gentler tone, 'I do not hate you.' He lifted the hand she had set on his sleeve and bowed over it formally. 'I hope you find a kinder life,' he said, and took his leave.

17

The settlement of Cynan ap Owain, April 1070

Cynan ap Owain stretched his arms above his head and gave a huge yawn. The hall as he sauntered down its length was flooded with yellow spring light pouring through the open shutters. An hour after dawn, the people of his holding were busy about their duties or else breaking their fast on rye bread and ewe's milk curds. Two women were preparing a stew in an iron pot and a small girl sat nearby, industriously spinning raw fleece into clumpy yarn. A dusty shaft of sunlight grazed the top of her head and made a red-gold nimbus of the curly wisps of hair escaping her plait. She glanced up as if aware of his casual scrutiny and eyed him solemnly.

Cynan took his seat on the high dais. A woman left the child's side and came to pour him a cup of mead. He watched her sidelong as she picked up the jug, for her body was ripe in the last stage of pregnancy. She ignored his stare, and having filled his cup, brought him a platter of the bread and cheese before returning to the girl.

Cynan drank and ate, and studied her through narrowed lids. Her movements were cumbersome; she no longer possessed the willowy glide she had when she first came among them. The sunlight gleamed on the rush work basket she held and dazzled the tips of her braids to white-gold. He wanted her and wondered if she would display more enthusiasm for his interest once she was lightened of the child she carried. It was difficult to pierce the wall she had built to protect herself. Sometimes he wondered if there was actually anything behind that wall. If he broke it down, there was a risk of no reward on the other side, but on balance he thought not. It might just take time.

He had taken her in at first because the little girl with her was kin to Siorl ap Gruffydd. He was amused to think that once he had dwelt under her roof as a hostage, and now she dwelt beneath his as a maidservant. The child and the baby in her womb would be his to do with as he pleased. Her own brother, Osric son of Burwald, had sold her to him in exchange for weapons and horses, and had ridden out without a backward glance as soon as the blizzard had abated. He knew who had the better bargain. If only she would set aside her grief and look at him instead of through him.

Christen left her spinning a short while later and took a drink to a man sitting on a straw mattress at the far end of the hall.

'How is the arm, Hrothgar?' she asked.

'A little improved, but I doubt it will mend straight, my lady,' he answered with a rueful shrug and a downward glance at the splinted injury which, fortunately for him, was on the same side as his missing fingers and he still had one arm and hand he could use. 'I was lucky to escape the last skirmish at all. If it weren't for a dead horse covering me, FitzOsbern's men would have seen me and hacked me to pieces. How goes it with you?'

Christen looked down at her transformed waistline and echoed his rueful gesture. 'The time cannot pass swiftly enough. I did not know until the baby first kicked that I was with child at all.' She placed her hand lightly on her womb. For several days now she had been aware of uncomfortable tightening and squeezing sensations and just now a low and persistent backache was making it difficult to find any position that was comfortable.

'It is the Norman's then?'

'Yes.' Her mouth tightened and the light left her eyes. She started to turn away.

'Do not think too harshly of Osric,' Hrothgar implored. 'He has wronged you thrice over, but it has not all been of his doing.'

Christen gave him a bitter half smile. 'I try not to think of Osric at all, and thrice is too many times to forgive or to mark down as unintended folly.'

'My lady, you are still fortunate and in a better case than the poor wretches in Eadric's camp.' He gave an involuntary shudder. 'FitzOsbern is doing his utmost to wipe them from the face of the land, just as the King laid waste to the north. The women and children . . . what his mercenaries do to them would not be permitted in hell itself.'

Christen made the sign of the cross on her breast. 'He is an evil man – indeed, they are all evil,' she said with a shudder.

The baby churned in her womb and she stroked the place where she had felt the kick. She had not thought that her child's father was of such an ilk, and perhaps that was the worst delusion of all. But it did not excuse Osric.

'While the Danes remain in the Humber and the rebels still hold out in Ely, Eadric will not surrender,' Hrothgar said.

'FitzOsbern has us between his fingernails, but our shell is too tough for him to crack.'

Christen glanced to the fire where Emma sat absorbed in her spinning. 'If I had the power to curse, then I would use it,' she said.

'So would we all.' Hrothgar followed her gaze to the little girl and then let his eyes venture beyond the child to the young Welsh prince sitting on his carved chair at the far end of the hall, drinking from a horn of mead and talking with a couple of his warriors. 'Are you content here, mistress?' he asked.

'As content as I can be when my heart is dead inside me,' Christen said bleakly. She knew what he was asking, and what he wanted her to say in order to assuage his conscience, but she could not do it. 'Siorl ap Gruffydd acknowledges his kinship with Emma grudgingly,' she said. 'Cynan treats me well – too well. I cannot respond to him in the manner he would best appreciate.' She winced as the pain in her lower back intensified and her womb constricted, feeling like a taut band under her palm.

'It seems a strange thing, my lady, that Osric would sell you to a Welshman for a handful of swords and that your husband's kinsman should give you to the lord Cynan to keep in his hall this way – I know you are not his mistress, but who knows what will happen once the child is born.'

Christen grimaced. 'Such a situation is not a dishonour in Wales,' she replied. 'A mistress has the same status as a wife, and I think that even if I refuse him, he may force me to a hand-fasting.'

Hrothgar cleared his throat. 'Perhaps it might be for the best?' he said, making the statement into a question.

'Best for who?'

She watched Cynan abandon his cup and his chair and stalk

down the hall towards them, a scowl on his face. He paused at Christen's side and gripped her shoulder. 'She is mine,' he warned Hrothgar, his tone deceptively mild, but his eyes burning with jealousy. 'Negotiated for with her brother, and payment agreed.'

Hrothgar returned Cynan's challenge with indignation. 'I have served Lady Christen's family all my born days, and I am too old to unlearn that loyalty now for any man.'

The young Welsh prince bared his teeth. 'Then go and serve where you will be most useful. Go to her brother and then you shall have two halfwits to make one whole.'

Hrothgar scowled at him in resentful anger. Christen stepped away from Cynan, and felt the hard imprint of his fingers still tingling on her shoulder. Picking up her basket, she murmured that she had to go outside to the latrine pit. As she departed, she felt Cynan's gaze boring into her spine and heard him warn Hrothgar again.

Once outside, she paused and rubbed her lower back to ease the ache as her womb tightened again. She had not realised that she was with child until beyond the midwinter feast. Distraught about what she had been told about the happenings at Oxley, unable to comprehend and disbelieving, she had been lying on her pallet, trying to sleep, when she had felt the flutter of new life within her womb. The light bleeds of earlier months had misled her, and she realised that she must have conceived soon after her marriage.

Whatever the ambiguity of her feelings towards her child's father, the miracle of new life had given her hope, and a fierce desire to protect the baby in her womb. She knew their lives would not be easy, but she was determined to survive if it was God's will.

A sudden gush of liquid down her legs saturated her gown and puddled the ground as her waters broke.

A serving woman who had followed her outside saw what had happened, took Christen's arm and, gabbling in Welsh, drew her across the compound to the women's chamber. Olwen the dairywoman, who performed the role of midwife when needed, came hastening from her butter churn, wiping her hands on a cloth. She reassured Christen in Welsh, patting her womb gently and indicating by gestures and tone of voice that all would be well.

Christen was glad of her reassurance. Olwen was in her middle years with rosy cheeks and a kindly manner. She spoke very little English, and Christen virtually no Welsh, but in daily life they got by with gestures and the few words they did know. Good morning, good night, yes, no, thank you.

Well aware from her previous experience that bearing a child could take many hours and in some cases days, Christen prepared to endure, and under her breath she prayed to God and Saint Margaret for succour in her time of travail.

The pains this time were relentless, powerful to the point of being excruciating and all-consuming. She writhed on the straw pallet, biting down on a rolled piece of cloth, as the surges broke over her body with almost no respite.

Another lady who spoke English was found to translate for the midwife. 'Quick as podding peas,' she told Christen. 'Olwen says a few more minutes and we'll have this one out.' She held up five fingers to a breathless Christen to emphasise her point.

Olwen was wrong, and it took the time of ten fingers before Christen pushed the baby into the world, all slippery and hot from her body, and fell back with a gasp. Almost before he was out he was filling his lungs and bawling his indignation to the world at being so precipitously forced from his warm interior bed.

'*Bachgen bach hardd*,' declared the midwife, smiling.

'A fine baby boy,' translated the woman. 'Listen to the lungs on him!'

Christen laughed and sobbed, overwrought by a flood tide of conflicting emotions as she held out her arms for her son. The midwife cut the cord and laid him in her arms, and Christen clutched him to her breast, wet, wriggling furiously, and alive. This time, alive!

Later, cleaned and made comfortable, she cuddled quietly with the child, and gazed into his tiny, crumpled face. The natal hair was fine and black, but would likely change in time, as would the eyes, which were the indeterminate slatey colour of all new-borns.

Hrothgar put his head tentatively around the chamber door, and seeing him Christen smiled and bade him enter. He tip-toed to the bedside and gently extended his good hand to touch the baby's fist, which immediately opened and then clenched around his finger and tightened. 'Strong,' he said with a wondering smile.

'He will need to be,' Christen replied. 'Even as Cynan's foster son, his life will be hard. Outsiders always have to prove their worth.'

'Foster son?' Hrothgar blinked, and then he reddened. 'Oh, I see, Welsh law.'

'To all intents and purposes, I am his woman, whether I will it or not. Who will feed and clothe us if not him? Osric? Siorl ap Gruffydd?' She gave a bitter grimace. 'Cynan will raise him as his own. Indeed, knowing him and the lord Siorl, it will give them a great deal of pleasure to see my son ride out as a young man to raid the lands that are his English birthright.'

'It is wrong, mistress,' Hrothgar said, staring down at his finger in the baby's tenacious grip, his loyalty demanded by a tug too great to resist.

'Is there a choice?' Christen blinked away the tears blurring her vision. In truth she wanted to howl with grief even amid her joy, but she checked the extremes as best she could. 'Do you think Cynan will let me go when he almost set upon you for daring a conversation? I am proof of his dominance over both English and Norman. The moment I am recovered from this birth he intends having me in his bed. He may not be my man but I am forcibly his woman and this child belongs to him even if he is not of his siring. Even if I did gain my freedom, where would I go? Out of this cage and straight into FitzOsbern's waiting jaws.' Her voice quivered. 'Do you think he will let us live to challenge his possession of Ashdyke and Milnham?'

'Did not your lord have a brother?' Hrothgar asked.

Christen shook her head. 'Do not look for succour from that direction. He went with Miles to the north and I do not know if he still lives. He is without lands of his own, and although he would cut out FitzOsbern's heart for Miles's sake, he does not have the power to do so without destroying himself.'

'William of Normandy then? I hear tell your husband was the best tracker he owned.'

'And FitzOsbern is his kin,' Christen answered bleakly.

She looked up as one of the other women entered the room, Emma tightly clutching her hand. On seeing Christen, Emma let go, ran to her, flung strangling arms around her neck and gave her a smacking kiss. Then she turned her attention to her baby half-brother with fascinated delight.

'Later,' Christen said softly to Hrothgar. 'We will talk of this later.'

Hrothgar took her hand, squeezed it, and returned to the hall.

18

Welsh Marches

It was a warm evening at the end of April. The moon rode the sky like a pale coin, its indigo backcloth so rich and deep that it seemed as if a man could reach up, grasp it between his fingers and snatch down the cool pinpoints of starlight into his cupped hands.

The reeds at the water's edge clacked together, swayed by a light breeze eddying in from Wales, a breeze that as it strengthened would bring the whisper of light rain, so typical of late spring and early summer in the Marches.

Standing beside the horse, Osric smoothed the grey's dappled neck and slackened the rein to let him drink at the pool. The bit chains jingled as the stallion muzzled the surface, and a startled frog plopped beneath the water. Osric inhaled and smelled the taint of smoke, a reminder that William FitzOsbern was scorching their heels. He had been harrying them throughout the spring without respite. They fled from one camp to another, and all the places that had formerly given them shelter had either surrendered or been destroyed. There was talk among the men that Eadric himself was preparing to yield for they could no longer sustain the rebellion. The Danish challenge in the Fenlands was fizzling out and the other revolts had been savagely quelled.

Osric knew he had no future in England. He was homeless and landless – an outlaw with the murder of a Norman baron on his hands. Cynan ap Owain might have taken him, but Osric did not want to live in the same hall as his sister and her Norman brat, perchance to have his throat cut while he slept.

The horse waded between the reeds, drinking his fill. Ireland, he thought. The only alternative was to go there and join King Harold's sons in exile, or perhaps hire his sword and his stallion to an Irish lord. The Irish paid well for a good fighting man, especially with a horse like this one.

Cloud lifted his muzzle and silver droplets trickled back into the pool and shivered the reflection of the sky. Osric glanced upwards and watched a wisp of purple cloud trail across the moon.

The knife at his throat and the hard arm that locked him against the blade came as a complete and terrifying shock.

'Softly if you want to live,' whispered the voice in his ear. 'I will spill your blood if I must.'

The hold on him shifted and Osric found himself divested of sword and seax. The grey, after a jerk of his head, showed no inclination to bolt but started to lip at the grass fronding the pool. A thin rope was efficiently looped over Osric's body, binding his arms to his sides.

'What do you want?' Osric croaked. 'I have nothing, only the horse.'

'And even he does not belong to you,' came the whispered retort. 'Turn around if you dare.'

The knife departed his throat, but Osric was acutely aware of its closeness as he pivoted to face the man he had left for dead. 'No! He shook his head. 'It is not true!'

'Shall I slit your throat to prove it?' Miles asked. 'Fortunate I am not scouting for FitzOsbern or I'd have dropped you at your post and led him into the heart of Eadric Cild's camp.' He removed the horn from Osric's belt and cast it far out into the water. 'You won't be needing this again.' He watched the horn splash into the moon's reflection and break it into hundreds of luminous shards.

'Why don't you kill me now, or do you want to gloat first as you did before you murdered my grandfather?' Osric sneered.

Miles shook his head. 'I have no intention of killing you just yet, nor did I murder your grandsire. I found him already dying. Oxley is hardly an estate to covet and murder for.'

'I do not believe you.'

'As you do not believe I am standing here now with nought but a scar to show for your incompetence. You are a master of the art of self-delusion.'

Osric made a sudden lunge but Miles was ready for him this time and swept his feet from under him with a well-aimed kick.

'On your feet, and no more tricks,' he said.

'Or what? You will kill me? I do not fear death.'

'I think you do,' Miles retorted. 'But even if you did not, there are many things worse than death and I can show them all to you if you desire. I am not alone and you would not get far.'

Scowling, Osric rose to his feet. Keeping a firm grip on the end of the rope, Miles mounted Cloud and patted the arched grey neck. 'I have my horse,' he said. 'Now all I need to make my life whole again are my wife and daughter, and I hazard that you know where to find them.'

Osric glanced around, watched four quiet wraiths rise from the sedges, and realised that he had been surrounded without knowing it.

Miles set off and Osric lurched along behind, stumbling over tussocks and uneven areas. Miles pondered what it would take to make Osric talk.

'If the Earl of Hereford discovers Christen's whereabouts, he will kill her because she stands in his way,' he said.

'So do we all,' Osric retorted. 'I have nothing left to lose. If I cannot drag you down to hell with me, at least I can make you suffer hell on earth.'

'At the expense of your own sister's life? Are you so steeped in your mire that you would do such a thing?'

Osric fell silent again, his lips pressed tightly together until the tense atmosphere got the better of him. 'Even if I did know where she was, it would be impossible for you to get her back,' he said.

'I never thought to find you an ally of FitzOsbern's,' Miles said scornfully. 'Dead or denied to me it makes no difference to the Earl of Hereford, save that I should be free for his purpose.'

'You talk in riddles!' Osric snapped, stumbling over a half-buried root.

'He wants me to wed his youngest daughter. She's fifteen years old and beautiful. A year ago I would have had her at the church door before you could blink. But that was before Christen.'

'Do not prate to me of love!' Osric spat.

'Why else would I be scouring these Marches?' Miles retorted. 'If I had sense or wits I'd be curled up snugly beneath the pelts with my new bride, not skulking about in the middle of the night with a surly, pig-headed Englishman as my prisoner. I tell you this, if I do not find Christen and my daughter, then you will die, and I will accept FitzOsbern's generous offer. I only hope you are granted the eyes in hell to witness FitzOsbern's blood inherit Oxley when my firstborn son comes of age.'

Osric cursed and struggled against the rope binding his body.

'Think about it,' Miles said. 'Use your brains for once – if you have any.'

They entered a stand of willow and blackthorn where his man Etienne waited with their horses. They had been tracking Osric's movements for a couple of days after picking up his trail, but had left their mounts behind as they came to the end of their stalk when silence was needed.

'You cannot have her,' Osric said starkly, 'because I thought you were dead, and as her closest relative I arranged another match for her.'

Miles stopped in the act of untethering a black palfrey with a white star marking between its eyes.

'It was the best thing for Christen and the child,' Osric continued brusquely. 'They would not have survived long among the camp followers,' he added, justifying himself with another man's arguments. 'He swore he would treat her with honour.'

'Who?' Miles demanded, his mouth dry. 'God's life, tell me!'

'Cynan ap Owain,' Osric said, and gave Miles a look filled with defiant triumph. 'Your kinsman Siorl ap Gruffydd brokered and blessed the match and Christen did not object. I saved her life. If she had been with the others, she and your daughter would be dead by now.'

'And if you had not been such a fool at Oxley, they would both have been safe at Milnham!' Miles contemplated slitting Osric's throat and leaving him for the foxes to devour.

'She did not object,' Osric repeated stubbornly.

'Probably because she would rather lie down for Cynan ap

Owain than for fifty of FitzOsbern's Flemings. A choice that is no choice!'

Hands shaking, Miles attached the black's leading rein to Cloud and mounted up again.

'Am I not to ride?' Osric demanded, pointing to the black.

'No,' Miles said tersely. 'You can walk the distance we need to cover and may your shoe soles wear out and your feet bleed.'

He set out, leading the black one side and dragging Osric the other.

'Here at last, I see,' Siorl ap Gruffydd said with a contemptuous grin as Miles dismounted in the small fortified compound that served Siorl's equally modest hall. 'I had looked for you sooner.'

Miles looped Cloud's reins around a tethering post. Behind him Leofwin and Dewi, one of his Welsh serjeants, also dismounted, the latter jabbing a footsore Osric with the point of his spear.

'How long have you known I still lived?' Miles asked flatly.

'Hah, who taught you to track? I have known since the end of March,' Siorl replied scornfully.

Miles swallowed the urge to leap at Siorl and throttle the life from him, for he could see that his uncle was ready for just such a move. 'Testing my Norman pride to see how easily it bleeds?' he said with a lightness he was far from feeling.

Siorl curled his lip. 'You deserved it.'

'Well, I am here now and suitably humble. Does Cynan know I am alive?'

'If he did, you'd not stay that way for long.' Siorl made a gesture of capitulation. 'You might as well come within. I owe you a horn of mead at least.' He added with a jerk of his head: 'I see you have found your woman's brother. Why don't you put a dagger across his throat? I would.'

'I don't know,' Miles replied honestly as they crossed the compound. 'Perhaps for Christen's sake. The first time I ever laid eyes on her, she ran out beneath Cloud's hooves to beg for his life. It may be that my conscience will not waste it now.'

'Hah, a Norman does not own such a thing.'

'Ah, but I am half Welsh, surely that makes all the difference,' Miles baited him as they entered the hall, and then said: 'I want you to help me get her back from Cynan.'

Siorl choked.

'He is not amenable to ransom or barter then?'

'You would be as welcome as the plague, and no, I want nothing to do with whatever enterprise you are planning. You advised me to stay at home and cosset my old bones, and that is precisely what I am going to do.'

Miles took the horn of mead offered by a serving woman. Another maid stood nearby, working at an upright loom with dextrous fingers.

'So you will ride out for the likes of Cynan ap Owain and Wild Eadric and deny your own kin?'

Siorl hunched his shoulders. 'I will not spill my blood for a *Saison* woman and a mongrel girl-child,' he said.

'But your life is already indebted to me,' Miles replied.

'I will not tell Cynan that you were here. Count that your repayment.' A muscle flexed in Siorl's jaw as Miles continued to stare at him. 'No, and no!' he shouted. 'I have too much to lose, and you are more that devil Norman's get than you are my sister's.'

'It suited you to claim otherwise last year.'

Siorl reddened. 'Aye, so it did,' he muttered, 'but a man will resort to any ruse when his life is forfeit.'

'Does the obligation of blood mean nothing to you?'

Siorl attacked his mead. 'About as much as it meant to your

own sire,' he said after he had swallowed. 'It is not my obligation to die for you. Cynan ap Owain welcomes me in his hall. If I help you snatch back your wife, then he will come for me. From what I hear, FitzOsbern has no reason to see you reunited with the woman, and will not love the man who helps you do it, so I shall be forfeit twice over.'

At the loom the female servant, unsettled by the acrimonious conversation, made a mistake, flawing the pattern. Miles stared at it, beginning to realise that he too had underestimated the level of Siorl's bitterness and his own ability to secure his aid.

'You are on your own,' Siorl said, his gaze hard, but avoiding Miles's. 'Let the bond be broken.'

'No,' Miles said with soft venom, 'let it stand so that all may see your dishonour.'

'Hah, you talk of dishonour!' Siorl's voice trembled with intensity. 'Your father seduced my wife, his own sister-by-marriage, and got her with the child that killed her! She was brought to bed within a day of your own birth. Your father bedded her while also bedding your mother. You are the spawn of the devil and I will not deal with you!'

Miles gaped at him, stunned. He had always thought that Siorl's antipathy for all things Norman sprang from being Welsh, not that it should be as personal a grudge as this. 'I did not know,' he said.

'Why should you?' Siorl dashed a hand across his eyes. 'A man does not crow his cuckoldry abroad. You may have your mother's blood in you and mine, but you have your father's eyes. Go on, get out of here and never return.'

Siorl turned on his heel and stalked away up the hall, disappearing behind a curtain into the private chamber beyond.

Miles stared after him and remembered running over the summer hills as a child with Siorl's son for a companion. A leggy, limber boy of his own age with dark auburn curls and bright eyes the colour of sea shallows. Swift as an arrow and agile as a young deer. But even young deer could slip and he had broken his neck the following winter on the iced-over River Monnow. His own half-brother and he had not known. Miles suspected the resemblance had been obvious to the adults though. He also wondered if the worsening relationship between his parents had been caused by his mother's suspicions. She had held her tongue until death, but sometimes her face had betrayed her emotions as she looked at his father, and they were not loving ones.

His father had sown the wind. Here in Siorl's hall, Miles reaped the whirlwind of that casual infidelity. Gazing at the loom with its flawed piece of weaving, he knew he was alone.

19

The settlement of Cynan ap Owain

Christen sat in the hazy sunshine of the ward with a group of other women, splitting rushes to extract the pith which would later be dipped in hot tallow to provide light during the long autumn and winter evenings. The baby, now a week old, slumbered in a basket lined with fleece, watched over by Emma, who was fascinated by him.

The women's mood was tense and pensive. Now and again they would look towards the barred gates. There had been a dawn report from one of the shepherds of the approach of a troop of men, not large enough to be an army but sufficient to be a threat. Normans, the shepherd had said; perhaps FitzOsbern's men coming to put an end to yet another source of Eadric's support. Lord Cynan had gathered together his warband and ridden out to investigate. The women had prepared their belongings in bundles in case they had to flee, and now sat at their work, ears straining for the alarm, their attention not upon their weaving but focused on the handful of spearmen on watch duty.

When the gates did creak open, two women half rose in fear, and Christen tensed, ready to run if she must. Four men astride good horses and leading a fifth mount entered the compound, and the women relaxed with wary relief that they had been admitted as allies. Christen's glance sharpened and her belly dissolved as she recognised Osric, then Leofwin, with Dewi and another man who wore a raised hood and reminded her for a moment of Siorl ap Gruffydd – except that he moved far too easily for Siorl. Her heart began to pound like a fast drum.

The gate guard said something to the hooded man and pointed in her direction. Christen stood up. He turned his head as he made a reply and she swallowed, made uncertain by the deep shadow of his hood. The guard's pointing finger became a beckoning one and her knees almost gave way.

'Go on,' said one of the women, misreading her hesitation. 'We will watch the children.'

Christen shuddered and stumbled across to the gate. She was within ten yards of the hooded man when he raised his head and looked at her. Again, she stopped, unable to move, struggling to comprehend.

'*Boro da fy arglwyddes*,' he greeted her in Welsh, and approaching her, bowed in deference, murmuring in English, 'They think we have come from Siorl ap Gruffydd to escort you to the safety of his hall. I have told them the truth, that I am Siorl's kin, come to take you out of here.'

'I thought you were dead!' she whispered, trembling. 'Osric said . . .' Her gaze flicked to her brother.

'He was wrong. There is no time and the guards are watching us. Go and get Emma and your things.'

He turned away to make a casual remark to the guard, and

took his horse to drink at the water trough without looking back at her although he was acutely aware of her presence like a breath over the fine hairs on his forearm.

Leofwin was talking to the guard, casually asking about Cynan ap Owain as if not an hour since they had hidden in a copse and watched him ride past at the head of his warband, and known that their chance was now or never.

Dewi stood beside Osric, close as a comrade, and pricked his knife warningly into the latter's ribs. The guard thought nothing of Osric's scowl because Cynan's woman and her brother had quarrelled violently in the past and were not on good terms.

Miles twitched Cloud away from the trough, not wanting him to drink a bellyful when they might need to make haste. His hand steady on the bridle, he looked towards Christen who was stooping among the women, busy with something at her feet. Her travelling bundle, he thought, for he could see that Cynan's people were organised for hasty flight. He was utterly shocked when she turned to face him with a swaddled baby in her arms, and Emma clutching her skirts.

Leofwin ceased speaking to the guard and stared.

'She birthed the child a week ago,' the guard volunteered. 'A fine, lusty boy.'

Christen walked across to the gate, another woman carrying her bundle which Leofwin took and strapped to the crupper of the spare horse before helping her to mount. Christen did not look at Miles and he avoided her eyes, intent on maintaining a courteous, impassive façade in front of Cynan's guards, although he was gravely concerned. A woman a week out of childbed was hardly fit to go riding over rough hill country at speed, never mind a tiny baby, but this was their only chance.

Emma cowered away from Osric, her eyes filled with stark terror, and Miles's mouth tightened. He cast a fulminating glance at Christen's brother – that at least did not have to be concealed – and scooped Emma into his own arms and placed her before him on the saddle praying that she did not know who he was. At least he could hide behind the beard he had grown during the northern campaign and not yet barbered off.

'If you need another man,' Christen murmured, 'Hrothgar is in the hall and I vouch for his loyalty.'

Miles and Leofwin exchanged glances. Miles gave a brusque nod and Leofwin went to fetch him.

After two hours of hard riding, their mounts were lathered and Miles noted with worry that Christen was as pale as bleached linen and swaying in the saddle. The baby, who had slept thus far, had woken and was whimpering fretfully with hunger.

Miles slowed Cloud to a walk and guided him along the narrow path of the woodland stream they had been following, and turned aside to a clearing made by a charcoal burner that was slowly returning to the forest. Reining in, he dismounted and lifted Emma down beside him.

'We'll rest a short while,' he said to Leofwin.

'Shall I make a fire, my lord?'

Miles shook his head. 'We dare not risk it. A brief respite is all we can take.'

He was too late to help Christen from her horse because Hrothgar had already done so. Emma ran to her and clamoured at her skirts for attention. The baby's wails had become long-drawn howls of furious demand.

Miles spread his cloak beneath the branches of an ash tree so that Christen could sit and feed the child. She would not meet his eyes and tried to avoid his touch, and he knew something was terribly wrong.

'I'll bring food,' he said abruptly, and walked away to let her settle the baby at her breast. Perhaps, he thought, she was finding it difficult to accept that he was alive when she had believed him dead . . . or perhaps she had grown accustomed to life in Cynan's hall – as Cynan's woman.

He unlooped the water costrel from his saddle and reached for their travelling rations – cakes made from flour, lard salt and water with the addition of a little honey. Also, small hunks of cheese. Hrothgar joined him and Miles gave him a hard look.

'Tell me,' he said, 'has your conscience decided to make amends for past crimes, or is there another motive for this sudden change of loyalty?'

Hrothgar reddened. 'I followed Osric out of long habit,' he said. 'But I have been laid up in Cynan's hall with this broken arm, and instead of riding hither and yon without respite I have had time to think the matter through.'

'I see,' Miles said sarcastically. 'So it was a waste of time to take off your fingers. I would have profited more by locking you up in your own company for a month to ponder your foolishness.'

'No, my lord. I was still collared by the yoke of folly then.'

'Then what caused you to slip that yoke?'

'The way Osric treated my lady. He might as well have been that whoreson in Hereford the way he sold her to Cynan ap Owain. He lied to himself until only the lies remained, and others have paid dearly for his indulgence – too dearly.' He paused, and drew a deep breath. 'I am Lady Christen's man now, sire, and yours if you will have me.'

Miles was briefly taken aback as Hrothgar knelt at his feet in homage. A bald patch spread outwards from his crown and his hair was threaded with grey. Hrothgar was no youngling to change his whim with the wind and this decision must indeed have been hard-reasoned.

'Gladly,' he replied, 'if only you will stand up. Ashdyke has need of a good bailiff. Do not smile at me like that. There are still several hours between us and crossing the Wye.'

'No, my lord.' Hrothgar's grin broadened.

Miles gave him Cloud's bridle. 'Here, give him enough water to take the edge off his thirst,' he said, and returned to Christen and the children.

The baby was suckling contentedly now, eyes half closed. Miles put down some hard cakes and cheese between him and Christen.

'Leofwin says you can use these for horseshoes in an emergency,' he said lightly to cover the silence.

Emma was looking at him wide-eyed. She had recognised him earlier while they were riding and had clung to him, fingers woven tightly in his quilted tunic, her small body quivering.

'Why have you got a beard, Papa?' she demanded.

Miles smiled at her. 'Because it kept me warm through the winter and I have not had time to barber it off. I have spent every waking moment searching for you and your mother.'

'And my baby brother.'

'Yes, and your baby brother,' he said, and had to swallow hard.

Christen prised the infant gently from one breast and shifted him, mewling in protest, to the other side. 'Osric told me you were dead,' she said. 'He also told me that you murdered my grandfather and plundered his holding. I believed him because Hrothgar said it was true, and I trust him more than I trust Osric. But now I see Hrothgar kneeling to you in homage of his own accord. What am I to think?'

Miles lifted his gaze from the suckling baby to meet Christen's bewildered brown eyes. 'I told you I would keep faith, and I did. Oxley was raided by English and Welsh rebels a few hours before we arrived, and your grandsire was mortally wounded while resisting them. I found him dying in a peasant's cot from a spear wound in his side.' He shook his head. 'Osric saw what he wanted to see and Hrothgar was nowhere near the place to be a reliable witness. All he saw was your brother's grief and believed his version of events. I freely admit that Osric saw me standing over your grandsire with a knife in my hand.'

'But I . . . you just said . . .'

'What reason would I have to murder the old man?' Miles said, and exhaled a hard breath. 'It goes against every grain of common sense. Besides, with my skills, if I really wanted to see him dead, there are cleaner ways of making an end than sticking him in the lungs. I had my knife bare to rip open his bed cover at his insistence. There was a brooch sewn into it that he wanted you to have.' He reached inside his tunic, withdrew the soft deer hide pouch and slid the jewel on to his palm. 'He gave his blessing on our marriage.'

Christen put down her food, wiped her hand on the grass, and tremulously took the brooch from his hand. Their fingers touched, and something that had been dead quickened within her. She looked down at the golden wolf with garnet eyes pursuing its own tail. 'I remember this from when I was a little girl,' she said. 'My grandfather would let me hold it sometimes, and he told me that one day it would be mine, because it had once belonged to my grandmother, and her grandmother before that.' She looked at Miles through a stinging blur of tears.

'Osric waited no explanation but attacked me in a rage,' Miles said. 'He thought he had killed me, and made good his escape on Cloud when my brother arrived. The rest, I suppose, you know.'

'The rest I know only too well,' she said bitterly. 'When he ordered his warband to burn Milnham and told me he had killed you for what you had done, a part of me died too because if I believed it then it was a vile betrayal, and I had no way of ever finding the truth . . .' She caught her breath on a sob and fought for control. Her son was almost asleep and she did not want to jolt him awake with her anger and grief.

Miles tilted her chin on his forefinger and kissed her wet eyelids, her cheeks, her nose, and finally her lips. 'You have it now,' he said, as he pulled back.

Christen drew a shaken breath and bit her lip. 'Guyon,' she said. 'I begged Osric not to do it, but he was blind to all reason. Did he die of his wounds?'

Miles's jaw tightened. 'No, but he was very sick with the wound fever. He will heal in time, but he will never ride to war again.'

'I am sorry. We did not see eye to eye at first, nor understand each other, but it changed with time. I shall do what I can for him when we are home.'

The last word filled her with sensations of warmth and fear. She wanted home desperately, but knew how easily everything could be taken away. It was not always for ever. She looked down at the baby who was now sated and sound asleep. Gently she prised him off her nipple and covered herself.

'At least I have done my duty by him and produced another male of your line to train up,' she said with a shaky smile. 'Hold him for me a moment.' She placed the infant in Miles's arms, and went to relieve herself in the trees beyond the clearing.

Miles gazed down into the tiny face of his sleeping son and felt a tender tug of emotion that brought tears to his eyes and forced him to swallow. Such a tender, vulnerable little creature, and his responsibility to nurture and protect.

'It becomes you better than a sword,' said Christen with a laugh as she returned to sit beside him.

'It is certainly less of a burden,' he replied with a smile that was not quite a smile. 'Sometimes in the north I began to think that I was but an extension of my bare blade.' Abruptly he changed the subject. 'Does our son have a name?'

Christen had not missed the bleak look in his eyes when he mentioned the north, but chose not to probe that particular sore until he was ready to speak. She lifted her head. 'Cynan said that he was to be called Gwalchmai, a good Welsh name from the old days. Gawain's the English version, like enough to Guyon for me in my ignorance to mispronounce, which I have done frequently and in defiance.'

Miles looked from the sleeping baby to his wife. 'God's life,' he muttered. 'When I said you must endure, I had no thought that it would be like this.'

'It has not been easy for you either,' she said. 'We have both been ground through the mill.'

Miles shook his head. 'I returned from serving the King in hell and discovered I was still there. FitzOsbern was only too happy to rake over the coals. I always knew he was a devious bastard, but it never touched me personally until now.'

'What has he done – beyond the obvious?' She reached for the water flask and took a long drink.

'What you would expect of a wolf like him. Took command of Ashdyke and Milnham as soon as he heard the rumours of my death, and when instructed by the King to disgorge them, did his best to maintain his influence by offering me the inducement of his youngest daughter in marriage. I was less than diplomatic in my refusal. He knows exactly where he stands.' He did not add that FitzOsbern wanted Christen dead in order to bring his schemes to fruition. 'It is time we moved on.' He gently returned the baby to her and picked up Emma to carry her to his horse. The sooner they were behind Milnham's defences the better.

Hrothgar helped Christen to mount her tethered gelding and Osric watched him with bitter scorn. 'First you go grovelling to the Norman whoreson who maimed you and now you fawn at my sister's skirts like a dog begging to be taken into her lap,' he sneered.

'Hrothgar has been more of a brother to me these past weeks than ever you have been with your blood claim,' Christen retorted as she settled herself in the saddle and arranged the baby against her chest.

'Oh yes, your "brother"?' Osric said with insinuation.

Miles, who had overheard the exchange, seized Osric's left wrist in a grip of steel. 'You cannot afford to lose another three fingers,' he said, 'and there is no one here willing to plead for you this time.'

Osric clenched his teeth as Miles tightened his grip. 'Then do it,' he said. 'Do it and be damned.'

'Sire, the Welsh!' Leofwin cried, pointing towards the trees at the far side of the clearing from which a warband of bowmen and lightly armed men was emerging, the former with arrows nocked, among them, mounted on a bay stallion, Cynan ap Owain.

Osric used the distraction to wrench free and ram his elbow into Miles's midriff, making him double over. He grabbed the bridle of the nearest horse, vaulted into the saddle and drove his heels into its sides. The startled animal shot straight into a gallop.

'Loose!' roared Cynan, pointing at Osric.

Arrows thrummed. Hrothgar clawed Christen from the saddle and flung her flat on the ground, pressing his body over hers.

Jolted and half smothered, the baby wailed. Miles seized hold of Emma and shielded her with his own body.

Osric cried out as an arrow winged him and for an instant he lost control of the horse. It plunged haphazardly through the trees, but he rallied enough to command the reins and flee the danger.

'Well, well,' said Cynan ap Owain, pacing the bay delicately forward to Miles. 'What have we here? A raiding party?'

'You cannot raid what is your own,' Miles said through clenched teeth. He released Emma, who ran to Christen.

'And you cannot die twice?' Cynan gave a contemptuous smile. 'Shall we see?' He ordered his men to take the horses and strip the weapons, dismounted and sauntered over to Christen. 'Does the thought disturb you, *cariad*? It will not do so for long, I promise you.'

He reached to touch her cheek and she jerked away from him, her eyes filled with loathing.

Cynan gave her a hard look. 'We might as well do it here,' he said with a glance around the clearing. 'There is no point in waiting.' He drew his sword. 'Madoc, hold her fast so that—'

He stopped and stared as hooves thudded at a tearing gallop and Osric returned, pounding into their midst, blood streaming from the snapped-off arrow in his arm. 'Normans!' he roared. 'It's FitzOsbern!'

Misconstruing his action, believing that he was returning to the attack, one of Cynan's bowmen nocked and loosed. The barbed tip punched into Osric's sternum and exited at an angle through his shoulder blade. He was dead before he hit the ground.

Christen closed her eyes and bowed her head over her swaddled son. The black horse galloped past her, reins trailing, stirrups swinging. Emma started to scream. More hoofbeats split the silence of the forest along with the hallooing cries in French of men hot on the scent of their quarry. Colours flickered through the trees, the dappled sunlight catching twinkles upon mail and shield bosses and the flashing tips of lances. Cynan barked commands and swung hastily to horse.

As the Norman troop surged into the clearing, Miles wrenched the short sword from his guard's scabbard and back-handed the hilt under his ribs. The man collapsed, retching, and Miles launched himself at the Welsh warrior who was struggling to mount and escape on a plunging Cloud. An arrow's wind grazed the side of Miles's head. He seized the Welshman's belt and dragged him down out of the saddle.

Hrothgar bundled Christen on to her gelding with Emma seated before. A Norman destrier shouldered past them, nostrils flaring, foam spattering neck and chest. The soldier astride pivoted the horse and spurred him at Hrothgar. Hrothgar cried a denial, cut off short as the soldier's lance rammed through his throat. Leofwin sprang at the Norman while he was still engaged in the killing blow, pulling him from the saddle, and used the spear, wet with Hrothgar's lifeblood, to strike him dead. He seized his shield and helm and leaped on to the horse.

Miles reined Cloud aside from the charge of another knight, caught the spear that Leofwin threw across to him, and, hefting it like a javelin, threw it. The soldier's horse went down. Miles grasped Christen's reins and, with Leofwin and Dewi hard on their heels, raced for the cover of the trees. A loose horse galloped with them – Cynan's bay, its saddle and withers drenched with blood.

They had ridden less than a quarter of a mile when they encountered the Norman rearguard, coming up fast to help their comrades, led by the Earl of Hereford himself. Miles swallowed, his throat dry as he stared into the iron face of death, for they were all dressed as Welsh peasants. It did not take a military genius to realise how simple it would be to kill them and to cover up.

FitzOsbern reined his stallion, making it dance and paw. Behind him, one of his mercenaries said something crude, and laughter ruffled the ranks. The Earl slowly levelled his lance, and smiled. Miles drew the short Welsh sword from his belt and turned Cloud to stand protecting Christen and the children.

'No!' she gasped, her face ashen. 'You cannot sacrifice yourself. Leave me. Without us you have a chance to escape.'

'Never!' Miles snarled, teeth bared. 'I have not come this far to fail.'

FitzOsbern's roan lunged and Miles tightened his grip on the hilt of the short sword.

The Earl was almost upon Miles when his stallion stumbled and went down in a tangle of hooves and tail, hurling FitzOsbern from the saddle to crash against the bole of an ash tree. As the horse threshed, striving to rise, Miles saw the arrow in its flank, and realised that the mercenaries with the Earl were being stung on all sides and that yet another wave of warriors had entered the fray.

'Go, run while you have the chance!' rasped Miles's Uncle Siorl at his shoulder. 'You might have your father's eyes, but I have seen you are not of his kind in the matter of honour. I'll wreak my spleen on this filth instead of bygones. Make haste, boy!'

Miles clasped Siorl's arm. 'Thank you,' he said simply, and taking Christen's horse by the the bridle he headed back into the trees.

A few hundred yards into the forest they came upon a stream. Miles urged Cloud across it and made a trampled mulch of hoofprints on the other side in all directions before forcing the horse into the undergrowth to create a false trail, eventually returning him to the water. Miles then led his party downstream, keeping to the middle of the flow so that the horses' flanks would not snap twigs from the bushes and trees lining the bank. Any pursuers would at least for a time be misled, and once they did discover their mistake and turn back, there would be no trail to follow.

Early in the evening, Miles and his party forded the Wye, and shortly before midnight, under the light of a bright full moon, came to Milnham and entered into safety . . . for the time being at least.

'FitzOsbern did what?' blustered Gerard. He had hastily draped a cloak around his shoulders and his ruddy curls stuck up in a crest along the top of his head. He had been snugly abed with Aude when a servant had come running to bring him the news of Miles's return. 'God's teeth, I'll use his guts to bind my hose!'

Miles sat heavily on the warm bed that Gerard had just vacated. 'If you have any sense you'll be out of here with the dawn,' he advised wearily, his voice pitched low so that it would not carry beyond the curtain behind which Christen was settling the children. 'To the Earl of Hereford, I am now as much of a rebel as Eadric Cild.'

'William is the King, not FitzOsbern. Go to him immediately, or send me in your stead.'

Miles pushed his fingers through his hair. 'And you reckon he will favour my cause above FitzOsbern's?'

'If he does not, then I will know the reason why. We have never swerved from our loyalty to him.'

Miles gave him an exasperated look. Gerard belted him with a meaty fist. 'Don't you glower at me like that! What kind of brother would I be to have you go through hell and high water to get Christen back only to desert you at the moment of greatest need? I will stand beside you whatever happens!'

'You would be the kind who stays alive,' Miles said. 'I doubt your sword arm, appreciated though it is, will hold back what FitzOsbern throws against me.'

'You reckon?'

Something in Gerard's tone brought Miles up short.

'William has granted me estates up at Ledworth, hard on the Welsh border, and some lands in the south rich enough to compensate for what it will cost me building a keep and brawling with the Welsh.'

'Hah, that is good news indeed – but even less cause for you to throw it away on me.'

This time Gerard's blow knocked Miles flat across the bed. 'No more!' he declared, face suffusing. 'Short of trussing me like a plucked fowl, there is nothing you can do to stop me – so just yield with good grace!'

Miles rubbed his abused shoulder. 'You are mad,' he said.

Gerard shrugged. 'It is in the blood.' He glanced up as Christen emerged from behind the curtain. 'We can begin stiffening the defences tomorrow. For now, I'll bid you both goodnight.' A wry smile twisted his lips. 'Perhaps the greatest indication of brotherly love is that I'm giving up my bed for you.' He stooped and kissed Christen tenderly. 'Welcome home, sister.'

She watched him leave. 'How long will our defences hold?' she asked softly, but without fear. She had seen so much death of late that she was inured.

Miles shook his head. 'I do not know. Come to bed; the dawn will be here soon enough – too soon.'

Christen looked at him. His eyes were dull with fatigue and

something else that was quenching his usual spark. It suddenly struck her that she might as well be in the presence of one of the corpses they had left behind them for all the animation she saw in his face. She was not as accepting as all that, and sitting down beside him, touched his springy dark hair.

'Come,' she said. 'What is wrong?'

Miles swallowed. He was seeing the future and it was black, no stars to light the way, and the Earl of Hereford waiting for them like Fenrir the wolf at the gates of Hel. He closed his eyes and buried his face in the curve of her neck, fingers tightening in her hair, his body racked by shudders as the reaction set in and he began to sob, and Christen held him, a rock battered by the storm.

20

Milnham-on-Wye, Welsh Marches, February 1071

Christen woke alone, the bed bearing Miles's imprint long cold. Slowly she sat up, hugging her knees, and stared blankly at the coverlet.

Grey light entered the room through the window cover of stretched ox membrane, dispelling the gloom enough for her to see the oak clothing chest in the corner and the pole beside it over which her gowns were draped. A separate, upright pole supported Miles's hauberk which, thank God, for once he was not wearing. Beyond the brazier warming the room stood her small portable altar where of late she seemed to have spent a great deal of time in prayer to the Virgin, asking for the strength to see her through another day.

It was February now and would soon be spring. In the herb garden, the cat's foot was flowering and there were some early clumps of archangel. Snow still threatened, but the bursts of sunshine between the showers were growing in strength and the evenings had begun to lengthen just enough to be noticeable.

There was a gentle tap on the door and Aude poked her head around it. 'You are awake then?'

'Is it late?'

'You have missed mass. The men were away at dawn with the huntsmen and dogs.'

Christen nodded and looked dully at her clothing pole. It did not matter what she chose to wear, Miles would not notice, or pretend he did not, which was worse. 'Where's Wulfhild?'

'In the hall with Emma and the baby. Shall I fetch her?'

Christen shook her head. 'No, I can manage.' She left the bed. 'It was good of you to come when you are so busy with the new keep.'

Aude shrugged a disclaimer. 'Not so busy that we cannot spare the time to visit.' She leaned against the door frame and watched Christen don her shift. 'How is it between you and Miles?' she asked. 'I could not help noticing last night at table that you were as distant as strangers.'

'Probably because we are strangers,' Christen said, tugging a working gown from the clothing pole. 'Ever since we came home and began preparing for war, we have grown apart. He bears up well in front of the men and his leadership cannot be faulted. To hear him with the garrison, you would think there was nothing wrong. He covers it too well.'

'Covers what?'

Christen shook her head. 'I should not be telling you this, but if I keep it stoppered inside me for one more day, I swear I will go mad.' She turned to her sister-by-marriage. 'Aude, it is like living with a corpse, as it was with Lyulph – but ten times worse. I cannot bear it!'

Aude firmly shut the door, and taking Christen's arm, sat her down on the bed. 'Tell me,' she said.

'He has terrible nightmares,' Christen said, her eyes dry. It had long gone beyond the easy stage of tears. 'He will writhe and toss beside me. If I waken him, then he laughs about it and says it is nothing, but I am not fooled. I hear the words he cries out. It is all blood and death and loss. If I ask him in the morning, he will not speak of it, avoids me lest I mention the night, avoids me altogether as you have noticed. It is the kind of marriage I expected at the outset, one of convenience, except that it is convenient to neither of us, and it tears me apart. We have not lain together since we came home. Either he cannot, or will not. He does not embrace me, yet he was keen enough when we stopped in the forest to rest after he rescued me from Cynan's hall and before that it was good between us.'

'So, what has changed since then?' Aude asked, frowning.

'FitzOsbern has become our enemy direct,' Christen answered bleakly. 'No more pretence or pretty fencing, it is out in the open. We came away that day with a price on our heads.'

'But FitzOsbern is away at war in Flanders. Surely your situation has improved!'

Christen stared down at her wedding ring. At first, they had prepared for war with frantic haste, raising the height of the mottes, deepening the ditches, garnering supplies and men, replacing wood with stone wherever possible. But then a Hereford merchant had stopped for the night at Milnham and had brought them the news that Eadric Cild had surrendered to the King and the Earl of Hereford had been temporarily recalled to Normandy to aid William's wife, Matilda, to govern there.

'It is the waiting,' Christen said. 'We are given a little more time that is all, or so Miles says.'

'He cannot shut you out like this,' Aude said, tightening her lips. 'Himself he may ruin with his brooding, but not you.'

'Words are easy,' Christen said bitterly. 'Open your mouth and out they come. How am I supposed to lighten this dark mood of his?'

Aude chewed her lip. 'Distract him,' she suggested after a moment. 'Take off that sack you're wearing. Have the maids prepare a tub, and comb your hair.' Her eyes sparkled. 'Lead him a dance.'

Christen regarded the garments she had just donned. The sleeves of the undergown were edged with grime. The smell of smoke from the central hearth hung pungently in the folds of the overgown. True it had been winter and no season to be finicky but it had never stopped her before. 'A thing cast aside soon begins to tarnish,' she said, lifting her eyes to Aude.

'He has not cast you aside,' Aude said, giving her a swift hug. 'Nothing else mattered to him when you and Emma were lost except having you back. I think perhaps it is more that he fears to lose you again and it is a high price to pay.'

Christen gave a thoughtful nod as she considered Aude's advice. 'I do not know what else to do.'

'It is certainly worth a try,' Aude said practically. 'You have nothing to lose.'

'You are right. As soon as I have checked on the household, I will do as you suggest,' Christen said, and rose to her feet.

In the hall, Wulfhild sat with her distaff, a keen eye on the quadrupedal wanderings of young Guyon of Ashdyke. He was supposedly confined to a rug of stitched fleeces but the rushes with their itinerant dog bones, scraps and general detritus were of far greater interest to the child than the soft, clean sheepskin and the intricately carved ivory rattle that Aude had given him as a christening gift. Emma sat beside Wulfhild with her little spindle, her actions dextrous now as she twirled the fleece into yarn.

Christen scooped up her son as he reached the edge of the rug, tucked him under her arm, and spun to face a rusty chuckle from the man sitting to one side, his leg propped up on a stool, his stick leaning to hand – his left one, for his right was missing.

'Nimble as a cat,' he approved, nodding at the baby. 'Won't be long before he's afoot.'

'Underfoot, you mean!' laughed Christen. 'It is easy for you. You do not have his care until he leaves my skirts for a saddle.' She cocked her brow. 'I hazard that such time cannot come too quickly for you.'

Guyon gave a reluctant grin of acknowledgement. 'About all I am fit for these days,' he said, 'teaching a babe to ride.'

'You set your worth too cheaply,' she admonished. 'I do not know what we would have done without your wisdom these past months.' Kissing her son, she set him back down on the fleeces.

Guyon mumbled an embarrassed disclaimer but his eyes met hers keenly. 'You fret for Miles, I see it in your face. A man when he is constrained by his ailments to watch instead of do sees far more of what goes on before his eyes. I admit that before I was blinkered. I did not want to accept you.'

'But it is different now?' She followed his gaze to the tenacious infant advancing again on all fours towards the dirty, winter-piled rushes.

'Yes, it is different now,' Guyon said with a rueful smile. 'We both bear scars, do we not?' He gave her a sagacious nod. 'He will come through this. It is the waiting that eats at him and perhaps the fact that you and the children are threatened. You should take up Gerard's offer and go to Ledworth with him and Aude for a little while.'

'No.' Christen compressed her lips.

'It might be easier for Miles if you did.'

'No, and no!'

'Who now is blinkered?'

Christen shook her head. If she left Miles now, she feared she would never see him again.

Her son began to howl in frustrated fury as Wulfhild snatched him away from a gristly, stinking bone that one of the dogs had dropped in its wanderings.

'You have a visitor, my lady,' Wulfhild said.

Christen turned to watch a young woman advancing up the hall, accompanied by her groom and Miles's knight Etienne, her pace long and graceful. Christen had no idea who she was, but went forward to make her welcome, grateful for the diversion.

'The lady Alicia FitzOsbern,' said Etienne, his blank expression more eloquent than a grimace.

Christen's stomach lurched, but she controlled herself, thanked and dismissed the knight, and invited her guest to sit with her and take a cup of wine.

'I thank you, no,' Alicia declined. 'This is only a brief visit; I dare not linger.'

'Then how may I help you?'

Christen eyed her warily. This must be FitzOsbern's youngest daughter, the one whom Miles had been offered in marriage. A graceful girl, with dark braids showing beneath her veil, and delicate features.

Emma skipped over to them, anxious to show off her skills with the spindle. Alicia FitzOsbern smiled and admired Emma's endeavours. 'Your daughter?' she enquired.

'Yes, by dint of my marriage to her father. Her mother is dead. Our son plays by the hearth.' She nodded towards Guyon.

'They are handsome children,' Alicia murmured.

'God grant that they are given the chance to grow up,' Christen said.

The guest lowered her eyes. 'That is why I am here,' she said softly. 'I have come to tell you that my father died in battle in Flanders two weeks ago. My brother Roger inherits the earldom. If anything, he is worse than my father, but the King's eye is on him and Roger bears no personal grudge against you. Indeed, he will seek you as allies, I suspect.'

'Your father is dead?' Christen repeated.

'Yes.' She gave Christen a defiant smile. 'Please, do not bother to offer your sympathy. I am not bereft with grief.'

Christen stared at Alicia while the words sank into her mind, sent a glow through her body. 'My husband must hear of this immediately!' she cried, almost adding 'God be thanked' before propriety asserted itself and she managed to bite her tongue.

'I will leave you then,' said Alicia, dipping her head. 'It would not be seemly for either of us to see the other dancing on my father's grave. I have no doubt you will feast in his honour tonight.'

'Why bring this news yourself?' Christen asked curiously as she saw her visitor into the compound and waited for her mare to be brought. 'We would have had it in a day or two from a merchant train or passing pedlar.'

Alicia turned. 'Your husband once paid me a kindness and I am but repaying the debt. I doubt when I wed Maurice of Ravenstow that I will be offered any consideration as his wife. You are most fortunate, my lady.'

Earlier that morning Christen would have disagreed with her, but now, suddenly, she felt as light as thistledown as she bid her visitor farewell and then hastened to instruct a messenger to take the news to Miles.

*

Miles reined in Lluched on the top of the hill. Six feet from the courser's forehooves, the weather-worn rock sheared away in juts and tumbles to the river bed below. Some of the exposed stone was this winter's frost-hewn debris, sharp and unpopulated; other lumps had mellowed to gather moss and golden whorls of lichen. February light, hoar but with a white circle of sunshine hazy behind the cloud, clothed Wales in a blurred mantle of misty air.

Miles stared out over the land and drew slow breaths of the piercing early spring cold. A sparrow winged past him wearing a moustache of straw. He studied his hands. They were steady and confident on the bridle. He held one out before him and the only movement it made was to the slow rhythm of his heart. His mind was clear and he could manage it so in public daylight provided that he did not let anyone come too close to shatter his defences.

Night was a different matter. If he slept, then his fears released themselves in horrific nightmares. If he did not, then he was assailed by shuddering and nausea. He could not even bring himself to look at Christen and the children for fear of what FitzOsbern would do to them should it come to the worst. He kept seeing the women of Yorkshire and remembering what the soldiers of King William's army had done to them, and he could not bear it.

FitzOsbern, as if to deliberately prolong the torture, had gone to Normandy and then on to Flanders, leaving his son Roger in command of the earldom. Roger, the watchful eye of the King upon his doings, had preferred to govern prudently thus far rather than stir up dubious feuds with neighbours whose goodwill he might need if the Welsh came seeking revenge for the lord Cynan. Miles, however, had no delusions. When FitzOsbern returned, Milnham and Ashdyke would be ground like corn between millstones.

'Brooding again?' demanded Gerard riding up behind him, a pack horse laden with a limp roebuck.

Miles turned Lluched, the smile on his lips not reaching his eyes, which were sombre. 'It is my grandfather's blood,' he said. 'I was staring at the homeland.'

Gerard glanced across the blue-grey smudge of the landscape lying beyond the dull glint of the Wye. 'Do you miss your mother's people?'

Miles shrugged. 'Sometimes. Most of the binding ties are dead – my grandsire and my mother. Between me and Siorl ap Gruffydd there is too much of the past for us ever to be at ease in each other's company.' He watched a hawk climb skywards on slate-dark wings. 'Our father was a fool with women. He never appreciated what he had because he was always sampling the grass on the other side of the hill, and usually it did not belong to him.'

Gerard lifted a ruddy eyebrow, but before he had more than opened his mouth a messenger's hail turned him in the saddle.

Miles went rigid, for the man was spurring his mount hell for leather and bellowing words that were half lost in the gusting hilltop wind.

'What does he say?' demanded Gerard, narrowing his eyes as if it would help him to hear.

'FitzOsbern,' Miles answered bleakly, tightening his hands on the reins. 'He is saying something about FitzOsbern.' Miles dug his heels into Lluched's flanks and galloped down to meet the man, his stomach wallowing.

'FitzOsbern is dead, my lord!' the messenger gasped, as if he and not his blowing horse had raced all the way from Milnham to bring the news.

Miles stared at him in incomprehension and the messenger had to repeat himself several times before Miles finally absorbed the news. Once he had finally grasped what he was being told, he spun the courser and spurred back towards home, leaving Gerard staring after him in bewilderment.

The hall was raucous with celebration, the mood light-hearted with relief and the effect of the wine and mead freely consumed by all. Servants scurried hither and yon bearing baskets of bread and dishes of sliced mutton from the sheep roasting over the fire. The air was pungent with the smell of hot fat and stung the eyes of those sitting near the spits, but any grumbles were good-natured.

Christen leaned her elbows on the fine linen cloth and nibbled a honey cake. The cup of wine at her right hand remained barely tasted and she was not sharing the mirth affecting everyone else as they held this wake feast for William FitzOsbern, Earl of Hereford.

She wore her gown of crimson-brown wool, cut in the Norman fashion so that it clung to her body, which was now embellished with roundels of gold embroidery around the neckline, hem and upper arms. She had pinned the wolf brooch on her breast above her heart. For all the notice Miles had taken of her so far, she might just as well have been wearing sack cloth.

He sat at the board wearing the expression of a sleepwalker. He answered queries when addressed but ventured no comment of his own, and he had barely touched his food or wine.

He had ridden into the bailey shortly after midday, his horse lathered and blowing fit to drop. When she had run to greet him, his eyes had been alight, vivid with triumph and elation. Upon dismounting, he had swung her round in his arms and kissed her soundly before bombarding her with questions, the half of which she was unable to answer, and then Gerard had pounded in and everything had started to fall apart.

Despite the joyous tidings, Miles's delight had gradually drained away to leave him sombre and thoughtful. He had looked at her in her finery as if she was part of the ordinary surroundings or not even there at all, and Christen's budding optimism had withered and died.

He rose now from his place at the table, sheathed his knife, caught up his cloak, and left the hall. A well-endowed kitchen girl crossed his path and, flustered, dropped the dish of roasted fowl she had been delivering to the side table. Uttering a cry of dismay, she stooped to retrieve the meat before the dogs could reach it, thus affording Miles a generous glimpse down the front of her gown.

Gerard, well lubricated with wine, nudged Leofwin. 'Perhaps that Flemish woman in York gave him a taste for such delights!' he said with a chuckle.

Leofwin grinned. 'He looked as if she had rolled on him the next morning, didn't he?' Belatedly catching Christen's eye upon him, Leofwin subsided into an embarrassed cough.

Christen rose to her feet. 'Pray swap your drunken soldiers' stories in the gutter, not my hall,' she snapped, and stalked out in her husband's wake.

'Cat among the pigeons,' said Leofwin, sheepish, but still amused.

'Precisely,' Gerard answered. 'You know how jealous women are. He will be so busy defending himself he'll have no time to brood.'

The same thought had occurred to Christen as her anger cooled, along with regret that she had not brought her cloak for the February evening was bitterly cold. The first hot moment of jealousy had swiftly evaporated. Whatever had happened in York, Miles had risked his life to find her and Emma after their capture when he could as easily have left them to their fate and married the graceful Alicia FitzOsbern. However, it would do no harm to confront him anyway.

She questioned a guard, who pointed to the wall walk and the solitary figure standing there, facing in the direction of Hereford. For a moment she stood watching him, and then she set her shoulders and went to join him.

'A Flemish woman in York, was it?' she said. 'I have just heard the tale from Gerard. And now your eyes stray to kitchen girls? I thought you were going to plunge inside her gown and join her!'

'I doubt there would be room for both of us without one suffocating – probably me,' he said, and pulled her against him. 'I prefer my woman as she is. Lithe as a weasel, graceful as a swan and brave as a lion.'

A guard passed on his round and looked studiously elsewhere.

Christen was both baffled and relieved to see that Miles's eyes were alive, sparkling with humour, and he was looking at her, not through her, and smiling.

'I confess to a woman in York. Gerard pushed her into my bed and said it was for the good of my health but he was very wrong and I eschewed such dubious delights after that for a life of chastity. I want you, not some substitute taken for one tawdry night of cheap release.'

'Then why have you been ignoring me?' she demanded. 'Why behave as if I do not exist?'

Miles looked over the wall walk to the new curtain wall edging the scarp and rubbed the back of his neck. 'I could see no future,' he admitted. 'FitzOsbern was prepared to murder us all and there was no way back. I would rather kill you than give you up to him. Call it despair. I could not touch what I knew I might have to destroy, and I knew he would come for us. It was only a matter of time.'

Tears blurred her vision. 'But today, even today you have been brooding. I wear my best gown, the one you bade me sew, and you say nothing. You leave the feasting to come up here and hunch like a moulting hawk. Why?'

'I suppose that I cannot believe it is true,' he said, testing the thought. 'I am still adjusting to the notion of living a lifetime with you – or at least for longer than tomorrow. When I saw the messenger this noontide, I thought he was riding to tell me that FitzOsbern was back and marching upon us but instead he brought the news that FitzOsbern was dead. Whichever side of the knife edge, it was still a long way to fall.' He pulled her against him again. 'Besides, I wasn't brooding like a hawk just now.'

'No?'

'I was thinking that these defences will not go to waste. FitzOsbern has left us a useful legacy. If the Welsh do come raiding, they will only break their teeth on stone, and Hereford's heir being the fool he is, it behoves us well to have strong defences between us and him for when our son grows up.'

Christen was very tempted to kick his shins. 'So, while I have been half out of my mind with worry for you, you have been thinking practical military thoughts!'

She shivered, for the February cold was seeping through her flesh and into her bones. Miles unclasped his cloak and swirled it around them both, drawing her within its fur-lined wings.

'You could always distract me,' he suggested.

'Hah, that is what Aude advised me to do.'

'Aude is a wise woman.'

His lips sought hers. They were cold, but warmth spread from their touch to fire Christen's blood. His hands roved intimately beneath the cloak, and so did hers.

'If you do not stop, it will be over before it is begun,' he muttered against her throat, and captured her hands in his.

'And you have been continent since York,' she agreed sweetly, and cast him a provocative look. 'Well then, my lord, the night grows late. Are you not weary for your bed?'

He gave a soft laugh. '"Weary" was not the word I had in mind – not yet, anyway. "Ready" perhaps . . .'

Miles rearranged the cloak so they could manage the stairs, and taking her hand, drew Christen back to the warmth of their chamber and the heart of their home.

A Note on the Historical Setting

In January 1066, the English King, Edward the Confessor, died and his successor, Harold Godwinson, a powerful, half-Danish earl, was chosen by the Witenagemot – a council of wise men who helped the ruling monarch make political decisions.

However, Harold's right to be king was disputed by Duke William of Normandy, who believed that England's throne should be his. He claimed that Harold Godwinson had sworn an oath to help him gain the throne and that it was Edward's wish that William should succeed to the English crown.

William duly began making preparations to invade England, deal with Harold and seize power. Harold made his own preparations and fielded an army to deal with the threat from across the Channel. However, adverse winds kept William from embarking his army. In the meantime, another threat had appeared in the north of England in the form of a Norse army led by Harald Hardrada, King of Norway, who was making his own bid for the English throne. King Harold Godwinson marched his army north and defeated the Norwegians at the Battle of Stamford Bridge. Hardrada died in the fighting and that particular threat was eliminated, but at a cost. Many of the English had been injured, and news arrived from the south that the winds had changed and William of Normandy had landed at Pevensey on the South Coast.

Harold turned around and brought his army south again, picking up troops along the way. The English and Norman armies faced each other on the 16th of October and fought the now-famous Battle of Hastings throughout the course of the day. Eventually, Harold was cut down and killed and William of Normandy gained the victory and a kingdom.

The next order of the day was securing that kingdom and apportioning the conquered lands to his followers. Some lands were taken at sword's edge, some were acquired because their lords never returned from the field of Hastings. Sometimes a marriage sealed the new order, with the incoming Norman knight or baron marrying a widow or daughter of the previous owner. It was a harsh and volatile time, where often survival was the hard-won bottom line that didn't rise much higher.

I chose the setting of the Welsh Marches around Hereford as my opening territory for *The Coming of the Wolf* because I wanted to write a romantic adventure story covering the period soon after the Battle of Hastings and the ongoing Norman Conquest of England. I had read several novels dealing with relationships between the Normans and the English, but I wanted to add something with a different slant.

I knew from my research that King Edward the Confessor had a particular affinity for Norman culture and had invited some adventurers and warriors to settle along the Welsh border in order to protect these volatile and disputed areas of territory.

This happened long before the events of 1066. Richard's Castle, for example, self-explanatory as a place, was the home of Richard FitzScrob, who came from Normandy at King Edward's invitation and built a castle there in 1050, sixteen years before the Norman Conquest.

I decided to make my hero, Miles, a son of one of these early Norman settlers and I gave him a Welsh mother to add to the complexity. The Norman barons dwelling on the border with Wales, known as the Marches, often made marriage alliances with the local Welsh lords and petty princes. Making Miles the son of a second marriage allowed me to bring in full-blown Norman relatives as well as playing the Welsh side through his mother's kin.

The villages and castles mentioned in the novel – Ashdyke, Milnham, Fletesbroc, Oxley – are figments of my imagination, as are my protagonists, but all of them are stitched on to a landscape of historical reality. I have enclosed a map to show the situation of actual places and my imaginary ones.

William FitzOsbern, Earl of Hereford, was an actual character from history and related to William the Conqueror. He was the dominant force in the Welsh Marches around Hereford and Chepstow in the years following the Conquest. In 1069, FitzOsbern was involved in dealing with the uprising of an Englishman known as Eadric the Wild, or Eadric Cild as I have called him in the novel. (He goes by other names too.) Eadric wreaked havoc along the border between England and Wales, attacking the Normans and then vanishing into the wilderness. One of his feats was to burn Shrewsbury, although the castle stood fast. He was a particular thorn in FitzOsbern's side, although his forces were defeated by King William's at Stafford in late 1069. At some point after 1070 he made his peace with William and may have campaigned for him across the Channel.

Another Norman baron mentioned in the novel in passing, Roger de Montgomery, was Earl of Shrewsbury and his son Robert de Bellême features in my novel *The Wild Hunt*.

William the Conqueror's efforts to deal with the insurrection in the north of the country are infamous today as a savage campaign to put down uprisings once and for all. While some historians have seen 'The Harrying of the North' as an act of genocide, others suggest that William did not have the troops to carry out such wholesale destruction and its effects have been exaggerated by the disapproving pens of the chroniclers. Whatever the truth of the matter, the campaign was harsh and brutal and left starvation and hardship in its wake. Parts of northern England would not recover for hundreds of years.

William FitzOsbern died fighting in Flanders, at the Battle of Cassel in February 1071, and was succeeded by his son Roger. FitzOsbern's daughter Alicia is another character from my imagination and one who has her part to play in the following novel, *The Wild Hunt*.

I hope you have enjoyed *The Coming of the Wolf*. I am delighted to have had the opportunity to revisit the novel. It's a work that has travelled with me for a very long time, and I am so pleased that at last it's out there!

Elizabeth Chadwick, 2020

Acknowledgements

I would like to thank everyone on the Sphere team for their support and hard work behind the scenes. I want to thank my editor at the outset of the novel, Viola Hayden, for being so keen to publish *The Coming of the Wolf*, and my terrific new editor Darcy Nicholson for bringing the novel forward to fruition. Thanks to Thalia Proctor for her editorial work during the later part of the process, and Millie Seaward in Publicity for organising my various talk adventures! A special thanks goes to Dan Balado for his sympathetic and perceptive eye at the interim edit stage. It takes a particular skill. Any mistakes that remain are my responsibility alone!

My thanks as always to the members of the Blake Friedmann Literary Agency, and my lovely agent Isobel Dixon. I would also like to thank Sian Ellis Martin and Tia Armstrong for their very useful and perceptive comments.

An enormous hug goes to my husband Roger, who was there

at the very beginning of *The Coming of the Wolf* and who undertook to type out the first draft from the sole paper copy I possessed onto a modern computer so I could then begin editing and rewriting.

And last but not least, thanks especially to readers Carole Turner and Sasha Wagner (Growlycub) for 'nagging' me to get on with it!

Publishing in September 2021

A MARRIAGE OF LIONS

An auspicious match. An invitation to war.

'Picking up an Elizabeth Chadwick novel you know you are in for a sumptuous ride'
Daily Telegraph